LOUISE WALTERS

◆

A LIFE
BETWEEN
US

Complete and Unabridged

CHARNWOOD
Leicester

First published in Great Britain in 2017 by
Matador
Kibworth Beauchamp

First Charnwood Edition
published 2018
by arrangement with
Matador
Kibworth Beauchamp

A catalogue record for this book is available
from the British Library.

ISBN 978–1–4448–3613–4

Published by
F. A. Thorpe (Publishing)
Anstey, Leicestershire

Set by Words & Graphics Ltd.
Anstey, Leicestershire
Printed and bound in Great Britain by
T. J. International Ltd., Padstow, Cornwall

This book is printed on acid-free paper

A LIFE BETWEEN US

Tina Thornton's twin sister Meg died in a childhood accident, but for almost forty years Tina has secretly blamed herself for her sister's death. During a visit to her ageing Uncle Edward and his sister Lucia, who both harbour dark secrets of their own, Tina makes a discovery that forces her to finally question her memories of the day her sister died. Who, if anyone, did kill Meg? As Tina finds the courage to face the past, she unravels the tangled family mysteries of her estranged parents; her beautiful French Aunt Simone; the fading, compassionate Uncle Edward; and above all, the cold, bitter Aunt Lucia, whose spectral presence casts a long shadow over everyone.

Books by Louise Walters
Published by Ulverscroft:

MRS SINCLAIR'S SUITCASE

For Emily and Amelie, with love

Prologue

JULY 2014

Lucia wandered from room to empty room. The house whispered to her, echoing with the sounds and colours of days gone by. The removal men hovered outside. The taxi she'd booked had arrived, and the driver tapped his steering wheel, looking hopefully at the house, the engine of his car ticking over. They could all wait. In the small bedroom at the back of the house she gazed for the last time at the green fields, the clouds gathering in the distance, the summer hedges in full flow. The cows grazed as they had always grazed, the sun shone over the fields like it had always shone and always would. She crept into the room that had once been her parents', then her mother's, then for many years her brother's. It was a particularly barren room, scarred by the removal of its furniture. The wallpaper had faded to a forgettable off-white, where it had once been a rich cream scattered with tiny rosebuds. This was a house that breathed its history; it sighed and whispered of its tragedies, of which there had been two. Unforgivable events that could not be undone, like all tragedies. But Lucia hoped they could now, at last, be forgotten.

In her bedroom, the sullen emptiness was hard to bear. She stood reluctantly at the window and heard once more, as she always would hear, those plaintive cries: No! Please! Stop! Forgive me! She looked down at the floor beneath the window and there was still the pale pink stain on the floorboards. She'd not managed to clean it completely, despite scrubbing and scrubbing, again and again. No matter. The house wasn't hers any more.

She slowly struggled down the steep narrow staircase, her gait awkward. Her leg had not been right for weeks. Since the day Edward — But she would not think of that. She would not think of him again, her handsome brother; the monster he had become, the monster he had in fact always been. She would never see him again. Her mind was set. Never. She would not see any of them: not Simone — especially not Simone — not even Tina. Despite everything, Lucia supposed she was indebted to her niece, and in her dark heart there lurked somewhere a solitary beat of gratitude.

Downstairs, she made sure to leave all the interior doors open. The house could do with an airing. The new owners would no doubt tear the place apart, rip up the carpets downstairs, put in new flooring. There had been talk of an extension and a conservatory. *In need of modernisation.* There had been a suggestion that all those over-grown plum trees at the top of the garden would need to come out. They blocked the afternoon light. The laurel hedge too, so thick and over-grown . . . She wondered at the destruction to be wrought upon this, the only home she'd ever known — Lane's End House. Many years ago her father had proudly chosen the name. Would that also have to be changed?

She pulled the front door to behind her and took her time in locking it. She made her way down the three front steps and walked across the lawn to the gate. She closed it behind her, taking care not to let it clang shut. That would be too much.

She opened the door to her taxi and slowly settled herself into the passenger seat. The removal men climbed into their cab, one of them throwing away the remains of his cigarette with obvious relief. The van's engine started, loud and raucous. Miss Lucia Thornton fastened her seatbelt and stared resolutely ahead. The van pulled away, the taxi followed; she did not look back.

Wednesday 29th October 1975

Dear Elizabeth

Thank you, thank you for being my pen pal. I have wanted a pen pal for a long time. Its handy that your dad is my Uncle Robert but its funny because I have never met him. He went to live in New Zeeland in 1963 my dad said, a long time ago but he lives in America now which you will know because thats where you live. You and me are cusins which is nice. My name is Tina Thornton (we have the same last name you see?) and I am 8 years old in 3 days, on the first of November, don't forget my birthday please but I know its too late for this year and can you tell me when is yours? I have a twin sister her name is Meg. She is one day older than me. Meg is bossy and sumetimes I don't like her but most of the time I do like her. Do you have any sisters or brothers? My proper name is Christina and Megs is Marghuerite but we dont like our real names much. We get teased about them. Other kids say they are posh names la-di-da. We live with our mummy and daddy. In our village we also have our granny and grampys house and our Aunty Lucia lives there too. She is your dads sister! My dad is your dads yungest brother! We have another granny and grampy but we dont see them much. Please write back, I am excited to get your next letter and now I will finish, Love from Tina Thornton nearly aged 8

PS my hobbies are writing letters. I love reading too. My Uncle Edward says I am a bookworm like him. I like playing with my dolls.

1

OCTOBER 2013

Keaton peered at his wife over the top of yesterday's newspaper. There was a question that ought to be asked, so he asked it. She looked up absently from her toast.

'Sorry, what?' she said, with that small shake of her head that he loved so much.

'Are you visiting Meg today?' asked Keaton again. It didn't do to lose patience.

'I . . . What?' Tina said, floating off to some strange and hidden place that only she could go. She was the most remotely self-contained person he'd ever met.

He had to repeat himself too often these days. There was nothing wrong with Tina's hearing. He put down the newspaper with a resigned rustle and looked at her squarely. 'I thought, with it being her birthday . . . ?' He left the sentence to drift untethered between them.

'Oh. Yes. Of course. Why wouldn't I?' Tina made a weak attempt at a smile. How he wished he could be more useful to her. He wished he could help.

'Are you taking flowers?' he said. All of this was the delicate subject between them, and always had been. They skirted it like timid ice skaters making their way around the edge of a rink, not daring to let go. Keaton was not

1

permitted into the twins' inner circle; that was understood. Had he been a weaker or vainer man this may have hurt his feelings. As it was, he felt nothing but a growing sense of unease on behalf of his wife. Life was not easy for her, despite his efforts. Her 'relationship' with her twin was . . . obsessive? He thought so.

'Oh yes, I'm taking flowers,' said Tina. 'Pink carnations, I think. I'll get them once I've finished at the Haynes's.'

'Ah, yes. I thought you would,' said Keaton. Then, as an afterthought, 'I'm sure she . . . if she could, I mean, she would appreciate these things.'

'Yes. Oh yes, she would.'

Keaton suppressed another frown. Tina was the most devoted of sisters. She had a glorious nature, really — generous and loyal and loving. Such things were abstract notions to most people, but they were manifest in his wife. He loved her so much, but he doubted that she fully realised this. She was a good wife. And he had no doubt that she would make a good mother too, even an exceptional mother. Sadly, this was something Tina also failed to realise, and Keaton's long-standing dream of becoming a father, of one day holding his own baby in his strong, trembling arms, was slipping away from him, year on year. Soon, too soon, it would not be possible for them to have their own child. It would not be possible for Tina to have her own child. It was something he tried not to think about. He had her, after all — his wife of eighteen years — and she was somebody to cherish, with or without a baby.

It was time to leave for work. His train left the station at 7:44am and he had to be on it or he would have to take the car, which he disliked doing. In many ways they were an oddly old-fashioned couple. He worked full-time, a career man, while Tina was mysteriously contented with her cleaning jobs. He wished she wouldn't undertake such work. She was bright and funny and well read. He thought the task of cleaning other people's homes unworthy of her. He wasn't a snob, oh no. He just wanted the best for his wife. Of course, she was an excellent cleaner and since she had taken up the occupation, she'd garnered several glowing references. He supposed it made her happy. She had her own income; he had no right to complain.

Tina always handed him his bag at the door, and if those things were still the norm, no doubt she would have also handed him a bowler hat, a briefcase and a black umbrella. It was a quiet, private joke, and there was something surreal about it: a touch of Reginald Perrin, Keaton often thought.

This morning, he gave Tina a tighter than normal hug, and told her she should try to have a good day. 'I love you,' he said. I understand, meant the hug.

★ ★ ★

It only took her a couple of hours to clean Mr and Mrs Haynes's home. She rarely met them, as they both worked full-time and their only child, a daughter named Poppy, aged about eight, was at school. Her weekly payment was always left on the kitchen table in an envelope for her: £20. Most of the work consisted of tidying away toys and piles of clothes and shoes, followed by hoovering and dusting. Repetitive work, boring, most people might say, but to Tina it was not boring. She loved to clean, to tidy. Often she was tempted to declutter the Haynes's overcrowded home. But it was not her place to do that, so she tidied things away as best she could, in the knowledge that all her careful work would be undone in a matter of hours — a day. Yet there was comfort in it. It didn't suit her, Keaton said, meaning the work was beneath her. It wasn't right for her. She had a brain, why didn't she use it? Tina, damn it, you're clever. Dear Keaton; such a caring, patient man, but quite blind.

Tina finished her work, collected her envelope from the table and carefully locked the Haynes's front door. She hopped into her car and headed for the shops. She wandered around in Waitrose, where besides flowers she bought a bottle of Prosecco, and just like that, most of the morning's wages were spent.

She thought Meg would have grown up to love flowers, particularly pink ones, although Tina couldn't pinpoint why she felt this. Meg had never been a 'pink' girl.

At the cemetery, Tina walked up to her sister's grave. She stood and looked at it for a while, assessing the work needed. She unwrapped the flowers. Pink roses today. There had been no carnations.

4

'Happy birthday!' said Tina. Nobody was around, nobody could hear. Not even Meg, she thought sadly. It was a chilly day, aswirl with red, orange and brown leaves. Tina put down her gardening mat and lowered herself onto her knees to begin work. Forty-six. She would have been forty-six! 'Happy birthday . . . ' she muttered to herself.

'You said that already.'

'I did?'

'Just now, when you first got here.'

'You're right.'

Tina cleared away last week's flowers. She trimmed the grass and rubbed down the gravestone with her scrubbing brush. She filled the urn with fresh water and arranged the roses to her satisfaction. As she worked, she felt Meg's presence, that certain feeling of being studied.

'Getting forgetful in our old age, are we?' teased Meg.

'Shut up,' said Tina.

'Shut up yourself, fattie.'

'I'm not fat!' cried Tina. 'And let me remind you, I am actually younger than you are.'

'Oh really? Time was when we both fought to be the oldest. And I won, ha!'

'Yes, you won. But times change. When you get to my age . . . '

'Do shut up, Tina. But yes. All right, I'll let you have that one. Happy birthday for tomorrow, anyway. I suppose your husband will wine and dine you?'

'No plans,' said Tina. She was taking her time with the flowers. She wanted them to look

5

perfect. There were no plans, it was true. A takeaway meal and a bottle of wine was their usual mode of birthday celebration. Tina and Keaton were not party animals, and each preferred the other's company to anybody else's. Tina stood up and took a couple of steps backwards to view the flowers.

'Bor-ring,' chirruped Meg.

'My flower arrangement or my lack of birthday plans?' said Tina.

'There's nothing wrong with the flowers,' said Meg.

'At least it's not raining today,' said Tina, looking around at the grey sky, the roiling leaves. 'Not yet, anyway.'

'I don't care about that. Listen. I have something to tell you.'

'What is it?'

'It's — it's rather important.'

'Oh. Sounds intriguing.'

'Stop trivialising,' said Meg.

'Well, it does sound intriguing.'

'Have we got our listening ears on?'

'Oh, for God's sake, get on with it.'

'I'm not fooling this time,' said Meg. 'There's something . . . there's something you need to understand.'

'Yes?' How Tina hated Meg in this mood: self-important and tedious.

'It's this. Just this. The day I died . . .'

Tina lowered her trembling knees onto her gardening mat.

'What about it?'

'I know whose fault it was.'

6

'Oh no, Meg — '

'And what's more, you know it too. Stop fooling yourself. And do something about it, would you? I'm so tired of waiting . . . '

'You're tired?!'

'Too right I am. I know you're going to bleat on now about how exhausting it is living with this burden and all this guilt and all this yadda yadda yadda but seriously, it's nothing. It's not your responsibility to feel this way. It's . . . hers.'

'Whose?'

'You know who!'

'Is it . . . the You Know Who?'

'Of course!' hissed Meg. 'I don't know why you've ever thought it was your fault.'

'Because it was!'

'No, it wasn't. Not for one second.'

'If it wasn't for me — '

'If it wasn't for you I'd be truly dead, Tina. You know that much don't you?' Meg's voice, unusually soft, drifted away, floated off, into the grey sky and the swaying, thinning lime trees. *Trust me*, rustled the leaves, *I know things . . .*

This was serious. Meg wasn't teasing. Tina stood up. She kneeled down again, and fiddled with the flowers one last time.

They had never spoken like this. In the last thirty-eight years, since that day, Meg had never once described herself as 'dead', let alone truly dead. Meg had never stated whose fault it was. It had been taken as read, always, that Tina was culpable.

'I'll drop by again next week,' Tina said, confused; struck, finally standing up to leave.

7

She gathered all her bits and pieces together. She thought her fellow forty-six-year-old sister would have probably shrugged and said, 'Whatever you think.' But she did not. The cemetery was cold and deserted. There was nobody there.

★ ★ ★

After Tina arrived home, she ate two slices of coffee cake and she pondered. She knew she spent too much time pondering. She knew she ate too much. Both of these things were aimless and unhealthy. She supposed she ought to get a grip. She was so lonely, although she dared not admit this. She had Keaton. She had her home. She had her books. She had her baking. She had her knitting. She had her cleaning jobs. But she wanted more. She had lately admitted to herself that she had 'issues', as Keaton called them. It was time to face up to them; work them out and shake them off. But of course it was easier said than done, and she had tried hard earlier in the year to find the help that Keaton thought she needed. But the help had not helped. She was no better off now than she had been then. In many ways things were worse because the 'help' had left things half-opened, half-faced. Half-arsed, in fact. Mess half-everywhere. Tina hadn't yet managed to stuff it all back into the deep vessel it had leaked from and seal the lid, so her life overflowed with gloop. And now this new thing, this new idea Meg had put into her mind . . . It was too much to contemplate. The events of the day on which Meg died were neatly arranged in

8

Tina's memory, or so she thought. The day was set, in her mind, if not in her heart. She knew what happened. For many years she had relived it, frequently, slotting things into place, arranging them to her satisfaction. But had she got it wrong? Nowadays she tried not to think about it, not to hear that day's words, its voices. And yet Keaton wanted her to talk about it: 'It would be good for you, darling.' He wanted her to pull it all apart, unpick the carefully sewn seams of her memory; as if that would help. And now Meg too, with her strange, unexpected . . . Tina supposed it was a revelation.

Tina considered cutting a third slice of cake, but resisted. Meg was right about one thing — she was getting fat. She placed the lid back on the cake tin and took an anti-bacterial wipe from its packet and slowly, methodically wiped down the work surface. A few of the cake crumbs found their way onto the kitchen floor. Tina picked them up and popped them into the bin with the wipe.

2

AUGUST 1952

Mum raised herself from her pillows and presented a hideous little creature to its sister.

'Lucia, this is your new baby brother. His name is William. Say hello to him!'

Lucia stared at the baby. He was ugly with a scrunched-up face. He barely looked like a person. Her new brother had been born in the early hours of the day, while Lucia had slept on in ignorance. She'd heard nothing — not the district nurse arriving, not the moans and groans of her mother labouring, and not the nervous whispered talk from downstairs as her father and Edward sat up for most of the night waiting.

Lucia finally said 'hello' to the baby in a flat and meaningless tone, but Mum seemed satisfied and gathered the creature back to her; Lucia watched in horror as her mother, her own mother, let this being suckle at her breast.

Lucia, six years old, and the darling of her family, ran from her parents' bedroom that smelled not of its usual violets, but of blood and baby and sweat. She ran down the stairs to get outside, and struggled with the awkward lock on the front door which she could barely reach. 'Damn this stupid lock!' her mother had cried hundreds of times. 'Tom, can't you see to it?' But Lucia was out now, out in the sunlight, out of that vile bedroom with that vile baby! Down the steps, and into the garden where she smelled honeysuckle and the blue morning sky, pure fresh flowing air that she sucked in as greedily as the creature upstairs sucked at her mother.

Edward rounded the corner of the house, whistling loudly and cheerfully like he always did. Edward was nice. She didn't need yet another brother. Especially, she didn't need a baby brother.

'What's up, Loose Ear?' said Edward, standing before her with his hands in his pockets. His smile was genuine. It was especially for her and she liked it. She felt special. She was special, damn it.

'I don't like the new baby!' she blurted, for once ignoring the objectionable nickname. Edward could have his fun, if he must. She didn't care any more.

'Oh, but he's sweet. Why don't you like him?'

Edward was sixteen today and he liked a particular girl in the village, and in the last few weeks Lucia hadn't seen so much of him. So here was a chance.

'He's horrible!' she cried, and covered her face with her hands, and sobbed loudly. Edward picked her up for a cuddle. He was warm and strong. When he put her down again he ruffled her hair and gave her a lollipop. Edward always had lollipops in his pockets. He had a sweet tooth, as did Lucia, and Robert and Ambrose, and since February all had been regulars at the village shop or the post office, buying hitherto unimagined or unremembered quantities of sweets.

11

Edward told her she should try to learn to love her baby brother, and not to mind her own feelings. And wasn't it nice that baby William shared his birthday? She tried to smile, but no, it wasn't especially nice. It meant something to Edward; it was fun for him, but not for her.

Lucia shrugged. 'I don't care about that and I don't love him,' she declared, 'and I never, ever will.'

'Nonsense,' said Edward, unmoved, and for the first time Lucia felt he was not completely on her side, and perhaps he was not to be liked or trusted too much. He chuckled at her, and she knew she was frowning and scowling and making herself look ugly, but she didn't care. How could he laugh at her? It was unfair and she hated him too! She sucked on the lollipop. Edward regarded her for a moment longer, then with a last ruffle of her hair, sauntered off, resuming his joyous whistling and letting the garden gate clang shut behind him.

Lucia, alone again, wandered up to the furthest reaches of the garden and sat down under the plum trees, and thought about her rotten life. She wondered if she ought to have wished Edward a happy birthday. Yesterday, she had made him a card using her crayons and a sheet of her mother's best writing paper. But she had not given it to him yet and now she didn't want to give it to him at all. She slowly and thoughtfully sucked on the lollipop, until only the stick was left. She searched the ground for plums, hoping to find some that were ripe but not ruined, and prodding at them with the lollipop stick, she found three or four. After checking for wasps, of which she was not terribly afraid, she ate her plums in succulent silence. How unfair it was that she couldn't reach the plums that still clung to the trees. Her brothers always got to the still-growing fruit before she did, leaving her only the fallen, wasp-addled and overripe.

Lucia concluded that she should be thankful that at least it was another brother her mum had given birth to, and not a sister. A sister would have been unthinkable; it was something she simply could not imagine. She was the sister. She was the only sister, and that hadn't changed, thank goodness. Even so, the new baby was a horrible thing and Lucia resolved not to love him. Edward could say what he liked. And Edward and Robert and Ambrose could love this baby if they chose to, but she had chosen not to, and that was her right, and she vowed to herself that she would never waver in this, not ever. She stood up, plum-gorged, and cried a little, spinning around in quiet fury, stumbling and almost falling over with dizziness, the wasps disturbed and angrily buzzing around her. She breathed quickly, and leaned back on the plum tree, feeling the solid, rough bark at her back. She turned to the tree and tried to shake it. She kicked it and pummelled it with her small white fists, but nothing happened. Her luck ran out then, as a wasp stung her on the neck and she fled towards the house, screaming in genuine pain and mock terror.

Monday 10th November 1975

Dear Elizabeth
I know I haven't heard from you yet but I
want to tell you about my birthday. I had a
book called Ballet Shoes which I have read
already and it was BRILIANT. I watched it
on telly and then I wanted to read the book
and I am glad I did. Uncle Edward and Tante
Simone gave me a book called A Child's
Garden of Verses which has lovley pictures. I
had another book called Heidi and a Heidi
T-shirt which has green sleeves and on the
front there is a picture of Heidi and a goat
and a mountin. Its a bit small for me but it's
OK and Meg said can she wear it sumetimes
she doesn't like the look of Heidi but she
does like mountins and goats. Heidi drinks
milk from the cow it is still warm when she
drinks it that makes me feel sick even though
I like cows they are gentle. We have milk at
school with a red straw and it is always warm
the milk I mean not the straw. We dont have
any pets. I would like a rabbit or a guinee pig
but we're not alowed. My mum says it will be
too much work and she will be the one who
ends up doing it. My dad says what harm
would it do its good for children to have a pet
to learn about life and deaf but that's not why
we want a pet why are grown ups so silly.
Anyway you are lucky to have your dogs and

14

there names are funny. Me and Meg wotch Laurel and Hardy on the telly and it makes us laugh a lot and its funy that one of your dogs is fat and the other is finn. Meg calls me Mr Hardy sumetimes but I dont care she cant help being mean. I like sweets best but cakes are nice too and I like frut when it is sweet. We have plums in our grannys garden that we can eat but only in the summer so not now and only if Aunty Lucia says we can because they are hers for jam she says, but actually they are Grannys not hers.

I hope you will want to write back to me. I will finish now from

Tina Thornton your cuzun aged 8 xx

3

NOVEMBER 2013

A few weeks ago, in his ongoing attempts at help or at least amelioration, Keaton had suggested, out of the blue, that Tina join a reading group. She loved to read, he said. She always had her head stuck in a book. Why didn't she hook up with other readers and make new friends? It would be good for her, he pointed out. He was a sensible man. She'd promised to think about it. She'd mentioned the idea to Judy and Sandra, her other cleaning clients. They thought it a marvellous scheme. Judy and Sandra were big readers — academics. Tina often found herself gazing in awe at their dense, intriguing bookshelves.

So a couple of weeks ago, she had gone to the local library. They had a reading group that met on the first Tuesday of every month, August aside. They were on the lookout for new blood, the librarian said, looking at Tina hopefully. Theirs was a democratic reading group, friendly and productive. Also, it was rather chaotic, but good fun. Members took it in turns to choose a book each month. There was tea, coffee and cake, sometimes wine. Did that sound like her sort of thing?

It did, Tina had to admit to herself. So she'd said she would join, and had watched Tess the librarian write down her name and phone number carefully on a notepad. Tina promised to turn up at the next meeting.

And now it was the first Tuesday in November and she had 'forgotten' to tell Keaton about her impending night out. The birthdays and the visit to Meg's grave and the baking and eating of cake had occupied her. Most of yesterday she'd been busier than usual at her Monday cleaning job — Judy and Sandra had asked her to 'turn out' their kitchen cupboards (and how she had thrown herself into that) and the reading group had slipped her mind. Or so she told herself. Of course, it hadn't. She just didn't want to tell Keaton about it too soon, in case it was a mistake; in case he made a big, thrilled fuss and got too excited. She had thought to tell him on her birthday, but he'd brought home Chinese food and a bouquet of yellow roses and somehow the opportunity to tell had not arisen. She'd wanted to eat in peace and enjoy her night with her husband. She'd meant to tell him. He would be so pleased, she knew. He would be relieved. She'd text him at work, that would surprise him. She didn't make a regular habit of texting, or telephoning, or in any other way communicating with her husband while he was at his workplace. His work was his world, as cleaning was hers.

She could imagine his deep brown eyes widening in surprise and delight. And in pride. He'd probably tell his secretary about it. Tina had never met Keaton's secretary. She had an odd name that Tina could never quite remember, and she'd once made Tina feel uncomfortable when she had rung Keaton at work. Tina wasn't sure why she'd been made to feel uncomfortable; perhaps she hadn't — it was probably just her and her silly tendency to paranoia. But something about the secretary's voice, the manner in which she had spoken, had made her feel uneasy. Tina had avoided phoning after that, making a point of never going to the offices or the firm's Christmas dinner.

Over the years, she had twice read the book which would be discussed at the reading group tonight. It was one of her favourites — *Birdsong* by Sebastian Faulks. She felt she ought to be able to join in with the discussions. But she knew she would not — she would say as little as possible, and quietly gauge the people present. That is what she would do; that is what she always did.

★ ★ ★

The library was bright, with all the lights on. Night crowded at the windows. Not all of the blinds were drawn, and Tina was unsettled. During the day, the library was light, airy and welcoming. Libraries and bookshops were second homes to her. Among books she was among friends, the best kind — silent, patient and undemanding.

Punctilious and nervous, she had been the first to arrive, and Tina took her time in removing her coat, hat, gloves and scarf. She'd brought with her an orange and apricot cake, baked that

18

afternoon. She shyly handed the vintage Peek Freans biscuit tin to Tess, the librarian.

'I made it myself,' apologised Tina.

Tess gushed a little over the cake, and placed it on a side table which gradually became crowded with other tins, plastic boxes and plates of cakes and biscuits, as one by one the members of the reading group arrived.

Tina studied the circle of chairs, and singled out the seat she guessed would be the furthest away from Tess's. She wanted to be as invisible as possible. Group members said hello, and nodded to her as they took their seats. Tess introduced her individually to each member as they arrived. There were many smiles. Tina fought the urge to push her chair further back, to disappear into the blackness crowding at the windows. She had always been shy and tonight she felt the pain of it more than ever.

By a quarter past seven, all the seats were filled bar one, on Tina's immediate right.

'We do have another new member joining us tonight,' said Tess, 'but she did say she would be a few minutes late. Shall we begin?' Tess rummaged around in her oversized yellow handbag, finally retrieving a battered copy of *Birdsong*. Everybody murmured in agreement: Yes, let's begin.

Tina didn't know what she was doing here. Why was she here? It was such a good idea on paper, like all her ideas, in her head, in advance. But in reality it was a mistake. And now that she was here, in the cool stench of reality, among strangers in the bright library inside the black night, she asked herself: why was she so stupid? What on earth made her think she could do this sort of thing? She realised how little she trusted people. Here was the proof. It was all so illogical. These people didn't know her. They knew nothing about her — about her secret, her shame, her guilt. She was perfectly safe here, sitting among kindly strangers, intelligent people, who meant her no harm whatsoever and who were, in fact, warm and welcoming. Her heart tripped its treacherous beats, her head pounded and she clenched and unclenched her fists, then clenched them again. She felt sweat forming in the small of her back. She was going to pass out! She began to push herself up from her chair and felt a few pairs of eyes flicker towards her, people aware of her movement, when the main library door opened and in flew a bright blue coat, a head of purple-ish hair and a flamboyant wave. The blue coat was removed and hung up with the others in the lobby and the hair was dramatically shaken about, and through the turnstile the woman came. She was tall, vibrant in her movements. Tina stared. She lowered herself down again.

'Ah, Kath, good evening,' said Tess. 'Everybody, this is Kath. Our other newbie.'

Kath took the empty seat alongside Tina and offered her hand. Tina took it, dumb. Kath's grip was brisk and firm and enthusiastic. Tina smiled. She knew she ought to smile.

'Sorry I'm late,' said Kath to the room. 'I had a bit of a debacle with the kids' tea. But I'm here now.'

The group murmured its greetings. It took up the discussion of *Birdsong* again.

Tina listened as members said what they thought of the book. Some liked it and some loved it, an awful lot. Like her, many had read it before. Tina remained silent, even though a large part of her was desperate to join in. She loved to talk about her reading and she supposed as a child she had bored people with her endless book talk, particularly poor Meg, who had not been much of a reader.

Kath cleared her throat and spoke up. 'I thought it was fabulous, all apart from the sex scenes,' she said.

Tess looked surprised. 'Oh?' she said, failing to disguise the defensiveness in her voice. Tina looked at the floor.

'They're not sexy,' said Kath in a mock whisper. A flutter of laughter flew around the circle, and Tess reddened. Tina smiled to herself. Kath called a spade a spade, obviously. Tina liked that. Tess said she found the sex scenes extremely 'successful'. Another reader chimed in, agreeing with Tess. Tina saw Kath redden. Oh, how awful, how embarrassing for her, and on her first night too. Nobody seemed to know what to say next. Oh God. She ought to . . . should she?

'Actually,' Tina heard herself say, leaning forward, a hard thudding at the base of her throat, 'I agree with Kath. I didn't think the sex scenes worked that well either.' She felt the sweat leap from her back to her neck. She knew she was reddening too.

Tina heard Kath sigh in relief. Tina leaned

back in her chair. The conversation about *Birdsong* continued, but Tina and Kath contributed nothing further.

Soon, much sooner than Tina had expected, the book discussion ground to a halt. A couple of kettles were boiled in the small, white kitchen off to the side; somebody peeled the lids from the tins and tubs on the table. Tina sensed that the true business of the meeting was about to begin.

'So . . . I'm sorry, I didn't catch your name?' said Kath.

'Tina.'

'Well, Tina, you saved my arse. I've a nasty habit of putting my foot in it. Thank you, and hello.'

'Hello,' said Tina.

'So, what do you get up to when you're not being a reading groupie?' said Kath in her confident drawl, stretching out her long legs.

'Not much really,' said Tina. What did she do all day? She read. She tidied her house, she decluttered it, she cleaned it. She baked. She knitted. She went to the shops. On a Thursday morning she cleaned Mr and Mrs Haynes's modest semi; on Mondays for four hours she cleaned Judy and Sandra's classy, capacious home. She visited Meg's grave. She ate. She ate some more.

'A woman of leisure,' said Kath, running her long fingers through her wild hair.

'I suppose so, yes. Apart from my cleaning jobs.'

'You can come and clean my place if you like! It's a pigsty. Do you have kids?'

'No. Oh, no.'

'Very sensible. I've got two of the little buggers. Boys. Hence the pigsty status. Need I say more?'

'That sounds nice.' Tina badly wanted to join in with the conversation and ditch the banalities she knew she was uttering, but she couldn't. She didn't know how to. The hair was incredible, so thick and purple. Purple-ish. Tina wanted to say something about it, but she thought that would be even more banal. It was the sort of hair that attracted regular comments, Tina decided, and Kath probably didn't need to hear any more.

'Most of the time being a mum is nice,' Kath was saying. She winked, and Tina liked her, she really liked her, and she was glad she had spoken up for her about *Birdsong*. Keaton would like her too. He was a quiet man, but he got on well with loud and funny people; he liked those who weren't afraid of things, and so did she. Tina and Keaton were afraid of too much.

And while Kath prattled on good-naturedly about her boys and their never-ending capacity for destruction, and how her part-time job made her feel human, although it was tough sometimes, Tina didn't really listen. She cowed inside as she thought of Meg and how she would feel — would have felt — about Kath. Meg would not have liked her. Kath was definitely not Meg's type. And Meg would advise her sister not to get involved, not to trust, not to cultivate this friendship which would be too distracting. For friendship it was, right there in the night-shrouded library, eating cake, chatting idly to somebody new and interesting and friendly, about a book both had (mostly) enjoyed. They sipped Tess's insipid coffee: 'I prefer it with cream, don't you?' whispered Kath. Tina did prefer coffee with cream, she had always done so, and she heard herself say, 'It's surprising how many people settle for milk, isn't it?' Kath nodded in ferocious agreement, eating up the last of her slice of Tina's orange and apricot cake. Kath told her she made a fine cake: sticky, gooey and fruity, just like it should be; Tina glowed with an emotion she couldn't describe.

★ ★ ★

That night she told Keaton about Kath and her purple hair, her boys (Zack and Joe) and her part-time job. She couldn't remember what Kath's job was although she probably did say, and she told him how funny she was, that they had swapped mobile numbers and planned to meet up again before the next book group meeting in December. They were 'going for a drink' one evening, probably food too. Things were on the up, Tina hoped. Perhaps this would be the beginning of a new chapter in her life? But the doubts piled in, as they always did. Perhaps Kath didn't really mean it when she said she'd like to hook up with Tina for a coffee or dinner. Perhaps she was just being polite. Perhaps she thought Tina was a freakish, socially inept weirdo? Tina tried to shake off these thoughts but they persisted, as they always did.

When Tina awoke on Wednesday morning, initially in the glow of the morning after the night before, her heart slowly sank at the prospect of needing to explain herself to Meg — to tell her about Kath and the reading group. Tina couldn't often hide things from Meg. It was nigh on impossible. Meg had vision, a sense, where her twin was concerned. Apparently, Tina had read somewhere, that wasn't unusual with twins. It was sometimes a comforting idea. All day Tina was apprehensive, dreading her Thursday visit.

Tina made her reluctant way to the cemetery after cleaning the Haynes's house. It was a chilly afternoon, a tart wind whipping about her every step as she walked from the car park up to her sister's grave. The cemetery was enveloped in a cloying grey light. Tina tidied the grave and she heard herself pour out the tale of the reading group and her new friend, and as she spoke, her terrible, misplaced guilt washed over her like a vat of warm slurry. Tina steeled herself for accusations, questions, tantrums. But Meg was silent and the silence was unexpected; it frightened Tina more than the tears, raging and dire warnings would have done. It was not like Meg, who never held back, who was never afraid to voice an opinion, who was naturally jealous as hell.

Tina fell silent too. She could not read her sister's mood. If only she could see her clearly, properly.

25

'She sounds all right,' Meg eventually said.

'She is,' agreed Tina.

'Do you think she could help us?' said Meg.

'Help us with what?'

'You know what. We discussed it last time didn't we? Well, I did. Seems I'm the only one around here who can sensibly discuss anything. Could this new friend of yours help us? We need to get our own back, remember?'

Tina closed her eyes and hummed loudly to herself for a while. It was a trick she'd learned in those first few days after Meg's death. Loud, tuneless humming, blotting everything out. She quietened after a while. She breathed hard and opened her eyes. Meg had gone, of course. Meg, wherever she was, was not there. Tina cleared her throat and glanced around. Mercifully she appeared to be unnoticed; nobody was near, apart from the woman in the green coat and the furry hat who was, Tina suspected, only pretending to take no notice. She looked like she was reading a book. Tina wondered which book, but she couldn't see from here. She had to go. She longed to be at home on her cosy sofa reading, eating, reading, eating . . . She stumbled, muttered goodbye to nobody at all and left. Yet she felt Meg watch her go. She felt the woman in the green coat look up and watch her go too.

★ ★ ★

The woman pulled her coat closer to her and shivered. Soon she would have to stop coming here; it could do her no good sitting around in

26

this cold. Poor Tina. How stressed she was. It wasn't surprising, when all was considered. She watched Tina leave, watched her place one foot in front of the other, stumbling like an injured soldier. All was quiet again now. She stood up to leave too. She should go and find warmth, some good coffee, and think, think, think. One day, she hoped, one of these days, and soon, she would get up the courage to approach Tina; to say hello, how are you, do you remember me?

4

AUGUST 1954

Lucia found it was easier than she had thought to harm her baby brother and get away with it. He was such a stupid, helpless little thing and he could not tell of her, which was the best part. And even if he could tell, Mum and Dad wouldn't believe him, because she was their little girl and they didn't ever think badly of her, not even when she was being bad. Mum especially saw no wrong in her, and this was something she had known ever since she could remember. So she inflicted upon little William regular pinches, slaps and smacks, which were hard enough to cause him anguish, yet soft enough not to leave obvious marks. She took his toys from him, and now, as he was going through that delightful toddler stage she broke his toys in front of him, laughing in glee as his little face crumpled, poking her tongue out at him as his tears flowed. She showed him little mercy, only occasionally feeling a twinge of pity or remorse. Then she could be nice.

The Thornton household was already over-flowing with three gruff boys and the attendant muddy boots, fishing nets, Dinky Toys, ice skates, books, Meccano, puzzles and paint boxes. William and his paraphernalia were not needed. Lucia may have realised, deep down, that she was the lucky one, enjoying a bedroom to herself (albeit the cramped, cold room above the kitchen) and having her own feminine and therefore uninteresting toys largely ignored and unmolested.

Edward came into the lounge just as she was smashing William's favourite toy car on the corner of the fire surround, hard, harder, grim determination giving her the strength to break it. He must have been summoned by William's cries. Mum was hanging out laundry in the back garden, Dad was at work. Robert and Ambrose were off out, fishing and roaming and probably getting up to no good, and wouldn't be seen again that day until they were hungry. Lucia, at eight years old, was a trusted babysitter, instructed to 'mind' William while their mother performed her many daily chores. Lucia revelled in her role, appearances suggested, and her mother had no qualms about leaving her youngest child in his sister's care for a few minutes here and there. Mum had the habit of seeing only that which she wanted to see, and this was useful. But Edward was clever; he saw things, all things, and made Lucia nervous. She had confided in him too much before, when she was little, when William was born. Edward was aware, where the others were not, of the firm boundaries of her love for William.

'What the hell are you doing?' said Edward, stepping into the room and staring down at her. He looked shocked and angry, and big and strong, so Lucia stopped banging the car on the fireplace and looked up at her tall, handsome brother and perfected her innocent face. But Edward was not fooled, as she had feared he wouldn't be. He advanced into the room and plucked William from the floor. He wiped William's nose and dried his tears with a large white handkerchief.

'I'm doing nothing,' said Lucia. She stood up and twisted a strand of hair in her fingers. About to put her thumb in her mouth, she stopped herself. Big girls didn't suck their thumbs.

'It's clearly not nothing, you little madam!' he said, glaring at her. She had not been spoken to like this before. Not by Edward.

'I don't want to be told off!' she cried, and stamped her foot and clenched her fists.

'Little girls who don't want to be told off shouldn't be so damned wicked towards their baby brothers,' said Edward. 'Does Mum know about this? I've noticed all these broken toys lying around. I thought it was William being too rough or too clumsy or too . . . something. It has to stop. Do you understand? It's not fair on him.'

'Don't tell Mum,' said Lucia.

'Why shouldn't I?'

'Because it would be horrid for her,' said Lucia. Her logic made perfect sense to her, and even to Edward sometimes.

'Oh,' he said. 'Yes, I suppose it would be. In that case, Loose Ear, you had better pack it in or I will have to tell Mum.'

'My name is Loo-Cheea,' she said. 'And another thing. Mum wouldn't believe you. She'd blame Robert and Ambrose. So there.' And she tossed her hair and left the room, leaving

Edward holding the now calmed William. Lucia stomped up the stairs to her bedroom, sat on her bed and looked down on her mother in the back yard hanging out the morning's laundry.

★ ★ ★

Edward crouched down to examine the broken car. He decided it was beyond repair, and gathered up the remains of it and put them in his trouser pocket to dispose of later. He resolved to keep a close eye on Loose Ear. She had always been a difficult child.

He wandered outside to reunite William with their mother. He pulled a lollipop from his pocket, unwrapped it with his teeth, and put it into William's chubby hand. The little boy was delighted. Edward handed him over to his weary mother, and offered to finish pegging out the laundry. Mum didn't receive many offers of help. She took her baby son in her arms.

'Did I hear him cry?' she asked. Edward said he just needed his mum. William nestled in her arms and sucked on his lollipop. Edward pegged out a dozen of his own handkerchiefs, followed by Lucia's white knickers and vests and slips. He reflected that his little sister was probably right — neither Mum nor Dad would believe that their daughter was capable of such unkindness towards her baby brother. They assumed she loved him. Everybody assumed so, because why on earth wouldn't she love him? In front of her parents she was a model sister, playing with William, wiping his nose, spooning food into his

31

clumsy little mouth. She was quite the little actress, Edward knew. It was a shame for his sister really, this nasty streak, because at times she could be a most likeable little girl. He glanced up at her bedroom window and saw her looking down sadly on him. How lonely she looks, he thought. She was such a silly thing. He raised his hand and waved. She didn't wave back.

Tuesday 18th November 1975

Dear Elizabeth
Thank you for your letter and the birthday
card that was nice of you to send one and it
doesn't matter that it was a bit late because
we didnt even know each other in time for
my birthday. I have written yours down and
I WONT FORGET IT that is a promise. I
would love to see a photograf of you thank
you and I will see if I can get one of me to
send to you. My mummy keeps photografs of
me and Meg when we were babys but there
are not many now we are grown up. I think
our letters will have crossed in the post so I
will write this one now and you reply to it
then we will be taking it in turns. It is better if
we take it in turns but my sister Meg wouldnt
agree she doesnt like to wait her turn but I
dont mind.
Love from your new friend and your cusun
Tina Thornton xxx

5

NOVEMBER 2013

After Tina arrived home from the cemetery, cold and despondent, her mobile rang, and it was Kath, breathless and friendly. Would Tina still like to meet up? The new American diner in town was supposed to be fun. What was she doing on Saturday? When's the last time she went out on a Saturday night? If Tina was anything like her, Kath was willing to bet she couldn't remember the last time she went out on a Saturday night. How about it?

The arrangements were made, but immediately Tina panicked about what she would wear and what she would talk about. She already knew that Kath was a confident talker, so Tina hoped there would be no awkward lulls or difficult questions. Mostly, she wanted this night out badly.

'So what exactly is worrying you?' Keaton asked, as he sprawled across their bed on Saturday afternoon and watched his wife try on yet another top. This one was orange with sparkly trimmings and floaty sleeves. 'No, that's no good,' said Keaton. 'Too dressy. And it's too cold out, surely?'

Tina knew he was right. Keaton judged these things unusually well. He was practical, with a good eye for detail. She peeled off the orange top and threw it onto the colourful and ever-growing floordrobe (as Mrs Haynes would call it: both

34

she and Poppy had one) under the window. Keaton passed her the last of the tops she had laid out earlier that day on the bed.

'I'm not really worried about anything,' said Tina, pulling the top over her head. It was one of her favourites, empire-line and tunic-length. It had three-quarter-length sleeves (flattering), a curved neckline, and a riotous pattern of purple, orange, pink and red; all good for disguising the burgeoning flesh that was becoming ever more obvious around her waist and on her hips.

'Oh, come off it,' said Keaton. 'Be truthful.'

'You know,' she said, putting her hands on her hips and swinging from side to side in front of the mirror.

Keaton leapt from the bed, stood behind his wife and snaked his arms around her waist. He kissed her neck. Tina knew he was aware she was gaining weight, gradually, year on year, but neither of them ever mentioned it. He kissed her cheek, her neck again. She twisted her head towards him and he kissed her mouth slowly; he clearly didn't want to stop when she pulled away from him and sighed.

'Later,' she promised.

'This is the outfit,' he said.

★ ★ ★

Keaton dropped Tina outside the diner at eight o'clock precisely. She wondered if she should just go in — it was beginning to rain — or if she should wait in the small lobby for Kath to arrive. Tina feared her new friend would be late.

35

'Go in,' said Keaton, and he leaned across and kissed her cheek. 'If she's not there just sit at your table and wait.'

'But . . . What if . . . ?'

'What if what?' Keaton said.

'Nothing. I'm being stupid.'

'That's what I thought. I'll pick you up at around ten, yes? Or later, if you like. Text me.'

She got out of the car and watched Keaton drive away, back home to their comfy sofa, the TV and a mug of hot coffee. Lucky Keaton. Oh, lucky, lucky Keaton with his simple life, steady job, fantastic temperament and sane secretary (who was not his secretary, but his assistant, as Keaton always insisted). Tina shook off the silly thoughts and as she turned towards the diner, saw a smiling, gesticulating, on-time Kath beckoning enthusiastically for Tina to join her.

★ ★ ★

Tina took a long time to make her choices from the menu and apologised to the more decisive Kath, who didn't care how long it took, she claimed, because they were going to make a night of it. They shared a bottle of house white. Tina chose her food and the food came. They ate, Tina modifying her pace to keep time with Kath. Tina was a fast eater. When Kath asked the inevitable questions, Tina replied as best she could. She felt herself open up like a flower in June. Kath was the sun, Tina thought dreamily, and the wine was the rain and the food the earth. The thoughts were poetic, she supposed, and she

36

reminded herself of her Uncle Edward. She giggled.

'So you've been married for . . . how long, again?' said Kath, glugging back her wine. Her polite little sips had long ago ceased.

'Eighteen years,' said Tina, as she popped a forkful of New York cheesecake into her mouth. She was full, but determined to finish. Cheesecake was one of her particular favourites. And she didn't like to leave food on her plate.

'And you don't have kids, I think you said?' said Kath.

She was a little nosy, but it was all right. Nosy people were interested people. Tina knew that there were those who would be interested in her. Psychological types. Psychiatric, in fact. Her brush with that sort of thing a few months ago had put her off forever. Her sessions with Virginia, her short-lived counsellor, had done little to help. Virginia had been very nice and very earnest, but the experience had left Tina broken and confused. It hadn't been Virginia's fault and Tina was wise enough to understand that. Yet the upshot was Tina was even more guarded and reluctant to talk.

Tina hesitated. Kath paused awkwardly with a forkful of her own dessert halfway between her mouth and her plate. 'Oh, I'm sorry. Me and my big fat mouth. It's none of my business,' said Kath.

'Oh no, it's fine. It's just . . . we . . . I . . . I don't think I'm ready to be a mother.'

'Oh. But you're older than me aren't you?' Kath laughed, and topped up both their glasses with the rest of the bottle. Tina wasn't offended; it was funny. She already knew Kath spoke her mind. She was also a good listener.

'Forty-six is getting on, I suppose,' said Tina, and it was strange to hear herself speak her own age. It did sound old. If not old, certainly not young any more. 'But I don't think I'm mother material,' finished Tina. It was lame. She was lame — pathetic.

Last month, for the first time in her life she'd missed a period. For a few days she'd wondered if she might be pregnant. She'd wondered so much that she'd popped to Boots to buy a test kit. Shy and self-conscious, she had left the shop with not only the kit — the last item she'd picked up — but also a can of body spray, a packet of hair nets and a tube of arnica tablets. She had used none of these things in her life, including the test kit. At home, she'd carefully studied the instructions, her hands and neck clammy. It had felt like the beginning of an adventure. She'd found herself in tears when the kit had revealed the truth to her. Yet she had felt relief too. She'd said nothing to Keaton.

'Why aren't you mother material?' asked Kath.

'I haven't got what it takes,' said Tina, lifting her chin.

Kath hesitated for a second or two. 'I bet you have,' she said. She took another swig of wine. 'What about your husband? How does he feel about kids?'

'Oh, he wants a child more than anything in this world.'

The pause was awkward, but not prolonged.

38

Tina had never voiced this thing before. She felt like a headmistress confiscating a wrongly accused child's favourite toy. But Kath shrugged. 'Do you have any nieces or nephews? I bet you're a good aunt to them.'

'I don't. Although that would have been nice.'

'I take it that's beyond the realms of possibility?' said Kath, smiling. She was certainly easy to talk to. She was a gentle digger.

'I'm afraid so,' said Tina.

'You don't have brothers or sisters?' asked Kath, and her ingenuousness was touching, and not new to Tina. She had fielded such questions before, and had a stock of set answers to draw upon, depending on the questioner and the circumstances. It was never easy to decide which way to go with it, which route to take. On more than one occasion she'd found herself denying Meg's existence, omitting her entirely from her story. On another, she'd talked about how close she and Meg were, how they had always been close, and how they were godmothers, as well as aunts, to each other's children.

'I have a twin sister,' Tina said, and took another sip of wine.

'Oh, you're a twin! Do you feel that you're two halves of the same person?' Kath drained her glass and beamed across the table at Tina.

'Not really,' said Tina. She looked out of the window, but all she could see against the backdrop of night was her own vague reflection and the lights of the restaurant, mirrored and multiplied. 'We were born on different days. A few minutes apart either side of midnight.'

'How lovely.'

'I don't know. It is what it is.'

'So does your sister look like you?'

'Oh, God no, she's nothing like me. She's taller and a lot slimmer and she's always been the pretty one even though she wasn't ever girlish . . . Actually, she's beautiful. She really is. But I don't see much of her these days. She's unwell.'

'I'm sorry to hear that,' said Kath. 'Do you mind my asking . . . is it serious? Tell me to shove off if that's too much of a question.'

'It is serious. Yes.'

'I ask because I've been there. My brother was unwell. He died four years ago.'

'He died?'

'He had cancer. He was only thirty-four. Sorry. I'm sorry, Tina. I still get upset . . . ' Kath rooted around in her handbag for her compact. She flicked it open and dabbed at her eyes with her napkin. Tina said nothing. She was paralysed and had nothing to say. How she feared for Meg. It was frightening, how much she feared for her sister. Death was all around, as dark and unavoidable as the night trying to push through the windows, trying to swallow her up in blackness.

Kath recovered, and smiled bravely. 'So, back to my original question, which I think was . . . ?'

'I was saying I don't want children. I still don't,' said Tina. Kath laughed and Tina was glad she was able to lighten the mood. 'I'm sorry about your brother,' she said, remembering the things that people said when an untimely death was discussed. Everybody was sorry, whatever that really meant. Kath glanced away from her, just for a second, and Tina feared she had done wrong.

But Kath's face softened and she smiled apologetically at Tina. 'No, I'm sorry,' she said. 'I shouldn't have brought it up. It happened. It's over. And whether you want kids of your own or not is none of my bloody business, right? So tell me to get stuffed. I'm too nosy.'

It happened. It's over . . . Tina wondered at the simplicity of those words, the minuscule philosophical statements that seemed to simply end the matter. She was envious of Kath, with her easy-flowing tears and her ability to accept. Why couldn't she feel like that? Tina knew she was blanking out, staring at Kath and thinking about what she'd said, it happened it's over it happened it's over and she needed to speak, to say something, to be normal. 'No, you're not nosy at all. It's just . . . we women should want a child shouldn't we, and I don't. I just don't. I think it baffles some people.'

'There's no such thing as 'should',' said Kath.

Keep going, Tina heard. Meg — her voice, insistent and pure. Don't give in to this woman and her questions. She is nosy, like she says. But she's all right, as her type go. Tell her to get stuffed, anyway. She said you could. It's not over, Tina. It's not over, not over, not over . . .

'No,' whispered Tina.

'What?' said Kath, and the waitress was at the table asking them if they would like coffee.

They had coffee, but Kath asked no more

41

questions about children and carefully avoided
any further talk about her own, although her
conversation had earlier been peppered with
anecdotes about ten-year-old Zack and eight-
year-old Joe. They were their father's sons
apparently, which Tina took to mean they looked
like him and behaved like him. They were good
kids, Kath had said. They fought at times, but
show her a pair of siblings that didn't.

At a quarter past ten, after most of their fellow
diners had left for home, Tina texted Keaton and
asked him to pick her up at half past. Kath
booked a taxi, despite Tina offering a lift with
her and Keaton. She liked getting taxis, she said.
It made her feel like a proper grown-up person.
Outside the diner they hugged each other
goodbye, and Kath promised to call before
December's reading group meeting.

★　★　★

Keaton pulled away from the kerb and glanced
at Tina.

'Are you all right, darling?' he asked.

'Not really. Not sure.'

'But you had fun?' Keaton changed gear. He
was good at changing gear. She liked watching
him drive. He was smooth and assured.

'Yes. Kath's great. We had a lot of fun.'

'So . . . ?'

Tina turned to look at her husband. She made
her movement definite, defined. She was usually
so slow and quiet — undecided in her actions.
But tonight she felt different.

42

'What is it, Tina?' Keaton asked gently, keeping his eyes on the road. He was ever the careful driver.

'It's high time I got over Meg, isn't it? Properly, I mean. She's dead, isn't she? She's long dead. It happened. It's over.'

6

SEPTEMBER 1954

Now that Edward had gone off to do his national
service, Lucia could relax again. Those last
couple of weeks of the summer holidays, he'd
watched her closely and she knew it, so she had
done the only sensible thing, which was to desist
in her hate campaign against William. She took
to being nice to him instead, playing with him
for hours — no toy-breaking, no pinches. That's
not to say she wasn't tempted, because she was.
But she knew Edward would tell of her, and she
might get into trouble. She couldn't bear the
thought of her mum and dad being cross with
her. They were proud of her. They were also
proud of Edward, but she knew he was the
eldest, so that made him special too. He was
clever, the cleverest of them all. He'd scored A
grades in all his exams. Robert and Ambrose
were nothing to him. Neither was William. Oh,
how it riled her that William was younger than
her, and therefore sweeter and more deserving.
But at least Edward had gone away now, and
when he came back he would soon go away
again to study at his precious university,
somewhere else far away and she would again be
free of his watchful eye. Eight years old, clever
too in her own way, not Edward-clever, but
Lucia-clever. Nobody would ever know all the

44

things she felt and thought.

She had few friends in school. Nobody liked her much, was the simple truth. She looked down her nose at most of the children, and those who she looked up to looked down on her. So she spent playtimes alone mostly, wandering around the yard, planning her next course of action at home. 'That girl is nothing like her brothers,' Lucia overheard one teacher say to another. 'The older one so bright, destined for great things, and the other two, such a pair of happy-go-lucky lads, active — not eleven-plus material of course, but to be fair, not far off it. But Lucia Thornton, she's an odd one.' The words had stung, and Lucia, agonised, had wrung from them every drop of their meaning.

Lucia couldn't even badger Robert and Ambrose at school. She might have asked them to play with her, even though she would have brought down upon her head a hard rain of scorn, but they were much older than her and had already left the village school by the time she started. And now Robert had left school completely and Ambrose was in his last year at their secondary modern, threatening to leave any day, and Dad insisting he stay put, at least until Christmas. Lucia was an embarrassment to her brothers, she knew, as little sisters were apt to be. Well, she'd show them, she'd show them all, even William. Yes, even the new golden child would one day see what his sister was like, what she could do, and who she could be.

Mum was in the back garden picking what remained of the rhubarb. Later, she knew her mum would ask her to help chop it. Mum would stew it for their tea and she wouldn't put in enough sugar. Being 'prudent' with sugar was a habit she'd learned during the war years and after, she said, and she hadn't yet let go of the custom. She would always watch in consternation as Tom, Edward, Robert, Ambrose and Lucia ladled more sugar onto their rhubarb, their apples, their goosegogs.

Lucia was at the dining table, colouring with William. In a surge of impatience, she snatched a crayon from his chubby hand.

'You little brat,' said Lucia as she snapped the crayon in two and threw it on the fire. William began to wail.

'Shut up, you nasty little boy, or I'll throw you on the fire.'

'Me not want to be in fire!' cried William.

'Then be quiet and don't tell Mum. I'm bigger than you, William, and much, much cleverer and Mum likes me best so don't forget it.'

'Me want Nedwood!'

'Edward's gone to be a soldier, so there.'

She wondered what her other brothers were up to. She barely saw them. During the last week of the holidays they had argued, and Ambrose had been punished and made to stay in for two whole days. Lucia had tried to play with him, to talk with him, but she had been brushed aside, and she'd cried until he had grudgingly given in and agreed to do a jigsaw puzzle with her. Her brothers had argued because Ambrose had been the ring leader of a group of boys who had, using sticks, beaten to death a fox cub. Robert had become upset and he'd eventually tried to stop the carnage, but too late. Then Ambrose had turned on Robert with his bloodied stick. Robert had told their father, and he'd asked Ambrose, was it true? And Ambrose had said yes, it was true, all of it, and what's more, it had been fun. Dad, furious, had taken his strap to Ambrose. Lucia had listened to her brother's yelps of pain. Their father had belted him three times. For a day or two the usually inseparable brothers had not spoken. Then they did speak, and Ambrose's sentence had been served; things were back to normal. Now it was the weekend, and the brothers were off out again, all day long, nowhere to be seen.

Lucia toyed with the idea of throwing another crayon on the fire, but she thought she had better not. So instead she coloured with William, and helped him to draw a robin, until Mum came through from the kitchen with her handful of rhubarb, her bowl and her chopping board. She sat in her favourite chair by the fireplace and began the topping and tailing. After a while, she began to cry. Lucia and William stared at her, uncertain of what to do or say. In the end William slid off his chair with a clumsy bump and toddled over to his mum and stood beside her. He put his hand on her knee. Lucia left the table, and kneeling beside her mum, took up the chopping knife and began, carefully and silently, to chop the rhubarb.

'I miss Edward so!' said Mum, after awhile.

'Miss Nedward,' repeated William.

'We all miss Edward,' said Lucia.

Monday 1st December 1975

Dear Elizabeth
I know you havent written back to me yet
because I havent given you enouth time but I
wanted to write to you because I am so exited
for Christmas. This morning I opened the
first door on our advunt calender and Meg
was jealus so she tried to open the second
door and mummy told her off. By the way my
picture was a star and we think Megs will be
a robin. But I will open it properly tomorrow
now because Meg was naughty. What do you
do for Christmas I wonder? You said it was
sunny and warm where you live, I cant
imagine that. Look out for sumething in the
post for you very soon I hope you will like it.
Thank you for saying my writing is good.
Nobody helps me I am just a good writer. I
read a lot. I am the best in my class at school
in reading and writing. I am finishing now
because it is time to get ready for bed. I am
going to give this letter to mummy to post for
me tomorow.
Love from Tina Thornton xx

7

DECEMBER 2013

Keaton arrived in his office at the beginning of December and found an advent calendar sitting on his desk. It was an expensive one with posh chocolates behind each window. It was his favourite brand of chocolate. Keaton looked at it for a while, and scratched his head. Did this mean . . . ? He hoped not. Sharanne (Keaton had long suspected the original spelling was Sharon) was a great secretary. No! She was a great assistant. He supposed she was pretty, but he wasn't sure. She was trim and petite. She wore neat clothes and kept her hair tidy and her fingernails clean and freshly polished. She typed dizzyingly quickly and had a friendly and efficient telephone manner. She was the ideal assistant. And she was in love with Keaton.

Sharanne pushed open his office door with her hip, smiled at her boss and carefully placed a mug of coffee on his desk. One sugar and a generous helping of cream, as Tina had taught him, and he in turn had taught Sharanne.

'Good morning!' she said. 'Happy advent, too,' and she shrugged, looking at the advent calendar.

'Hello, Sharanne,' said Keaton, as he took off his jacket and slung it over the back of his chair. He removed his lunchbox from his bag and

49

placed it in the small fridge in the corner of his office. 'Thank you for the calendar,' he continued, pulling out his chair but not sitting on it. He rested his hands on the back, and tried to look nonchalant. It was too bad of Sharanne, really. 'I think . . . actually it might be better if you . . . if you have this on your desk,' he finished in a rush, feeling his cheeks reddening. Damn it. He wanted to look cool and laid back. But it was impossible. Sharanne, in a brave effort, smiled to show him she was unperturbed, and plucked the calendar from his desk.

'Pre-Christmas detox?' she said, and tried to giggle. He felt dreadfully sorry for her.

'Something like that,' said Keaton, and he sat down to begin his day of work. Sharanne backed from the office and closed the door carefully; Keaton felt he had been reproached, but wrongfully so, and he wanted to ring Tina, to hear her voice. He longed to hear her say, 'It's high time I got over Meg, isn't it?' again, but she had not. 'Properly I mean. She's dead, isn't she? She's long dead. It happened. It's over.' On the Sunday morning after her night out with Kath, Tina had been quiet. Hung over, he'd suspected, so he'd made her breakfast in bed and tried to talk to her, but she'd been unresponsive. So he'd let it go, and days and now weeks had passed. He would have to bring it up again and remind her of what she'd said, before he came to believe that she hadn't said it at all, before the words, the intent behind them, passed irretrievably into memory and imagination. He would do an hour of work, then ring her, by which time she would have showered and dressed, and cleaned up the kitchen. He had not forgotten those words of hers and he never could. They were the most sensible, real thing she had said to him in years. They were words of hope. He had grown to believe he would never hear Tina talk about Meg in such a way. His lovely wife was so under her sister's thumb, her toxic spell, even after all these years, even though she was dead. Decades had passed since the tragedy and drama of their childhoods, yet she could not seem to let go of any of it. It was ridiculous, except it wasn't that simple, because it was much worse than ridiculous. But now . . . perhaps now Tina was ready to turn a corner.

★ ★ ★

Tina had seen Keaton off to work as usual, then sat with her second mug of coffee and finished reading December's reading group choice. It was a book new to her: *A Clockwork Orange* by Anthony Burgess. It was all right, she decided, but she didn't care for the violence. After she finished reading it, she placed the book on the end of the kitchen counter by the backdoor, where she always kept her mobile phone and keys: the things to remember, the things not to lose, the things to take out. The kitchen was neat and tidy and shiny. In the utility room, which was equally neat and tidy and shiny, the laundry basket was empty. The washing machine had been dusted. Last week she had decluttered their bedroom yet again, although Keaton had objected.

51

'We'll have literally nothing left in this house if you carry on like this,' he'd said, carefully removing from the bulging bin liner an old but particularly favourite cowboy shirt (circa 1990), and his old Swiss Army knife. 'It's a useful knife, Tina,' he said, and when she'd protested he'd shown her what it could do, all the gadgets: the efficiency of the bottle opener, the handiness of the corkscrew, the sharpness of the small blades. It was his special toy, clearly. She'd apologised and had given in, and watched him as he'd carefully put his shirt back in his wardrobe, and his knife at the back of the second drawer down of his bedside cabinet.

Her numerous bookshelves in the living room were dusted and her books (the only possessions she refused to get rid of) were stacked in strict alphabetical order. There was really nothing else to do. *Thank goodness*, she thought, *for my cleaning jobs.* She would be lost, utterly lost, without them. She wandered around the house for a long while, cogitating, and opening each door with renewed hope, only to find, over and over, nothing in the rooms but neatness and air. Eventually it was time to head over to Judy and Sandra's house. Three floors, lots of rooms, paintings, books, plants, rugs, well-chosen ornaments, more books, and two cats named Monty and Winston. Much was expected of Tina's time, but she was paid well, sixty pounds for the four hours. Judy and Sandra also encouraged her to borrow their books, which was an undeniable perk.

★ ★ ★

Keaton was disappointed when Tina didn't answer her phone. He supposed she was busy at her cleaning job. He could never remember her working hours. He ignored the infernal answer machine as he always did, and carried on with his work. Sharanne brought in more coffee for him at eleven and placed it on his desk with a small half-smile. The 'thing' Sharanne seemed to have for him had become more than awkward and it was increasingly difficult to ignore. Could she be dismissed? He'd have to refer it up, of course, and get agreement, but it was difficult these days to sack anybody. And did she deserve to be dismissed, truly? It didn't seem fair. She'd get over it, eventually, this stupid crush that Keaton trusted was essentially meaningless. It was nothing to worry about because nothing would ever happen and he thought Sharanne realised that, because she wasn't stupid. She was single, Keaton guessed, and a bit lonely. He didn't understand why she was single, because she was generally regarded as an attractive woman. Certainly their boss Alistair thought so, quite obviously. Keaton had overheard the crude remarks. Sometimes they were directed at him. He always laughed along and said nothing, embarrassed for Alistair, feeling uneasy.

He sipped his coffee and gazed out of the window. Had it been entirely wise of him to have told his wife about Sharanne's apparent attraction to him? He'd mentioned it to Tina back in the summer. Sharanne had been flirty with him all that particular day, he recalled, floating around the offices in a pretty turquoise frock and high-heeled sandals, and Keaton wondered if he hadn't flirted back, just a little bit, just for fun — maybe it had even been to spite Alistair — and he'd gone home that evening feeling hot and bothered, feeling guilty. So after tea as they'd sat out on their patio with a glass of ice-cold wine, he'd told Tina. He'd asked for advice on how to deal with it. He'd played it down, of course. But he'd been as honest as he could be. Tina had appeared calm at the time and laughed it off, they both had. 'Just ignore it,' Tina had said, unconcerned. It had felt the right thing to do, to discuss it with his wife and get her advice. Yet all those secrets she held close to herself, all those feelings she never laid bare . . . It had been a mistake to burden her with his silly problem. It wasn't even a problem, then. He should have known better. But it was too late now.

* * *

The December reading group meeting was uneventful. *A Clockwork Orange* divided the readers. Again, Tina didn't join in much with the discussion. Kath did, and this time there was no need for Tina to pipe up and save her. Half the group seemed to agree with the points Kath made, and she had plenty of support. Tina had little to contribute, apart from the mince pies she'd made that morning. Kath chatted with her as they enjoyed their coffee, into which Kath poured brandy from a miniature bottle — 'It's Christmas!' But Tina could not be cheered. She prepared to leave early, blaming a headache. Everybody was kind about it, and Tess asked her to choose the book for January's meeting. If she could let her know within a week Tess would cascade the information to the other members. Tina and Kath glanced at each other, ghosts of smiles hovering about their lips. Cascade was just one of those words.

★   ★   ★

When Tina arrived home she was soaked through; the rain was falling hard and relentless, a wailing wind tossing it in all directions. Keaton insisted she towel-dry her hair and put on her pyjamas, while he made her a hot water bottle and a mug of hot chocolate, topped off with abundant swirls of cream and chocolate sprinkles, just as she liked it.

'Drive next time, Tina. I know you wanted to walk for the exercise, but it's dark out too, and there's no point in getting caught in downpours. You should at least have phoned and I would have picked you up. Darling?'

Tina said little and let him prattle on. He was the gentlest of naggers and she quite liked him to fuss around her. He finally sat down with a mug of hot chocolate for himself, and turned down the television. The wind howled around their house. It was trying to get in, Tina thought.

'Well?' Keaton said. 'How did it go?'

'It was great. Kath was there again.'

'Are you getting together over Christmas?'

'We might meet up for a shopping trip in town

next week. Then go for a coffee . . . '

' . . . and a natter,' Keaton finished for her.

'Kath will do most of the nattering,' said Tina.

'Ah, I see. Good, good. I'm happy that you've . . . I'm happy.'

They each paused to take a sip from their mugs. A log hissed and bubbled in the wood burner. The wind screeched outside.

'Tina?'

'Hmm?'

'Do you remember . . . Can you recall what you said after you went out with Kath last time? As we drove home?'

'I don't think so.'

'I remember. You said, 'It's high time I got over Meg.' Don't you remember saying that?'

'Ye-es,' she said.

'Did you mean it?'

'Oh, Keaton.'

'I think it would be good if you meant it, if you could try to do . . . that.'

'She was my sister.'

'I know, darling.'

They sipped at their hot chocolates. *Keaton has no idea*, Tina thought. And he clearly wasn't going to give this up, not just yet. He had more to say.

'Tina?'

'Yes?'

'I know we've touched on this before, but I think you need to see somebody.'

'What do you mean?'

'I think you still need professional help.'

'Another shrink, you mean?'

'If you want to call it that, yes.'

'We more than touched on it once before. I tried once before. It was a complete waste of time, if you remember.'

'I can't see how else you're ever going to get over all this. How are you going to be . . . free of her?'

'Has it occurred to you that I don't want to be free of her?'

It hadn't. And he didn't believe it. 'Then . . . why did you say you ought to get over her?'

'I don't know why. I honestly don't really recall saying such a thing. Maybe I said something else.'

'No, you definitely said, 'It's high time I got over Meg, isn't it?' I heard you very clearly. It's all so unhealthy, this . . . obsession? Your sister's death . . . Meg's death is a big thing to live with. I do see that. It's not your fault. But it's having a terrible effect on you. You mustn't spend the rest of your life blaming yourself, Tina.'

'You don't understand . . . ' He'd never been this frank with her before. Poor Keaton. How she deceived him.

'Explain it to me, then,' said Keaton, curling his hands earnestly around his mug and leaning forward. 'I'm listening, I'm here. I want to help.'

'I'm beyond help,' said Tina simply, staring through the wood burner's little window where the logs glowed like mercy. Keaton knew how to make a good fire. It was one of his numerous talents. She was so lucky.

'Nobody is ever beyond help, unless they make it so for themselves,' pronounced Keaton, a little

57

loftily, but Tina wanted to believe this. She knew these words were designed to comfort her; she knew they were wise and true words. Keaton meant well and he spoke with common sense and he spoke from the heart. But he didn't get it, nobody did, not even the counsellor last year who had been supposed to know about these things.

'It's complicated,' said Tina, turning to look at her husband's uncomprehending face. She couldn't tell him the truth because if she did she would lose him forever, and really, he was all she had in this world, her one true and complete friend. The truth would destroy everything.

'Look,' he said, carefully placing his mug on the lamp table. He moved from his chair and crouched at her feet and took her hands in his. He pushed her hair back off her face. He tucked it tenderly behind her ear and smiled his most persuasive smile. 'Why don't you try the counselling again? For me, if not for you? I'm finding I'm not coping too well at present. I mean, I am coping . . . but I'd rather not. I wish we could iron out these . . . issues and be happy, I just want us to be happy. I want our . . . our family to be happy.'

Ah, poor Keaton. Poor Keaton Fathers. How he longed to live up to his name. What a silly name, but a nice one too, distinguished and a bit posh, like Keaton himself. Distinguished and posh and switched off. Turned off, turned away, by her. What to do, what to do? She started to hum, but not out loud — no need, mustn't frighten Keaton, mustn't scare him away — only

58

in her head where she knew she spent too much time. But Meg lived there now. Only there. Nowhere else did she exist, and Tina lived there too with her, keeping her company, occasionally foraying out into the world around her. But always coming back, always coming back to her.

Keaton was obviously disappointed.

'Promise me one thing?' he said, standing up. 'Try counselling again. Please? What was her name — Virginia? I thought she was beginning to help you, and I'll pay, you know I'll pay. Think about it. Don't say no again. Please, Tina. We can't go on struggling like this. Neither of us is properly living.'

Tina tried to smile at her husband; she reached out and took his hand in hers, but it was hopeless, and she thought she heard the distant, familiar, girlish, mocking laugh that never left her alone.

8

DECEMBER 1963

The New Year's Eve party beckoned, and all that went with it: the choking smoke-filled air, the music and dancing and fondling, the feuding, the sweating, the kissing, the gossip, the spilling of secrets. Parties were not usually Lucia's favourite pastime, but tonight's was going to be different. She spent all afternoon choosing, and choosing again, her outfit. It had to be perfect. Her favourite, Clive Stubbins, had finally asked her out on a date and she was determined to look the best she ever had. She'd hardly eaten since Christmas Day and as a result she was light-headed and weak. Mum had tried to get her to eat, but Lucia couldn't face food. She told her mother not to bother cooking for her. Her days at work since Christmas had been long and boring, with few customers to fill them, most people choosing not to venture out into the cold. And who had any money left after Christmas anyway? Lucia and Sheila had been set to tidying, cleaning and dusting the shop, restoring order to the stockroom, and making cups of tea in an attempt to stay warm. The days were long and dark, and not even the candy-coloured lights on the Christmas tree in the shop window could brighten them.

Edward had arrived yesterday to spend a

couple of nights at home. His fiancée, Simone, had gone to France to see her family for the New Year. Edward, seasick always, had elected not to go. Lucia wondered if the couple had in fact argued. When he'd arrived he'd been out of sorts. Lucia was just glad he was at home. Since his departure all those years ago, Lane's End House had become rather a drab place. Mum and Dad were not exciting company, William she did her best to ignore, and Ambrose did his best, it seemed, to ignore her. Robert had left for New Zealand a year ago, hungry for travel and adventure after his national service.

Edward and Simone had met at university and they had been boyfriend and girlfriend ever since. They lived together in their rented flat in Primrose Hill in London, an arrangement Mum and Dad had not commented upon. Lucia wondered how they might react if she were to 'live over the brush'. She could only imagine, for she had not once heard her parents discuss the matter. Lucia alone, it seemed, doubted the morals of her brother and soon-to-be sister-in-law. Simone was modern. She was charming. She was French (half-French, as her mother always corrected her). She was also beautiful, and really she should have been easy to like, and perhaps she was. Yet Lucia did not like her.

Clive had asked Lucia to go to the New Year's Eve party on the day after Boxing Day, popping into the shop, it seemed, solely to ask her out. He didn't buy any records. Lucia thought he'd seemed a little awkward. Sheila had listened intently, pretending not to, and Lucia had thrown her a smug look, a haughty smile. Sheila had not smiled back. Something was not quite as it should be. Clive had not seemed thrilled when she'd agreed to go to the dance, and half of her wondered why he had asked her at all. But she'd put these thoughts aside.

She finally chose her favourite and most expensive outfit, which was her black dress that made her look like a blonde Audrey Hepburn; she also picked out her string of fake pearls and her red lipstick. She would go easy on the mascara, as she knew heavy eyes didn't suit her, which was disappointing. But red lipstick did, so she took great care to practice applying it well, blotting and powdering several layers. She chose the right handbag to go with the ensemble, and the right shoes, in fact, her only evening shoes, because she was still saving up for a new pair. She listened to her Helen Shapiro records and sang along with gusto; she washed her hair, she shook talcum powder all over herself, she hummed and danced and preened and sang and made up all that afternoon, ignoring her mother's appeals for her to try to eat something for heaven's sake, to turn down the music, please. She waved away a slice of toast with plum jam that her mother timidly brought upstairs for her. She brushed aside her mother's suggestion that the dress was perhaps a little too . . . summery? Could she get up to the village hall in those shoes? What about the snow?

'It's the fashion,' Lucia said, looking hard into the mirror as she touched up her make-up. 'I'll wear what I like. I couldn't give a fig about the snow. Besides, Ambrose said he'd walk up there with me.'

Finally ready at eight o'clock, she made her way down the steep stairs. Ambrose waited by the front door, anxious to leave. He was going to be meeting a girl at the dance. Mum offered Lucia her winter coat. Lucia declined, despite the heavy snow falling. She had her own coat, thanks.

'It's too thin . . . ' muttered Mum. 'And those shoes . . . '

'Leave it, Mum,' said Edward and he gave his mother's shoulders a gentle squeeze.

'She looks like a princess,' sighed Mum. 'All grown up.'

'She does,' said Edward and he took out his wallet and with a flourish he handed Lucia a ten-bob note. 'Enjoy your evening,' he said. He winked at her. Lucia blushed.

'Really?' she said.

'Of course! Take it. Have a good time. Mum and I will keep the home fires burning for when you get back.'

Lucia reached over and kissed Edward's cheek. She took the money.

★ ★ ★

She left her (too thin) coat hanging with all the others in the foyer. After almost slipping just trying to get down the front door steps, Lucia had been forced to admit she couldn't walk through the snow in her shiny black court shoes, with or without Ambrose's help, so she'd

63

trudged up in her wellingtons, and left them neatly paired on the floor beneath her coat. It was like being back at school. She knew that her boots would no longer be neatly paired when it was time to go home. She was relieved to see she wasn't the only partygoer who'd felt the need for more suitable footwear. No need to feel silly. She quickly put on her party shoes. When she looked up, Ambrose had already gone in, leaving her alone in the cold, damp foyer. She straightened up, breathed deeply, smoothed back her platinum hair and faced the wooden doors with the large round handles. This was it.

She didn't want to walk into the hall on her own, but when she swung open the doors and walked in, nobody took any notice of her. The village hall was thronging with young people from miles around. It was festooned with paper chains, lanterns and streamers. She looked around for Clive, and saw him at the bar, which was already three people deep. She waved, and he half-waved back and mimed drinking. She nodded and mouthed, 'Babycham.' He nodded, and looked away from her. He looked at the floor. *He doesn't took happy*, she thought. And it would have been better if he had picked her up at home and walked her here, so they could have arrived together, and everybody would have known. It hadn't felt right, walking up with Ambrose. Lucia looked around for a table, and saw two chairs free at one end of a long trestle. She sat down and spotted her brother, standing with a pretty girl in a corner up by the stage. She watched, fascinated, as he kissed her. Lucia

noted the girl's simple ponytail, her dark blue pencil skirt, her short-sleeved blouse, her sturdy arms. Lucia stared as the arms snaked around her brother's neck. Mum was worried that her third-born son was going to get some poor young girl 'into trouble' one day. Carousing like he did. Lucia had shrugged. It was up to him, wasn't it? It would be his fault. Mum, you worry too much. We're grown-ups now.

Clive eventually joined her, bearing two Babychams and a large tankard of something dark. He didn't want to have to go up to the bar again, he said, not for a while. Lucia wondered if he was trying to get her tipsy. She didn't get tipsy. Unlike William, who was now regularly sneaking drinks from the cabinet at home, and watering what remained down. He thought he was being so clever.

Clive carefully placed the drinks on the sticky table. He sat down opposite her. Lucia waited. The room was unnaturally hot. It was noisy. Yet Clive was quiet and restrained and she didn't know why, and she wasn't about to ask. Something was amiss. The romantic date she'd anticipated was melting away. Out of the corner of her eye she was aware of Ambrose's hand sliding up and down the girl's thigh. Which girl was it? Lucia didn't know. She had lost touch with almost everybody in the village. But for Clive's invitation, she wouldn't even be here.

'I like your dress,' he managed in the end.

'Thank you.'

'You look a bit like Audrey Hepburn but with blonde hair.'

'Thank you.'

And their silence grew monstrous, amid all the noise and music and jollity, and she feared she was going to cry. This wasn't how it was supposed to be. This was no date. She caved in.

'What's the matter?' she asked, taking the horrible maraschino cherry in her mouth and chewing, then swallowing it. It was the only thing she had eaten all day, and it was revolting. She took a mouthful of Babycham. Her head span. She felt a wave of nausea flow into her. Ambrose and the girl were kissing, cuddling. Lucia looked away, fascinated but embarrassed.

'I don't know what the matter is,' said Clive.

'You must know what's eating you?' she said. It was difficult to make herself heard above the din, but he had heard her.

'I do know,' he said. 'Yes. I know. But I can't — we can't — look, I really like you.'

'I really like you.'

'But I can't take you out.'

'Why not?' she asked, chilled at last. The snow and her unheated bedroom and the inappropriately sleeveless dress had not chilled her. But now she was frozen. She didn't understand. She took another sip of Babycham. Her head span.

'You're only engaged, Clive,' she said, hoping he would hear her. The music was becoming ever louder. 'That's not the same thing as married. Besides, didn't you tell me and Sheila that you didn't like your . . . your fiancée that much and it's your mothers who want you to get married and not you or even her?'

'I'm not engaged any more,' he said.

'But that's good, isn't it?'

'No, it's not good. I'm a bastard, Lucia. I really am.'

'No. You're nice,' and she leaned across the table and placed her cold white hand over his warm, strong one. It was a pity he'd felt the need to swear, but she could ignore that.

'Shall we go outside?' he said, pulling away his hand and standing up. 'Bring your drink if you like.' She picked up her glass, and looked across towards the stage, but Ambrose and the pencil-skirted girl had disappeared. She thought she saw some billowing of the thick stage curtains.

Snow was still falling. She had liked snow, the soft ease of it, as a child, but not any more, not tonight. She hadn't been able to find her coat as she'd followed Clive from the hall. She'd spotted one of her Wellington boots, kicked around and jumbled up in the melee of outer garments and boots. So she shivered in her party shoes and her little black dress, clutching her Babycham, as she and Clive stood quietly together around the side of the building, beneath a window that beamed the pulsing hall's yellow light out into the night. Mostly Clive talked, while she listened. His talk was rapid and earnest and to the point, leaving her in no doubt. Lucia's teenaged heart hardened there in the ice and snow. It hardened against Clive, against Sheila, and it hardened against the world, every last inch of it. Something in her, small and quivering, closed up for good.

'You creep!' she shouted once he had said

what he needed to say, and after his silence had become one with the soft-falling snow. She smashed her glass into the wall and bits of it flew all about, performing a strange dance with the snowflakes, glinting treacherously in the hall light. She had to go home, get out of there. How could he, how could she!? Lucia failed to stifle a sob. She turned to go from Clive and with no warning at all she vomited, all over her dress, all over her shoes, all over the snow, and her humiliation was complete.

Sunday 18th January 1976

Dear Elizabeth
Thank you for the lovely Barbie doll you sent me for Xmas (that means Christmas) she is a beatiful doll and I've never seen a Barbie before. Meg is jelous but not very jelous because she doesnt like dolls much. Meg says Hello. In England we have Sindy dolls. I will try to send one to you for your birthday in March, I havent forgoton you see. I love my new doll so much. Iv'e named her Elizabeth because you sent her to me. I am glad you liked the bath cubes but its a shame that some of them got crumbled up in the mail. (We would say in the post.) Some of my Sindy cloths fit Elizabeth but some dont because the dolls are diffrent shapes. For Christmas Meg and I were given a big jar of aniseed sweets. They are orange and deliciuss. We are back at school now. I like the holidays and I am sad to be back at school. My teacher is called Miss
Tyson. She is nice.
Love from your cousun in England,
Tina x

9

DECEMBER 2013

Meg was in a sulk, Tina could sense. Tina had not visited the grave for nigh on a month. But the last couple of visits had been so upsetting, so disappointing, so . . . frightening. Tina managed to ignore the echoing twin-voice in her mind that never let her go. She'd decided to let her sister sulk. She had to get over it. Tina had a life. Tina had a new friend. Kath was nice and she was funny. She sent text messages. Meg had never sent a text message.

On the morning after December's book group meeting, as she drank her coffee and ate four slices of toast spread thickly with peanut butter, Tina decided she would give in and go to the grave today. She owed it to her sister. December was not an easy month. Apart from August, and the birthdays, Christmas was the hardest time.

★　★　★

Meg was definitely in a sulk. She answered questions in monosyllables. On visits like these, it seemed to Tina that the eight-year-old Meg was present, not the forty-six-year-old. The eight-year-old Meg was disconcerting. She was a little girl who didn't get it, who didn't understand what it was to be an adult.

'I went to my reading group again yesterday,' Tina said. Perhaps it was unwise to mention the book group. To talk about these sorts of things ... they were boasts, really, weren't they? Luckily, the group was something of a departure, because Tina rarely socialised, and she felt reprieved. Meg would have to try to understand. Tina had a life. That was just the way it was. She glanced around. The few people present were quietly going about their business. Only the woman in the green coat was near, reading as she often was.

Meg said, 'What exactly is that anyway? A 'reading group'?'

'It's kind of a social thing. We all read the same book, then get together once a month to talk about it.'

'It sounds am-maaaayz-ing.'

'It's all right. Actually, it's fun. I love talking about books. I've been asked to choose January's book. I've picked *I Capture the Castle*.'

'Stupid.'

'It's not stupid. It's brilliant. It's by Dodie Smith.'

'So what?! Stupid name.'

'I always wanted to be Cassandra Mortmain. Once upon a time I suppose I was her. Well, like her anyway. Sort of.'

'What are you blathering on about?'

'Nothing. Doesn't matter. I made a cake yesterday.'

'Most of which you consumed yourself, I presume?'

'No, I — '

Tina winced before she even heard Meg's unkind words; she knew what the words would be, in essence: 'You're getting fatter and fatter.' It was nastily said, and it was ill-meant. Tina was never sure how to handle this sort of remark. Should she ignore it? Or try to be nice? Meg was so juvenile!

'I like food,' was all Tina could think of in reply. She did like food. It was one of the biggest pleasures of her life, and one of her surest refuges, along with books and cleaning. She had always hoped that Meg might understand that, but she had never seemed to. 'I like food, that's all,' repeated Tina, and it sounded no less pathetic the second time.

'You eat far too much,' said Meg. Tina knew she ate too much. It was a habit cultivated over many years, and nobody was surprised by it and nobody even thought about it any more. Certainly nobody ever mentioned it, apart from Meg. Christ, she was annoying today. Why on earth had she bothered to visit? So what if it was December? There was no good will in Meg, none at all.

'Leave me alone,' said Tina. 'I came out here to visit you today. How about a little kindness?'

'You're going to burst one of these days,' said Meg. 'What a nice mess that will be!'

Before Tina could prevent them, her words flew out, each one a poison-tipped arrow arching towards the crumbled ramparts of her sister's soul.

'It's better than not eating at all!'

The silence was solid, invincible for a few long

moments. Tina was flooded with instant regret. She burned with shame.

'Let's not talk like this,' Meg said in such a whispered voice that Tina barely heard her. 'Please.'

Tina found herself gabbling an apology to her sister, who did not hear it. There was no point in staying any longer, not today — Meg was beyond her. Tina backed away, whispered goodbye, and left. Driving home, she reproached herself. She shouldn't have been so unkind. There should have been a proper goodbye. As she pulled up on the drive at home and switched off the engine, Tina wondered if Meg didn't sometimes deserve the loneliness. She hadn't always been a kind sister. But Tina hated that thought and let it go. She felt she could see it, her bad thought, a thing, lifted up on a breeze, floating away across rooftops and treetops and oceans, and landing in someone else's life, a long way away. And that was forgiveness, Tina thought.

★   ★   ★

The woman in the green coat sat alone. All was quiet again. Just when she was beginning to understand Tina's routine, the routine had been broken. The visits were weekly, most weeks. Thursdays often, Wednesdays occasionally, like today. But not recently: one, two, three, almost four weeks had passed with no sign of her. She'd considered giving up her vigil entirely. But that would not do. She could not give up. So she continued her visits to the cemetery, hoping to spot Tina. And today Tina had come, and stayed a while, and shouted again, and stumbled off.

And was she partly to blame? Yes, of course she was, partly. But it was too late to change what had already gone, too late to alter what was in the past. You could only look forward and plan ahead. So she came here, Wednesdays, Thursdays, Fridays, waiting, trying to get up the courage to speak.

It was simple. If you felt guilty, you had to do something about it, before it was too late.

10

DECEMBER 1963

Lucia struggled home through the thick snow, slipping many times. The village hall wasn't so very far from home, a matter of yards on a sunny day, but tonight, it may as well have been miles. In the end she carried her shoes and struggled on in stockinged feet. The lane that led down to home was particularly arduous. She slipped and fell, five, six, seven or more times. She felt drunk, although she wasn't drunk, as she hadn't even finished that first Babycham. She tasted vomit, she smelled of vomit, she was in the worst mess she had ever been in, in every way. She just wanted to be at home. So she forced one foot in front of the other, sunk her feet into deep cold snow, and clenched and unclenched her fists in a futile attempt to keep her hands warm. She may as well have been naked. If she passed out and fell down, she could die, her body frozen and undiscovered, perhaps until morning.

'Keep . . . going . . . one . . . foot . . . one . . . foot. Keep going'

When she finally arrived home and let herself in at the kitchen door, Mum was there in her mauve house coat, preparing cups of tea. She stared at Lucia.

'My God! Lucia? Oh, Lucia! Tom! Edward!'

Mum ran the bath, boiling the kettle and saucepans in the kitchen to top up the water. She and Edward trailed up and down the stairs a dozen or more times between them. William was summoned from his bedroom by the commotion and Lucia, undressing in her bedroom, heard him ask what was going on. Mum assured him it was nothing to worry about and shooed him back to his room. Mum took Lucia's clothes downstairs, 'to soak'.

In the bath at last, any part of her that wasn't submerged was horribly cold. She lay back and sank herself into the water, right up to her chin. Mum had been generous with the bath salts and Lucia could no longer smell vomit. The bathroom was silent. Condensation formed on its pink walls. She could hear muffled voices from downstairs; no doubt her parents and eldest brother were speculating about what had happened to her. Soon the long-drawn bath worked its magic, and the water's heat penetrated first her skin, then her guts, then her bones. She closed her eyes. She felt the hot tears forming. If she kept her eyes closed could she keep them in forever? The bath water steamed, lapping at her body even with her slight movements. This must be how it felt to be truly warm, from the inside out. She stayed in the hot bath, trying not to move, for half an hour, until the water eventually became too cool. She got out, dried, brushed her teeth, and dressed herself in her nightie and house coat and slippers. When she opened the bathroom door, William was sitting at the top of the stairs, apparently waiting for her. He stood up.

'You all right?' he said. His lip wobbled.

'Yes. Thanks. I'm fine.'

'You must have been so cold.'

'It's horrid out there.'

'But now you're home and safe.'

'Yes.'

'Can I use the loo? I want to go back to bed. I'm knackered.'

A *little tipsy too*, she thought. He must have had a tipple with Dad and Edward. She didn't think it entirely wise of them. But it was sweet of him to have waited patiently for her; he'd not pounded on the door, yelling at her to hurry up, as he might have done.

'It's all yours,' she said.

She went downstairs and Edward insisted she take the seat nearest the fire. He stoked up the blaze, piling on the coals. Dad prepared to go to bed now he was satisfied his daughter was restored.

'Where's Ambrose?' Dad asked. Lucia looked at Edward, he looked back at her.

'Right,' said Dad. 'Lock up before you go to bed. If he hasn't got his key that's his look out. You bits of kids . . . '

Mum insisted on making cocoa for Lucia. She needed it, she said. She bustled off into the kitchen and returned a few minutes later with her favourite tray laden with two mugs of cocoa, one each for Lucia and Edward, and a tea plate of artfully arranged Nice biscuits. 'For heaven's sake, eat something,' she remonstrated with her daughter.

'Go on up, Mum,' said Edward. 'I'll wait for Ambrose.'

After a minute or two of further fussing, Mum was finally persuaded to go to bed. She stroked Edward's shiny brown hair. She kissed Lucia and held her hand for a moment. Then she left them and they listened as she made her slow way up the steep staircase.

The cocoa was hot and thick, and Lucia leaned back in her chair and stretched herself out. Her house coat slipped away, leaving her thin white legs exposed to the warmth of the fire. She felt like a child again, cossetted and loved. Edward sipped his cocoa. They each ate a Nice biscuit. For a long while they were silent. Then Lucia recalled her struggle home, the reasons for leaving the dance, Ambrose and the girl who had disappeared behind the curtain together, Clive's handsome face . . .

'Don't cry, Loose Ear,' said Edward, and he put down his cocoa and came to her. He gently eased her mug from her thin white hands. His hands shook. He smelled of booze. *He is*, she thought, *trying very hard to appear sober.* It wasn't a bad effort. He kneeled before her. 'You're still so cold!' he said, and he placed both his hands over hers and chafed them, rubbing gently, and Lucia stared at her kind, graceful brother in awe. He looked handsome in his pale blue shirt, his slacks, his brown hair slicked back, his eyes so blue, such a nice deep blue.

'You're only seventeen,' he said, out of

nowhere. He continued to rub her hands, back and forth, fast, then slower, then he stroked her hands, her wrists, gently, absent-mindedly. 'Don't set too much store by the likes of Clive Stubbins,' he said, almost in a whisper. 'Isn't he engaged anyway?'

'Like you,' said Lucia.

'Like me,' said Edward. He laughed mirthlessly.

'Are you excited about the wedding?' Lucia said. 'Simone must be.'

'Oh yes, she can't wait to be princess for a day,' said Edward.

'Me too,' said Lucia.

'Of course. And you will make a very beautiful one, I'm sure.' Edward continued to stroke her hands. He stared into the fire. 'And I suppose I shall be the prince.'

'You will make a fine prince.'

'We'll see.'

'Have you and Simone had a row?'

He looked at her, looked away, looked back. 'A little one,' he finally confessed. He shrugged.

'What about?'

'Oh, nothing much. It's me. I think I'm getting cold feet.'

'I know all about that,' said Lucia, and they both chuckled. He still stroked her hands, and she thought it might have been as much for his comfort as hers. He was clearly upset, despite the matter-of-fact words, the chuckling. He gazed into the fire, his eyes moist.

'Seriously,' he continued, 'yes, we had a row. I told her to stop pestering me with wedding talk.

It wasn't nice of me and she flounced off to France to visit her parents. She'd half-decided to go anyway. I must have pushed her over the edge, if you like. The truth is she didn't even ask me to go with her.'

'I see.'

'Heigh-ho. These things happen. I'll iron it all out when she gets back.'

'I don't think Ambrose will be home tonight,' she said, staring now at her brother's smooth hands as he continued to stroke hers.

'I thought as much,' said Edward. 'He's a law unto himself, that brother of ours.'

'I am too,' said Lucia, struggling to keep any defensiveness out of her voice. Just for once, couldn't they talk about her?

'That's true!' he said, and laughed. Lucia didn't laugh. Why was he laughing? Why was he laughing at her? She was not a laughing stock. She was not. She would show him. She would! Almost midnight now. She took hold of his hands in hers and held them still.

'Happy new year, Edward,' she said softly.

'Happy new year,' he said, and he leaned across and kissed her forehead.

Up on the main road a car horn blared, there were distant shouts and woops. A firework went off. And the house so quiet, the fire beginning to smoulder, just the two of them, up and waiting for their wayward brother who, they both knew, would not be home tonight. Her whole body was glowing, aflame. She slowly placed her brother's hands on her naked knees. His hands were warm; he made to pull them away but she made

80

them stay, pressing them to her using all her feeble strength. She leaned upwards, forwards, and she kissed his mouth. He tasted of rum, hot and sweet. He tried again to pull away, he might have said no, but his hands ran up her thighs. He kissed her. Properly. Mum and Dad and William were upstairs, asleep she hoped, mere yards away, but worlds away, and even Ambrose could come home at any moment, and with the thrust and scrape of the kitchen door all would be lost. But she knew he would not come. He would spend the night elsewhere, with that girl at the dance. Edward was warm and strong. She was perfectly safe. She could hardly be any safer, at this moment, in this house, with this man. Her time had come. This was how it felt to be truly warm, from the inside out.

Sunday 15 Febuary 1976

Dear Elizabeth
Thank you for the Valentines Day card, it is
so sweet and I like it a lot. Meg says it is the
only Valentines Day card I am ever going to
get but she is just jealos because she did'nt
get one at all and I did even though I know
its from you it still counts. I am sorry I didn't
send you one but in England we send them
to people we secretly love. You do'nt write
your name you write a? so the person you
send it to has to guess who you are. Our
Grampy died at the end of January. He was
71 years old which is very old and he was'nt
ill he just woke up dead one morning and I
cried but Meg did'nt and Aunty Lucia did'nt
ether but Granny cried a lot and kept saying
he worked too hard he worked so hard and
poor Tom, poor Tom and she cried such a lot
and kept going on about how he missed
Robert (thats your dad) and Ambroze, poor
Ambroze, I do'nt know who that is, and poor
Toms disapointmunt and he never got over it
and Aunty Lucia said hush before too much
is said and she looked at me and Meg and
opened her eyes wide at Granny who nodded
and went quiet. Granny is old too and she sits
in her chair with a blankit on her knees
watching things like Pebbul Mill which I
think is boring because its just people talking

82

but through the windows you can see cars going past on the road. My favourite programme on telly is Bagpuss. A little girl called Emily has a cuddly fat stripy toy cat he is Bagpuss and she has her own shop with things in it that she finds. Do you get Bagpuss?

Love from your couzun in England,

Tina xx (these are kisses in case you wandered)

11

DECEMBER 2013

It was a Friday in mid-December and busy everywhere, even at the cemetery.

'You decided to come back then,' said Meg. Tina had tidied the grave and was sitting on the nearest bench. Meg was beside her.

'I came back,' said Tina. 'As if I wouldn't.'

'As if,' agreed Meg.

'I had a row with Keaton,' said Tina, and she burst into tears. Meg said nothing. She waited for Tina to stop crying. 'Well, it was a sort of row. The closest we ever come. We had words.'

'What were the words about?' said Meg.

Meg was so nosy. Yet Tina herself had brought the subject up, so obviously she wanted to discuss it. Didn't she? 'I don't really know,' she said.

'You're such a fibber,' said Meg.

Tina thought her sister tossed her hair. It's what she would have done. 'He wants me to go back to that woman,' said Tina. 'It's all he talks about at the moment.'

'What woman?'

'Virginia,' said Tina, guarded now and wishing she'd said nothing. Meg didn't hold with counselling any more than Tina did.

'Who the hell is Virginia?'

'You know. The . . . shrink woman.'

'Oh, not that crap again? Honestly, some people . . . ' and Meg lapsed into a disapproving silence, until, 'And?'

'And what?'

'Are you going back?'

'I don't know.'

'Oh, for Christ's sake!' and nothing further was said for a moment or two. Tina thought Meg had closed her eyes. As a child she'd closed her eyes and smacked her own forehead in frustration, or disgust, whenever Tina said or did anything stupid, which was often.

'You know why he's doing this don't you?' said Meg, leaning forward and staring at Tina, who tried to stare back but found she couldn't. It was hard to focus sometimes, hard to see through the fug and fog and bleariness of her mind; her inner life, which was more real to her than anything around her, more real than Keaton and coffee cake and graves and logs hissing in wood burners.

'Yes, I know why,' said Tina.

'No. You don't though. It's because he's fed up with you being nutty and he's thinking of running off with that secretary of his. He's trying to put the frighteners on you.'

'Rubbish,' said Tina, picking lint (that may or may not have been there) from her coat, and sitting up straight. She wasn't going to listen to such nonsense. 'Meg, honestly . . . '

'You'll see,' said Meg, with malicious confidence. Keaton's secretary — assistant — was somebody Tina tried to ignore. The thought of her, the nagging doubts that lingered in her mind, even though she knew Keaton was a man to be implicitly trusted. Tina did not feel threatened. She knew Keaton could handle such things, and nothing terrible would come of it. She had felt light about the whole thing, that evening last summer when Keaton had . . . confessed, almost, to his assistant's feelings for him.

The sisters were quiet for a few moments.

'Tina?'

'What?'

'Don't bother with counselling. It's a waste of time and they'll crush your soul and make you believe in all sorts of nonsense.'

'Oh, Meg, come — '

'And they'll steer you away from me. You'll stop believing in me and we'll never — '

'Meg . . . ' warned Tina, but Meg was not listening.

'And we have things to do, right? We have unfinished business to attend to.'

'No. I do, apparently. Me.'

'That's the way it is. I can't help that any more than you can.'

'That's not quite true. I could have helped it. I could have done more. It would have been all right but for me.'

'What the hell are you talking about?'

'Forget it, Meg,' said Tina.

'Shan't. What are you going on about?'

'*That day.*'

'I thought we didn't talk about *that day?*' said Meg, mocking, and Tina knew it was time to end the conversation but she couldn't, not this time, she had more things to say and she felt she ought

86

to say them. Rarely had it been sensibly discussed, if at all. If it was all right for Meg to say startling things, it was all right for her as well.

'I know you think it wasn't my fault, but it was,' Tina said. 'It truly was.'

'You are joking?'

'No. I'm not joking.'

'You know good and damned well whose fault it was!' cried Meg, and she reached out her hand, and Tina took it. Meg's hand was cold, so cold, and so light it may not have been there, resting in Tina's larger hand, which was strong and sturdy and warm by comparison. 'And we don't talk about *that day*,' continued Meg. 'Remember? And until you face up to the truth of it — '

'No, no!' Tina snatched her hand away, and stood up. 'I won't listen to this. I can't any more.'

'Chicken,' said Meg.

'What did you say?'

'I said 'chicken' because that's what you are!' cried Meg. 'And you're stupid too. You actually believe in your philandering husband and your tiny, tiny life!'

'How dare you? At least I have a life, at least I haven't — '

'Shut up!'

'Well, don't you dare bring Keaton into this! He'd never cheat on me, never. He's not that kind of man.'

'We'll see,' said Meg and she chuckled, cruel and derisory.

'Fuck you, Meg,' said Tina, shocked at her

87

own words. Meg had wound her up before, of course, thousands of times, but rarely did Tina swear. It wasn't her style.

'Fuck yourself,' said Meg. 'Better still, fuck Keaton before that secretary of his does.'

'Assistant,' said Tina quietly, her voice floating away from her, taken and lost. These arguments with Meg were exhausting; ephemeral. They were impossible to win, and perennially circular. Why couldn't Meg just let it go? It happened. It's over.

Kath had said those words with such confidence, such conviction and simplicity. Kath was a good person. Perhaps she was somebody Tina could talk to about all this? Perhaps Kath could help after all, like Meg had hoped, just not in the way she had hoped. Perhaps Kath could help Tina, if not Meg, who was beyond help, but refused to know it. Damn her! And now something else, another crazy idea, this new but not-new idea, that Sharanne was in love with Keaton. Was Keaton in — ? No. No. Some thoughts were unthinkable. She mustn't take any notice of Meg's nonsense. She rose from the bench. She muttered goodbye to her sister, who of course did not reply.

★   ★   ★

Keaton arrived home from work to find his wife sprawled across their sofa. She appeared to be drunk. She'd evidently opened one of their bottles of wine they'd been saving for Christmas, and it languished on the floor next to the sofa.

He picked it up — almost empty. Defensive and short-tempered, Tina said she could drink if she damn well wanted to and she'd had a bad visit with Meg. She'd had a bad day. You know, like he did sometimes, and came home and had a glass of wine? That was supposed to be that, Keaton could tell, but he wasn't satisfied. Had she forgotten it was his work's Christmas do tonight? The thirteenth of December? This year she'd said she'd join him. Had she forgotten?

She had forgotten. She couldn't go now, she claimed. She felt dreadful. She'd eaten already and she wasn't hungry any more and she felt like she could throw up. He'd have to go without her. She was sickening for a cold too, on top of everything else. She'd been so chilly visiting Meg. Why did she even bother? Keaton shook his head and withdrew from the lounge and took the stairs two at a time. He stripped off his work clothes and jumped into the shower. He had about forty-five minutes. Had Tina remembered to book a taxi? He doubted it, and what did it matter now anyway? She clearly wasn't going to join him, not in that state, so he'd drive himself there and take a taxi home. He might even walk back. The hotel was only five miles or thereabouts from home, not so far. He liked to walk, especially on cold, clear nights. He could get a taxi back to the hotel in the morning and pick up the car. He'd known deep down that Tina wouldn't go, because she never did. But he had hoped, and he certainly hadn't expected to arrive home and find her drunk.

He tried not to imagine what had happened

89

this day to his wife. It was becoming boring, this way of carrying on. Her mental state was an increasing worry to him, but he was running out of ideas. What more could he do? If she wouldn't go to counselling, he couldn't force it. She was a grown woman and she could make her own decisions. It seemed to him, as he showered, that the only thing he could possibly do was to give up trying to help her, and give up on his dream of being a father, and let Tina carry on as she was. He would be there for her, of course. He loved her, absolutely and without conditions. But he couldn't change anything and he was tired. He was tired of nagging. This time, she would just have to deal with it in her own way. He was going out for once, and he was going to have fun.

He turned off the shower, stepped out and wrapped the towel around himself. Fleetingly, so fleeting he was barely aware of framing the thought, he wondered what Sharanne would be wearing to the party.

12

JANUARY 1964

Lucia thought she heard Edward leave on the morning of New Year's Day, but she wasn't sure. She was in bed, and could not get out. The chill her mother had foretold last night was upon her. 'Walking home barefoot in the snow, Tom! She'll catch her death' — and she had. In her night-mare visions she saw her brothers. They were monsters, all. Even William, in truth a harmless soul, but there he was, looming over her, breath-ing fire, wielding an axe. She closed her eyes. They were already closed. She heard a voice.

Did she cry out? Had she cried out? Had she dreamed it?

She thought she heard her parents and William say goodbye to Edward as they stood at the foot of the stairs. She thought she heard his car struggle up the lane in the snow. That must be why he had gone earlier than planned. The snow. It's stopped snowing at any rate, she thought she heard her dad say. The snow was in her mouth. She was choking. His hand covered her mouth. Be quiet, oh be quiet.

She'd made love to Clive Stubbins. But it wasn't Clive. It was never Clive.

Mum was at her bedside. She worried — 'Should I call the doctor?' 'She's caught a chill that's all. Stop your fussing, Anne.' Later,

Helen Shapiro was at her bedside, crooning a lullaby. Lucia reached out her hand to her; she wanted to tell her what had happened, but she knew she could not. Helen was singing, just singing and smiling. And soon she was gone.

They wouldn't understand. Nobody would ever understand. But had she dreamed it? There was stickiness all over her. Perhaps it was sweat. Perhaps it was blood. Perhaps it was something else. She was on fire yet she had snow in her mouth; she was lying in snow. But the snow was hot. Oh, what had they done? He was gone. Back to his London flat and his half-French fiancée whose name was Simone and who would be coming home from France, when of course they would kiss and make up and get married. And in the early days, the university days, when Lucia used to stand in the corner and stare at her, Simone came for tea twice and Mum had made buns the one time and scones the other and she had thought Simone marvellous: such a nice girl! But Mum was wrong. She was frilv . . . frivolv . . . what was it? Frivolous! Simone was frivolous.

Simone must never know. Nobody must ever know what they had done. What had they done? There was one person she could tell wasn't there? 'Mum? Mum?! I — ' 'Hush, Lucia, sleep now, dearest.' Coldness on her forehead, her mother's cold hand, a cold flannel smelling of bath salts. Her brother's hot hands. Her hot hands, their hot mouths together. The stickiness between her thighs. The life she might have led. Nobody must know.

Monday 1st March 1976

Dear Elizabeth
I got your letter and I really like the paper
and matching envelope you have nice things
in America. I wish I could live there. It is still
cold here even though it is supposed to be
springtime now because it is March. Wow-
wee, you are so lucky to have a new baby
sister, and I like her name. My grannys house
is changeing. Aunty Lucia has taken over, it is
more or less her house now she says and she
is throwing things away. She says a clutered
house is a clutered mind and no wander
Grampy was sumething, but I cant remember
what she said. It was'nt very nice about her
own dad. Granny got upset and cried but
Aunt Lucia tutted and told her to keep out of
it and not interfeer, she knows what she is
doing. Meg and me went there for tea after
school today. Mummy went to see her frend
and she was'nt back in time to make our tea.
Aunty Lucias food is dry and it tastes funny,
a bit like old bread. At school we are going to
have baby chicks, we have an incubator and
its warm and I cant wait to see the babys
when they hatch. Miss Tyson says we will be
able to cuddle them if we are carefull. I am
always careful with little animals but Meg
and me are still not allowed to have a rabbit.
I'm reading a good book called The Diddakoi

93

by a writer with a funny name it is Rumer Godden. It is a fantastic story, please read it if you get the chance. The girl in the story is called Kizzy and she's a bit like me and Meg except we're not gipsys. Its been on telly too which I watched and so did Meg and we really liked it. It was called Kizzy on telly. If it is ever on your telly PLEASE WATCH IT! I am sending you a card for your birthday and a packet of my favourite sweets which is Tooty Frooties. I hope there are a lot of purple ones because they are the best.
I have to go now, Meg wants me,
Love from Tina xx

13

DECEMBER 2013

Keaton wondered as he drove home if it might be worth getting a pet for Tina. A cat, possibly? A dog might be too much, and besides, he didn't like dogs. But really, the idea was soft — it was silly. He was clutching at straws, he knew, just casting around in the darkness for something to hold on to. He was driving home from the Christmas do with a head full of empty and useless ideas, yet he couldn't wait to get home and talk to Tina about them. Two cats, maybe? A little cat family? Like that historian couple who Tina cleaned house for on Mondays. She was fond of their cats. Surely she would love a pet of her own? He opened the car window and breathed deeply, wanting cold fresh air in his lungs and in his head. He'd had only the one drink, an ill-advised gin and tonic, and hadn't enjoyed it much; in fact, he'd thought himself in some kind of danger as he'd felt the alcohol begin its hideous dance in his blood.

And a holiday, he thought. They should take a holiday somewhere nice, somewhere exotic, perhaps before they got the cat? Tina needed a break, and so did he. Something had to give, something had to change. A cruise, maybe? Time to relax, see the world, swim, read? An exotic holiday followed by their very own little pet family. It would be just the ticket. Maybe. It was something, at least.

The images of the party and the images of Sharanne intruded at last, despite his efforts to ignore them. She had been so pretty tonight and slim, dressed in a black dress and high-heeled shoes — simple, a classy look. Red lipstick. And they'd pulled a cracker together and she'd put on her purple paper hat and read out her motto in her sharp, confident voice and everybody had laughed. And that was the trouble. She was highly regarded at work; she was efficient and bright. She was funny. Alastair and everybody else thought a lot of her. It would be difficult to undo this, to speak to her, but he would have to try. He couldn't do this thing that she clearly wanted him to do. It was beyond doubt now. But it could not happen. Even if he . . . which he didn't. He absolutely did not. He was in control, utterly. Maybe the purely male part of him, the part of him that drifted aimlessly somewhere between his brain and his bollocks, the part that physically assessed women whether he wanted it to or not, that part that decided yes or no in a second, less than a second, maybe that was beyond his control, maybe that part of him was attracted to Sharanne. But he was married and wasn't marriage all about ignoring that part of your being? Isn't that what decent men did? He was married, and not to just anybody, but to Tina, his suffering and tortured wife, his good friend.

He arrived home. He sat for a few moments in the silent and rapidly cooling car, composing himself. He knew now what temptation tasted like, and it was bitter.

★ ★ ★

Tina was awake when he got in, which surprised him. She was hung-over, she said. Why on earth had she drunk so much that afternoon? She was sorry not to have made it to the dinner. Anyway, how was the food, the disco? Did he have fun? Did Alastair get drunk and make an exhibition of himself on the dance floor again? And would Keaton get a hot chocolate and come and sit with her? She'd made a decision.

'What's this decision, then?' asked Keaton, after he'd made the drinks. He sidled along the sofa to be next to his wife. She smelled nice, she smelled reassuring — she smelled like Tina. Of course, she was Tina, and it was good to be with her again. It had been too long. Just a few hours, but so long. She smelled of clean skin, fabric conditioner, and faintly of her regular shampoo. He couldn't think which one she used, and that was bad, wasn't it, surely he should know which shampoo his wife used? The bottle sat there in the bathroom and he saw it every day. Attentive husbands knew these things. He usually thought of himself as an attentive husband. Tonight she also had the effusive scent of wine about her, but he could ignore that. Tina was no drinker. She must have had a very bad day. Perhaps he should have been kinder after work instead of impatiently showering and dashing off out again. It really hadn't been worth it.

'I've decided to go back to the counsellor,' said Tina.

'Really? Oh, darling, that's wonderful,' said Keaton, straight away deciding not to make too much of a fuss; not to treat this as the biggest thing ever. He needed to play it cool. But he wanted to grab her, pick her up and twirl her around the room.

'I rang Kath while you were out,' Tina went on, eager, like a little child, 'and I told her a bit about . . . only a bit . . . about things . . . and she knows . . . I told her I actually do want a child and she thinks . . . she says you're right and I should try counselling again. She said she does counselling herself. I think that's what she said. Something like that. Anyway, I'm going back. I will.' She paused for breath and added, 'I didn't tell her everything. You understand.'

'Of course, sweetness, I do understand.' *Tina wanted a child? Had she just said that? Did she mean it?* He shook himself clear of his thoughts. 'I think you're right and this time it will help you, I'm sure. The counselling. I think you're ready now.'

'I am. I feel that too. I've had enough.'

'I know.'

'I need to get it off my chest once and for all.'

'Indeed,' said Keaton, but feeling vaguely uneasy. There was nothing to get off her chest, was there? There were just feelings to conquer, thoughts to set free and watch float away downstream. This is what he wanted for Tina.

'I need to confess, if you like,' said Tina and he noticed then the look in her eyes, the twist of her

98

hands in her lap, the excitement — unnatural — in her voice. 'It's time.'

'Tina,' he began. *Tread carefully,* he told himself *This could go either way. This could go horribly wrong.* 'Tina, darling, it's not a case of confessing, is it? It's talking and being listened to and getting help with coming to terms with what happened.'

'Oh, Keaton. Do you think anything is ever that simple?'

She was silent then, and leaned her head on his shoulder, and soon she was asleep, so he manoeuvred himself from the sofa, laid her head down gently on the cushions, kissed her, cleared away her untouched hot chocolate, and went off to dig out a couple of blankets from the box in their bedroom. He left her to sleep on the sofa after tucking her up and kissing her forehead. He went to bed, and had no idea how he felt. He had no idea how his wife felt, which was even worse. Was she crazy? This was something he'd asked himself over the years, more frequently in recent months. She suffered from delusions, certainly, that much was obvious. She carried around with her, at all times, a huge burden of guilt, and it was high time she gently placed that down forever, and walked away from it. If only she would talk about it, open up and tell him the whole story. Did she mean it, the baby thing? Would they . . . ? Could they . . . ? As he slipped into sleep he thought that Tina was a bad, miserable drunk and he would have to hide the rest of their Christmas bottles away before she got hold of them, and anyway with a baby on the way she shouldn't be drinking; these dreamy ideas entwined with thoughts of how nice Sharanne had looked . . . how glamorous in her black dress, and her cracker joke so awful, and how everybody had laughed, everybody, and Tina the loudest.

14

APRIL 1964

Lucia knew her parents wanted her to get out from under their feet and get a job. It wasn't even as if she was helping at home much, if at all. Mum knew something was amiss; she'd clearly guessed something had gone wrong back in January, but Lucia wasn't telling, batting away her mother's tentative enquiries. Mum was quietly unconvinced that Lucia had grown 'bored' of her old job, and Mum was right. Lucia hadn't been bored at all. The job had been fun. All those records, all those exciting, young customers: Clive Stubbins among them. And Sheila, her workmate and, she'd thought, her friend. Now, Lucia had no friends, and no money, apart from the amount she had been saving for new shoes, and that had almost all gone, with no new shoes to show for it. And she wasn't handing over keep any more, because she had none to hand over. So Mum and Dad were supporting her while she swanned around, or moped around, depending on her mood during any given hour.

'That girl needs a job,' Dad said, with his knack of talking about his children in front of them as though they weren't in the room. 'No child of mine is going to be a layabout.'

But she was a layabout, and despite the hints

and uneasiness, her father's mild threats, nothing was done about it. She was their girl, after all. She'd get a job in good time. Lucia had suffered with a bad cold for much of the winter. Mum knew it was better not to make too many requests, but she had tried. 'Could you give me a hand with this laundry, please, love?' or, 'Are you bored? I've got a remedy for that,' and she would indicate the large ironing basket brimming over, largely with Lucia's clothes. Lucia preferred to ignore hints, and rarely did she respond reasonably to requests. She chose to ignore her mother's increasing fatigue and her worn, yellow-pale face, her breathlessness while sitting perfectly still. Mum was in her fifties and, as she frequently complained, she wasn't getting any younger and she was tired, tired, tired, so tired that some days it was all she could do to drag herself down the steep and narrow staircase. She was thin and grey and told Lucia that she had given up looking in the mirror, hating what she saw there.

Mum loved to sew, and over the years she had taught Lucia to embroider and patchwork and make simple toys for William. Lucia had never been that keen, but she had sometimes enjoyed sitting with her mother: the two females of the household keeping each other company, having quiet little talks during which nothing was said. There was plenty of mending to be done. William had turned out even rougher on his clothes than Robert and Ambrose had been at the same age. He was a nice lad though, Lucia admitted to herself, quiet but happily quiet, a good healthy eater who loved the outdoor life. She had worse brothers.

She gave in and sewed with her mother that morning. She knew she ought to, for once. And she was bored, if the truth be told, and lonely, and she was in the mood for talking today. Her mother was the only female left in her life, because Helen Shapiro didn't count. Besides, she was going off her music. She was going off all music. The Beatles were changing everything, nobody seemed to want to listen to anything else these days. And even her dad, who professed to hate 'hooligan' music, joyfully whistled 'I Saw Her Standing There' when he thought nobody was listening.

Lucia patched a worn-through knee on William's school trousers. She was a good seamstress, she knew, despite her natural aversion to it. She made neat little stitches, just as Mum had taught her.

'I do miss Robert so,' said Mum, frowning at her work and holding it up to the window. They were sitting at the dining table, a gentle coal fire glowing in the grate and the family cat Horace licking his paws, sprawled on the clippy mat in front of the fire. Dad and Ambrose were at work (although nobody was entirely clear where Ambrose's 'work' was these days). William was at big school now, the secondary modern, where he was doing all right, although both his parents had been disappointed that he hadn't quite done well enough in his eleven-plus to get into the grammar school.

'I wish he would write more often,' said Mum,

103

and Lucia saw a tear fall onto her mother's neat work.

'It's selfish of him not to,' said Lucia. She hadn't written at all to Robert, who had made a big fuss of them at Christmas, sending a long letter and cards and gifts for them all. They had heard nothing from him since, but Mum had sent two letters, short and sweet, with news of the family.

'New Zealand is so very far away. Will he ever come home, do you think?' said Mum.

'I don't know and I honestly don't care,' said Lucia, finishing off her work, snapping off the thread precisely with her mother's tiny, sharp, pearl-handled scissors. Mum dabbed at her eyes with the sleeve of her cardigan, knitted by herself last winter. Mum was a good knitter, although she described it as a chore. She had long made pullovers for her boys: plain grey ones suitable for school, more fancy designs too if she had a mind to; if she found an interesting pattern at the haberdashery shop in town. Cardigans for herself and Lucia, in baby pinks, powder blues, mint greens, lemons. Lucia had grown to feel half-irritated, half-comforted by the constant click of her mother's knitting needles. She had told her mother, before Christmas: 'Please, no more homemade cardigans. Not for me. They're not fashionable. They're ugly.'

'You're a strange girl,' said Mum.

Lucia swallowed these words, chewed them up, and spat them out. 'I don't have to care about Robert,' she said, taking up a second pair of William's trousers. 'He doesn't care about us.'

'Nonsense. But I do hope he doesn't miss Edward's wedding.'

'That's up to him,' said Lucia. Christ, the wedding. Next week she was supposed to be meeting Simone in town to get measured and choose the material for the bridesmaid dress. It was all arranged. It was April and the wedding wasn't until August, but Simone was a planner. She was a fusser. Lucia was not looking forward to the shopping trip. She had put on a little weight recently. She was embarrassed. It was Mum's fault, trying to feed her up all the time. Mum's fault, yes. Always.

'I dare say it is, but it would be lovely if he could make it.' So much in Mum's world was 'lovely', or could be.

'I don't suppose Simone will care either way,' said Lucia. 'She's only got eyes for Edward, the rest of us don't matter. She's so . . . frivolous. Because she's French I suppose.'

'Half-French,' corrected Mum, in that quiet faraway voice all mothers have during conversations with their children when they are really thinking about something else. 'You must try to like her, Lucia. I wonder when I'll have my first grandchild?' she asked, sharp and bright, warming to her theme. 'That would be nice, wouldn't it?'

'I suppose so.'

'Babies are so lovely.'

'I hadn't noticed.'

'And you, Lucia? How do you feel about being a mother one day?'

'I'm not ever going to be a mother.' She

thought of Sheila, who must be getting disgustingly fat, and she dwelled, just for a moment, on how hideous she would have looked on her wedding day, which, she'd heard on the grapevine (Ambrose had heard talk in the pub), had taken place a month ago. Clive's former fiancée's father had, she'd also heard, reimbursed Clive for the cost of the engagement ring. Then the ring had made its way back to him, because his fiancée didn't want it. Clive had pawned it. Or had Lucia made that bit up for her own satisfaction? She wasn't sure. *No matter, those two were married now, and a baby was very much on the way, and they were happy,* Lucia thought with spiteful glee. *Well, they could keep their happiness.*

'Oh, you'll change your mind one day,' said Mum, patting her daughter's arm.

'I doubt it. Shall we have more tea?' said Lucia, and Mum murmured, 'Yes, let's.' Lucia rose from the table. She swayed, couldn't stop herself, as blood surged into, out of, all around her head. She slumped down, clattering into the teacups as she fell forward.

'Lucia?' Mum's voice was distant, echoing. 'Lucia?'

Sunday 11th April 1976

Dear Elizabeth
Thank you for your letter. You have used
more pretty stationry. I am sorry about my
plain paper but its all we have at home at the
moment. I prefer lines on paper else my
writing goes wobbley. I'll do my best to keep
it straight. Something has happened at home.
I have another Uncle, his name is Uncle
Ambrose. He came yesterday. He had a cup
of tea with granny and Lucia. He ate a lot of
biscits. He was a bit sad and asked if he could
stay for a while and Aunty Lucia said he
could'nt stay long. She made up a bed for
him in her old bedroom. He did'nt know our
grampy was dead and he was very quiet when
he found out in fact he wiped his eyes and
granny rubbed his back and said it was all
right. He said why did'nt anybody let him
know and Aunty Lucia said how on earth
could they nobody knew where he was for the
last eleven years. He said some things I didnt
understand then he started talking about how
S.H.I.T. it was IN JAIL and why did'nt
anybody visit? Aunty Lucia told him to mind
his languidge and she said it was a long time
ago and he should stop wining about it he
was'nt in jail for long was he and why should
anybody bother when he was a common thief
and a nare do well who brought shame on his

107

family. So now we know. Our new Uncle was a criminel but we like him. Me and Meg sat in our den in the laurel bushes and we dicided we would ask Uncle Ambrose to come into our den for a visit. We do'nt let many grown ups into our den so far only Uncle Edward who sat with us once even though it was a bit small for him.
Love from Tina xxx

15

DECEMBER 2013

The drive to Lane's End House took twenty minutes or so, but to Tina, wanting to put off the laborious visit, it seemed as though the drive was taken in a matter of seconds. In the footwell she balanced a poinsettia between her feet. She had made a Christmas pudding for her uncle and aunt, and she clutched the bowl all the way, chatting sporadically to Keaton, who understood her dread, and rested his hand on her knee for much of the journey, removing it only to change gear and turn wipers on and off. A mild, unseasonal drizzle fell.

As the car wound down the lonely lane that lead to Lane's End House, Tina tried not to notice the mess of the garden, sparse and straggly, with only winter nesting in its wayward branches. Anne had tried to keep the garden after Tom's death, and Uncle Edward had taken over for a year or two after he'd returned there to live, but he was not a natural gardener, preferring to spend his days reading, walking, thinking. His questionable enthusiasm had waned, and he'd fallen to performing only the more basic garden tasks. He'd turned the beds and borders over to grass to reduce the workload. Lucia had never gardened, for fear of getting her hands dirty.

Keaton pulled the car to a smooth halt. How

did he do that? Tina's driving was erratic and spiky, unsatisfactory. She wondered how she'd managed to pass her test, but she had at her first attempt, a rare moment of triumph. She climbed from the car, pulling her coat around her, chilled. She must look on the bright side, she told herself Uncle Edward was a dear, and she was about to spend some time with him.

Keaton opened the gate for Tina and closed it carefully behind them. Together they reached the front door. Tina climbed the steps and knocked. The ancient knocker was as loud and portentous as ever. As a child, she had hated it. The noise and reverberation had seemed to permeate the entire house and everything in it.

The door opened. Tina drew in a deep breath and perfected a smile.

'Oh. It's you,' said Lucia.

She was as thin as ever, wearing a mustard-colour, polo-neck jumper, a brown shapeless skirt, thick skin-tone tights, and a grim expression; none of which did anything for her. She was old before her time. Tina stepped into the tiled hallway. The steep and narrow staircase rose before her like the road to hell.

'Rain again,' Lucia commented to nobody in particular as she closed the door behind her guests. 'Well, come on through. I've made tea.' Tina and Keaton followed her into the dining room, in truth also the sitting room, the room where the fire burned, where the television blared, where Uncle Edward's many books lined the walls. Tina half-fancied she saw the ancient ginger tom, Horace, licking his paws before the fire, but of course he was long dead. There was no cat at Lane's End House. But the clippy mat she and Lucia had once made together was still there, threadbare in places and scarred by years of flying sparks. It was all so homely, but this was not her home, and it never had been. She had simply spent too much time here.

'Hello, Uncle Edward!' she cried. He sat in the chair closest to the fire, a blanket on his knee. There wasn't any central heating at Lane's End House. She stood next to her uncle's chair, and kissed the top of his head. He liked that, she knew. He looked up at her and smiled weakly.

'Well, niece,' said Uncle Edward, 'sit yourself down. Pull up that pouffe and warm your toes.'

'Oh, I will, but let me just put the pudding in the kitchen.'

'I'll take it,' said Lucia, and Keaton raised his eyebrows at Tina as he seated himself on the small, high-backed sofa. It was furthest from the fire, but Keaton rarely felt the cold. Lucia took the pudding, muttering a thank you. Tina was left holding the poinsettia. She put it on the dining table. She took her place on the old, dark-green leather pouffe by the fire, opposite her uncle. She smiled at him, and reached across and took one of his hands in hers.

'How are you?' she said. She wasn't sure how loudly she should speak. She didn't want to shout and be rude. He looked tired, and frail. She couldn't remember him looking this frail last year. She hoped he wasn't ill, but she couldn't ask. You didn't talk about illness at Lane's End House.

'There's nothing wrong with me, my girl,' said Edward as he pulled a clean white handkerchief from his pocket and blew his nose loudly. 'Just a silly cold.'

'There are a lot of colds doing the rounds at the moment,' Tina said, nodding reassuringly. 'Keaton's secretary's got one, hasn't she, Keaton? She's been off work for a few days.'

'Yes,' said Keaton. He looked into the fire. 'She's back now. Feeling a bit better. You know.'

'When I was at the doctor's yesterday the waiting room was full of people coughing and sneezing,' said Tina, and immediately she wished she hadn't spoken. Keaton looked at her. She'd have to think up an excuse for later. He was bound to ask. Damn. She'd meant to keep it to herself for now. She was serious about wanting a child, but she didn't want to get Keaton's hopes up too soon. Her doctor had been patient, understanding, thorough. She had explained the pitfalls, the things that could go wrong; she had talked about the possibility of pregnancy never occurring.

'Aye,' said Uncle Edward in that wearily philosophical manner of the elderly. He clearly hadn't been listening, or just hadn't heard.

Lucia came back through from the kitchen with a tea tray, bearing the old brown teapot, milk jug, and the cups and saucers that Tina remembered from her girlhood, along with the heavy-handled, tarnished tea spoons. She shuddered, but told herself she was chilly, and she pulled her coat closer across her chest.

'Sugar?' said Lucia to Tina, and Tina nodded, mute, as the older woman took a sugar cube in

112

the tiny tongs and dropped it into Tina's cup. Tina dared herself to look at the wrinkled pinched skin on the thin face; the pale, veined hands that vaguely shook as their owner leaned across from her seat at the dining table and passed Tina her cup. Lucia then handed a cup to Keaton, and finally, via Tina, to Edward, who took it in his own shaking hands. Tina slowly stirred in her sugar lump. She didn't like tea. But there was no coffee at Lane's End House.

'Biscuit?' Lucia rattled the old rusty tin that had housed biscuits for as long as Tina could remember. Longer. Inside the tin were malted milks. Tina politely shook her head. Why were there no mince pies? Not even shop-bought? It wouldn't hurt Lucia, would it, to make even a small effort?

Keaton gamely took three biscuits and slurped at his tea. 'So,' he eventually said, 'are you all ready for Christmas?' Keaton winked at Tina. It was one of their private jokes, asking this inane question that everybody seemed to ask.

'We don't have much to get ready,' said Uncle Edward. 'I don't suppose we'll hear from Robert again this year.'

Lucia shifted in her chair. It creaked. She took a sip of her tea. She snapped a malted milk in half — snap! — and the crumbs flew off in tiny random directions. She put one halfback into the biscuit tin.

'Are you still in touch with his daughter?' said Uncle Edward. 'What's her name?'

'Elizabeth?' said Tina. 'No, not really. Only on Facebook, you know, on the internet. But that

113

doesn't really count. I send her a card every Christmas.'

'Oh, I don't know about this internet stuff,' said Uncle Edward. 'They keep on about it on the telly. Elizabeth. Yes. That was her. I don't suppose we'll ever meet her, will we? What's all this fuss about face . . . what do you call it?'

'Facebook. But don't worry about that,' said Tina. Uncle Edward nodded. 'But you're right,' she continued, 'we probably won't get to meet Elizabeth or her sister. Although it would be lovely if we did.' Edward didn't respond, his eyes closing, his head drooping towards his chest. Then he jerked himself awake again.

'She must be in her twenties by now, that Elizabeth?' he said.

'You silly old fool,' said Lucia. She shook her head and tutted, and sighed melodramatically.

'Oh, Uncle Edward, she's only a few months younger than me,' said Tina. Edward looked at her blankly. 'I'm forty-six!'

'Are you? Really? Oh, bloody hell, I don't know where the years get to . . . ' and Uncle Edward slipped into another quiet contemplation, staring into the fire, his still-bright eyes watery as though filling with tears. *Perhaps they are,* Tina thought, and she looked away. They all sipped their tea, apart from Edward. Keaton scrunched on his third malted milk. The fire hissed. All was stillness. It should have been so cosy.

'We had a card from Clive and Sheila,' Uncle Edward said, snapping back into life once again. 'That one there on the mantelpiece. Don't mind the dust.'

'Dust?' said Lucia. 'There is no dust! We have a card from them every year.' She sounded clipped and weary. She put down her tea cup, a. small clash against the saucer.

'Do you remember them, Tina?' said Edward, ignoring his sister. He possibly hadn't heard her.

'No, I'm afraid I don't,' said Tina, and she saw her aunt's face settle into a sneer. Tina could remember talk of Clive and Sheila Stubbins, many years ago. She recalled it as bitter talk, their names uttered in hushed voices, and Lucia more than disdainful. Tina had been at the same secondary school as their youngest daughter, Bella. They had not been friends, being three school years apart, but Bella Stubbins had been a mature, sensible girl and had once kindly helped Tina out with a private matter in the school toilets. Tina was tempted to say she could remember Bella, but she decided not to. It was clear that Lucia was uncomfortable when the names of Clive and Sheila Stubbins came up. It was sensible to say nothing. Hadn't Meg once said that she'd heard that Sheila Stubbins had been Lucia's particular friend when they were teenagers, but they had fallen out? Meg wasn't sure why they had fallen out. But that was all Tina could remember, and quite likely none of it was important. Lucia, with an imperious sigh, rose from her chair. She looked out of the window.

'That rain is set in. We won't keep you here, Tina. Before you go could you give me a hand with something?'

'Oh. Yes, yes, of course I will,' said Tina. What

could it be? Lucia rarely asked for help.

Keaton took over the TV remote control and started to flick through the channels. Uncle Edward dozed, and snored, his head gently nodding up and down, the remains of his tea becoming cold and forgotten. Tina followed her aunt into the kitchen.

'I want to get something down from on top of the dresser,' said Lucia. 'But my balance isn't . . . well, I can't manage. It's the old blue teapot that your granny used to use. Her best.'

'Oh, yes,' said Tina, her heart beginning to thump.

'Do you remember it?'

'Yes,' said Tina.

'If you could climb up the steps here . . . ' Lucia drew the old kitchen steps closer to the dresser.

'I . . . I can,' said Tina.

'I know you don't like heights much.'

'No. I don't like heights.'

'But it's not so very high, is it? Should I have asked Keaton?'

'No. Oh no, I can do this.'

Tina took one step on the ladder, then a second. She reached up, on her tiptoes, and could just see the dusty blue teapot. 'I see it,' she said. She couldn't reach it.

'Take another step,' said Lucia.

'I can't . . . OK. One more . . . ' Just look up, reach out for that damned teapot and grab it, and go. Get out of here. You should not be here. What is this? What . . . ?

'Can't you reach?' said Lucia, her voice, it

116

seemed to Tina, no longer the wavering speech of a woman in her sixties who needed help to get a dusty old forgotten teapot down from on top of the dresser, but a woman of thirty, scarily thin, bossy, and — in all that heat! — wearing flared brown slacks and a stripy yellow and brown knitted tunic with wide gaping sleeves and a thin knitted belt, and smelling of . . . what was it? Panache? And ordering her about, bossing her and Meg about. A woman in charge. Irritable, red-faced. 'Should I ask Keaton?' said Lucia.

'No. I can do it.' Tina breathed quickly and stretched out her trembling hand. She felt the cool touch of the porcelain and curled her fingers around the brittle handle. But it was too late. She caved in. Everything turned grey, then black, and only her aunt's voice remained.

'Reach up. You can reach.' The voice reverberated around the kitchen, harsh and forlorn. Later, Tina thought she could remember hitting her head on something hard as she fell; she thought she heard the smashing of the teapot as it met the floor, as the steps wobbled and slid from under her, as the kitchen receded and the woman's voice, her Aunty Lucia's voice, young again, echoing through the swaying branches of the oak tree, through the pitter-patter of the longed-for rain on the parched leaves, 'Tina, what have you done?'

16

APRIL 1964

The haberdashery shop in town was quiet. It was a pretty shop, Lucia had to concede, newly renovated. She had been there before with Mum, of course, many times, but not recently. The colours and patterns dazzled Lucia. The odours of fresh fabric, new carpet and cigarette combined to assault all her senses. Simone flitted from one bolt of material to another, exclaiming over the colours and patterns, rubbing fabric between her slim, elegant fingers, crumpling the material and bringing it to her nose, beckoning Lucia to come and look. Lucia was exhausted even before the shopping trip had properly begun. Simone had taken a day off from work and travelled by train up from London to meet Lucia. Simone said, when they met up, 'I hope we shall get to know each other better.'

Simone settled, after much decision-making, on a peach nylon. Lucia thought it nasty, both the colour and the feel, but said nothing. It was a surprising choice. Simone was usually très chic. Lucia watched the assistant cut the required amount of fabric and carefully fold it and wrap it in paper. Lucia felt hot, queasy. Her dress was a little tight across her chest and around her neck, the collar too high. She needed to sit down but knew she couldn't ask. She was seventeen, not seventy. She yawned, rubbed her temples. Simone paid for the material.

'Are you well?' asked Simone as she picked up the parcel of fabric. 'Would you like a cup of tea? We are not due at the dressmaker's until midday.'

'Oh, yes please,' said Lucia. She tried to smile at Simone, who looked doubtful.

They found a café and ordered tea, and fruit scones. Simone chatted about the wedding and this, that and everything, while Lucia tried to listen. She was going to be the only bridesmaid and at any other time in her life she would have been thrilled and excited. Simone talked about hairstyles. Lucia nibbled at her scone. It was acceptable, but a bit dry. The sultanas were too squishy. She avoided the butter.

'I'm sorry,' said Simone at last. 'I'm talking too much about the wedding aren't I? Eddie says, 'Enough now. Let's talk about something else!' I think I'm driving him mad . . . '

Eddie? No. Edward was Edward, most definitely not Eddie. It sounded all wrong. This woman knew nothing about him! And she was going to be his wife in a few months. Oh, she was so tired. Another yawn. Perhaps Simone would imagine she was bored. She was, in fact, bored. But —

'I'm expecting a baby,' said Lucia, and burst into tears.

★ ★ ★

Simone held Lucia's hand until she stopped crying, which she did after a minute or two. She

119

had said it now. She hadn't meant to say it. But at least the hard part was over. Somebody else knew. There could be no going back. Simone urged her to finish her tea. The café was almost deserted, but Simone nudged her chair closer to Lucia's so they could talk quietly.

Since last week's faint at the dining table, Lucia had felt bleached, all her colours bled out of her. She had been feeling sick, mostly in the afternoons, for weeks. She was constantly tired, a hefty fatigue that couldn't be fought. Nobody had cottoned on. Yet. It had taken her long enough — for weeks she had ignored the signs. She had denied her suspicions, but finally she'd had no choice but to succumb to disbelief and horror. She was well over three months now and had a tiny bump, her waist thickening day on day. She hadn't been to see a doctor. She would need to do something, soon. It was hard to think straight. She couldn't think at all, most of the time. It could not be. But it was. Yet it could not be. She'd been paralysed, all these weeks. She hadn't known what to do or who to turn to. Until now, until Simone.

'Who is the father?' Simone asked. She was pale. Incredulous. But not unkind.

Lucia thought for a moment. No. Some things were unsayable, even to silly French women who didn't deserve the man they were going to marry.

'His name is Clive and I . . . I thought we were going to get engaged. I thought he loved me.'

'Ah. I see.'

'But he's married to somebody else now.'

'Sheila, isn't it?'

120

'Yes. How do you know that?'

'Eddie told me. I think Ambrose mentioned it to him. But let us not worry about that. We need to concern ourselves with you, yes?'

'I think so.'

'You want to have the baby?'

'No! No, I can't.'

'Why not?' Simone truly was modern.

'Why . . . I can't.'

'Think about it. It won't be easy but there are ways. Homes for unmarried mothers? Your own mother will probably help you anyway. Anne is desperate for a grandchild, isn't she?'

'I'm not keeping the baby,' said Lucia, pushing her half-nibbled scone away from her. 'It has to go. There's no . . . no question of me keeping it.' She started to cry again, and Simone patted her shoulder.

'I see. I understand. In the circumstances . . . as long as you're sure.'

'I am sure. I'm more sure of this than anything else, ever. Will you help me? I don't know what to do.'

'All right, it's all right, Lucia. Don't cry. Of course I will help you.'

Lucia took a few shaky sips of her tea. It tasted revolting, but she was thirsty.

Simone thought for a long time. 'Shall we . . . ask Eddie what to do?' she said eventually.

'No!' Didn't she understand? No, she didn't. How could she? It wasn't her fault. Nobody would understand.

'All right. It's all right, Lucia. We shall keep this to ourselves. It's women's business, no?'

'Yes.'

'You are a woman now.'

'I know.'

'Don't be ashamed. Don't worry. And above all don't be frightened. I'll help. I promise.'

122

Saturday 1st May 1976

Dear Elizabeth
Thank you for your reply it was quick! I
wonder how soon this will get to you? I am
going to walk to the post office and post it as
soon as I've written it. Daddy has given me
and Meg some pocket money so I can post
your letters myself. Uncle Ambrose has gone
to live with sumebody he knows in London.
He wrote to Granny and asked her for money
but Granny is not to send even a penny Aunty
Lucia says. I asked if I could write to Uncle
Ambrose but the grown-ups say I cant. It is
absolutly forbiddon. Uncle Ambrose is naughty
so maybe its right he was in prison because
that is where naughty grownups go. Uncle
Ambrose smelled bad and he messed up the
house and did'nt lift a finger. He smelled a bit
like our dad sumetimes and Aunty Lucia says
this family has always enjoyed drink too much
and look where its getting us. I thought she
was going to cry when she said it but she
looked out of the window for a while and
when she looked back in she was'nt crying.
Before he left Uncle Ambrose bought an easier
egg for me and Meg. They were Smarties
eggs. Do you get Smarties in America? They
are chocolate sweets with bright colours on
the outside and when you buy a tube of
Smarties theres a letter under the lid. Meg

123

collects them. She still needs an X and a B. I am reading a good book at the moment it is called Ballet Shoes. I've read it before because it was my birthday present I told you about and its still BRILIANT and its about three sisters who are'nt sisters in real life and they do'nt go to school apart from ballet school and they are poor and I wonder if you have it over there? I wish I did'nt have to go to school as I am not good at school work apart from reading and writing because I love them both. In Ballet Shoes I like Posy best even though she is silly and annoying. She wants things and I think it is good to want something very badly and to try to do it. Petrova is nice and she reminds me of my sister Meg. Pauline turns into a big head but she is mostly nice. It is a really good book.

Before Uncle Ambrose left our house but when he was talking to us in our den about going Meg said why does'nt he take Aunty Lucia with him then we would all be happy. Uncle Ambrose laught when she said this and he told us not to let her boss us about she is spoilt he said. He said when she was young she was a little b-word, a bad word. A girl dog, Meg says. He said Aunty Lucia is a rotton apple I think I know what he means and so does Meg. We liked Uncle Ambrose and we will miss him even if he was a bad man. We do'nt know how bad he was. I wish we knew because we wander a lot about it.

Love from your English cousen,

Tina xx

17

DECEMBER 2013 — JANUARY 2014

The Christmas visit to Lane's End House came to an abrupt end. Lucia was apologetic, Edward confused by the fuss. Keaton drove his wife home and insisted she go straight to bed for a proper rest. It was a nasty fall, and, 'Why on earth didn't you call me through to the kitchen? I wouldn't even have needed the ladder and if I had, it wouldn't have made me dizzy or faint. And the damned teapot would still be intact. Will you never learn?' Tina thought to herself, sadly, no, she would never learn. 'I thought it would be all right,' she said. 'I thought I could manage it.'

'But you know you can't handle heights.'

'I need to be able to handle Lucia though.'

'I know, I know. But be sensible.'

Keaton closed the curtains, plumped up the pillows and insisted once again on checking the bump on Tina's head. It was sore but there was no cut, and only a little bruising; Tina refused to go to A & E. 'It would be a waste of everybody's time,' she claimed, and Keaton stopped nagging. She took an arnica tablet.

'Keaton?'

'Yes?'

'I think I learned . . . I think I might have discovered something today. About me, I mean.'

125

'Tell me.'

'It's silly really but I think I may have misunderstood something. All these years.'

Keaton stiffened. He slowly sat down on the end of the bed. 'What do you mean?'

'I think . . . *that day* . . . '

'*That day?*' a voice shrieked — Meg's, loud and angry and just behind Tina, there but not there, loud but silent. 'Only *we* talk about *that day!*'

Tina ignored the voice. 'I think I may have got things wrong. Something happened in the kitchen . . . her voice . . . it was her, Keaton. She made her do it!'

'All right, darling. Don't get excited. Why don't we talk about it later? You look exhausted.'

'Shut up. Just shut up!' screeched Meg, and Tina feared that Keaton would hear Meg and her soulful fury, but of course, he could not.

'All right,' said Tina. 'I am tired, rather. But I meant what I said about the counselling. I am going back. Even more so now. Something . . . something else happened. I know it did. I'll ring them after Christmas.'

'I can't tell you what a relief it is to hear you say that,' said Keaton. 'It's truly marvellous, it really is. Now, I'll get you some coffee. Then I'm going to track down your numerous rolls of wrapping paper and wrap your presents, so you mustn't come downstairs for at least two hours.'

Keaton left the bedroom and all was silence. Tina felt alone; she was alone. She would not listen to Meg, and Meg was gone. Keaton brought Tina's coffee. She sipped it, thinking, trying to . . . remember? Put things in order? It

126

was hard to say. It was hard to think and she was tired, so very tired. Her head hurt, but not much. When she finished her coffee she huddled down under the duvet and slept an exhausted sleep.

★ ★ ★

Christmas day passed uneventfully. They stayed in bed until ten o'clock, enjoying their customary champagne breakfast. They opened their gifts. They cooked dinner and ate all of it, and dozed on and off for the rest of the day, watching television, reading a little of their new books. They went to bed at eleven o'clock. They both silently regretted their grown-up Christmas, bereft always of the distant trappings of childhood: glittery homemade cards, bulging stockings, the household raised at five in the morning. Maybe, Tina allowed herself to believe, maybe one day that would be their Christmas. It could happen. In a way it was a good thing she had fallen from the stepladder in Lucia's kitchen. Keaton seemed to have forgotten about her letting slip she'd been to the doctor.

Tina didn't visit Meg on Christmas Day. She'd done that on Christmas Eve, against Keaton's advice, ignoring his pleas for her to look after herself and wait a day or two more. She'd taken a nasty knock to the head, he'd reminded her. Surely she needed to rest? But Tina had gone to her sister's grave. Meg had not been around. Tina had left a poinsettia, which Meg would not have appreciated any more than Lucia did. But there was nothing else to give.

★ ★ ★

Keaton took himself off to work on the day after New Year's Day and felt that strange, empty, post-festivity sadness. Yet he was also glad to return, for he liked routine. Sharanne greeted him with the usual cup of coffee and a smile he couldn't read. He was more nervous than usual around her, but he couldn't tell why.

'How was your Christmas?' Keaton felt he ought to ask.

'Oh, you know.'

Keaton guessed hers had been rather lonely.

'How was your Christmas?' Sharanne asked.

'Similar to yours I should imagine.'

He thought of Tina, who was, he hoped, making her nervous phone call this morning, arranging her appointment with Virginia, who, Keaton believed, had been making progress with Tina last year, until Tina had decided to quit the weekly sessions. They had cost a small fortune, but he didn't begrudge the expense. He would do anything, anything at all, to help rid his wife of the tyranny of her memories, the plague of the trauma that dominated her life. What happened, he wasn't entirely sure. He wasn't convinced his wife was sure either. And now this new . . . 'discovery' of hers. What exactly had happened in the kitchen at Lane's End House before Christmas?

He knew, he thought, the bare bones of what had happened all those years ago when Tina and Meg were eight-year-olds. The memories weighed Tina down, but sooner or later, surely, you had

128

to get a grip and move on with your life? He was convinced that his wife was stuck in the past and could not escape it. Her sister, even though she was dead, had a lot to answer for. How he wished Tina could get over her. All that had happened, happened a long time ago. Nobody should mourn for that long. And the accident in the kitchen, Tina's fall, it had awakened something in her; some memory was alive again where once it had been dead. But she didn't seem to want to talk about it, and he didn't want to keep on.

'Penny for them?' said Sharanne, her pretty face showing genuine concern. Her pretty face? He shuddered at his creeping fear. Her eyes were blue and sharp, yet disconcertingly pale. He had not noticed this before.

'Oh, no,' said Keaton. 'I wouldn't . . . it's all right. Thank you.'

Sharanne sat on Keaton's desk. Keaton froze. He didn't know where to look so he kept his eyes on the small patch of desk next to her thigh. She was wearing a short skirt and black tights. There was a coffee ring on the desk. Next to that, an indeterminate stain; perhaps ink.

'Poor old Keaton,' said Sharanne. Her voice wasn't as soft as the words. She smelled of hand cream, but it was not like Tina's. Sharanne's hand cream was cloying, a rich smell that invaded him. Her nails were perfectly manicured and painted a deep red. He looked up at her face and their eyes met and he was pierced, pinned to his chair. He felt like a hapless victim. But he wasn't hapless.

'Sharanne, I — '

'No. Please don't say anything. I just want you to know that I'm here for you, if you need me. I'm happy to help, as a friend. I mean it.' She slid off Keaton's desk, as a mermaid slips into the sea. She swayed towards the door and he refused to watch her, and turned his face to the window. Tears pricked at his weary eyes. He was being worn down, and he knew it. *Tina had better ring that counsellor today*, thought Keaton, as his assistant retreated from his office. *She really better had.*

★   ★   ★

It was a normal Thursday — time to clean the Haynes's house, time to visit Meg again. Was it Tina's imagination, or had Keaton seemed happy to return to work? After any holiday he was usually burdened by feelings of regret, lethargy, reluctance. But this morning he'd seemed wide awake and enthusiastic. Skippy, which was not like Keaton.

Tina had not read much of *I Capture the Castle* over Christmas. Of course, she had read it before, three times (it was one of her teenage favourites), but not recently. She knew she ought to refresh her memory so she would be able to speak about it. It would be incumbent upon her to introduce the book, to say why she had chosen it and what she loved about it. But now she was running out of time. She knew in her heart she probably wouldn't even go to the meeting this month, which wasn't really fair. It was nice, the group, but . . . that was all it was. Sometimes

130

these things were too much of an effort.

The cemetery was surprisingly busy this lunchtime. The sun was struggling out from behind dark grey clouds. How she longed to take her sister home. How they both hated it here! If only things could go back to how they used to be.

How they used to be? Is that really what she wanted? Even if it were possible? Her thoughts turned to Uncle Edward, how strong he'd once been; how fresh and funny and fine. She recalled his kind face, his kind actions, his mysterious, never-ending supply of lollipops, his clean white handkerchiefs. Seeing him before Christmas had saddened her — the wizened and resigned-to-his-fate old man, huddled in his chair, lost to Tina as much as Meg was lost to her.

'Tina?'

'Oh! I didn't hear you. Sorry. I was thinking.'

'I didn't know you could think,' said Meg and she sat beside Tina, she really did. Tina felt that if she reached out she would meet flesh — a body, something tangible. 'Actually, you think too much,' Meg said crisply. 'That's your problem, sister.'

'I see. Not 'Hello, thanks for coming, it's good to see you' or, dare I suggest it, 'Happy New Year?' Just more insults. Thank you so much.'

'Stop whining. What went on between you and Lucia before Christmas anyway?'

'I don't recall discussing that with you.'

'Oh, shut up, sis. You know how it works by now. You could have told her to get stuffed. I don't know why you didn't. I wanted to mention

131

it on Christmas Eve but I thought I'd better not.
I kept out of sight. You were so uptight!'

'For God's sake!'

'Shush. I — '

'No, you shush. Just for a moment. Please? I
have something to tell you for once.' Tina leaned
forward; she wanted to feel assertive. 'My mind
is made up. I'm going back to counselling.'

'Ha!'

'Don't scoff. Please.'

'You're the scoffer around here, not me.'

Tina imagined the eight-year-old Meg sticking
out her tongue. Tina ignored her.

'I just don't understand why you think you
need 'counselling',' said Meg. 'It should be clear
enough what needs to be done by now. How old
are you?'

'How old are we.'

'Right. We're big girls now. Well, you are. By
the way, how's Uncle Edward?'

'Why don't you tell me as you seem to know
everything that goes on in my life?'

'I know the things a twin should know. That's
all.'

Tina closed her eyes and hummed for a few
moments. Then: 'Meg? Don't you hate all of this?'

Meg shrugged. There was a pause during
which the young Meg seemed to melt away and
the latter-day Meg, an up-to-date Meg, took her
place. Tina thought she could see her sister's
pale, gaunt face. Tina gazed at it, trying to focus,
trying to see the mischievous smile, the arched
eyebrows. In a whisper Meg said, 'You know
what needs to be done.'

'I'm going to counselling,' said Tina. 'What needs to be done is I go to counselling and get it all straight in my head.'

'You make me laugh. 'Straight in your head'?'

'Yes.'

'Just don't let this counsellor person talk you out of things.'

'What things?'

'You know what things.'

'But that's probably what I need. To be talked out of things.'

'Rubbish.'

'I'm going,' Tina said. 'I'm going to ring up and do it this time. You are not going to talk me out of that. I'm going to these sessions for as long as I need to regardless of what you say.'

But Meg had gone.

★   ★   ★

The woman in the green coat watched Tina. Tina shook her head, sighed, waved her hands around and hummed, loudly. She stood up, she sat down again. Eventually she left the grave, looking tired and frustrated. It was painful to watch. Once again the woman had sat in silence, saying nothing, doing nothing. She had to make up her mind. All this dithering was getting her nowhere, all this careful observing. So what? What was it achieving? Nothing. It had been all right to begin with, she'd got the idea, could see the situation clearly enough, had confirmed her growing suspicions.

God, January was a hateful month, so long

133

and dark. Yet it was the New Year, and time for a new start. Time for action, no? The woman got up to leave, and wrapping her coat closer around her, pulling her scarf up over her chin, she too left the cemetery.

18

APRIL 1964

When Lucia arrived for her 'day out' in London, 'wedding shopping' with Simone, she wondered how on earth her young life had come to this. She was intimidated by London — just getting off the train at Paddington was fraught. The hustle and bustle was difficult to escape. So she was relieved when she spotted Simone coming towards her along the platform, waving and smiling. The day's pretence, Lucia could tell, was going to be absolute. They embraced. Lucia asked to visit the toilet.

The underground was hot and the rough swaying of the train made her feel sick. They had to stand up for most of the journey. Lucia felt sweat forming all over her body. Simone put her hand on the small of Lucia's back in a protective gesture. Lucia was dizzy on the escalators, and breathless climbing the endless steps up to the street. It was a relief to be above ground again, in sunlight, breathing warm city air. They walked for some minutes, Simone an expert guide in the labyrinthine London streets.

The house was inconspicuous, with no outward signs of the horrors waiting within. There were three steps up to the front door, just like at home. The front door was smart, a pristine red, with brass trimmings. Simone knocked on the door. Lucia started to cry as they waited for somebody to answer. Simone put her arm around her. 'It's all right,' she said. Lucia wanted to believe her.

Eventually, the door was opened. The woman was small, neat and bespectacled. She wore a nondescript skirt, a high-buttoned blouse. Unseen petticoats rustled as she moved. She seemed respectable, vaguely Victorian. She called Lucia 'little one' and appeared to regard her with great pity. She was French, Lucia thought. That didn't surprise her. Simone must know people, women, in the French community, if there was such a thing in London. Lucia didn't know. But there were French restaurants, she supposed, therefore there were French people. The woman led them along the unlit corridor towards the rear of the house. Down a short flight of steps there was a door. Lucia counted the steps. Eight. A cellar. The woman asked Simone to wait at the top. She opened the door.

'Can't she stay with me?' asked Lucia, crying anew, stopping halfway down.

'No, little one, it would not be right.'

'But . . . but . . . '

'I'll wait here,' said Simone. There was a ladder-backed chair against the wall at the top of the stairs with a round, worn, patchwork cushion. *Mum would have liked the cushion*, Lucia thought. But the colours were dull browns, yellows. Simone nodded and smiled at Lucia.

'Est-elle ta soeur?' said the woman to Simone. Lucia guessed the meaning; she knew the words elle and soeur. She wished she'd had the chance to learn French properly. Perhaps with a French sister-in-law it might yet be possible.

Simone and Lucia locked eyes. 'Yes,' said Simone. 'She is my English sister.'

The woman nodded. 'Elle ne sera pas blessée.' Simone nodded gratefully. The woman smiled at Lucia. 'I will not hurt you,' she said. She stepped into the room and switched on a light. Lucia looked up at Simone, Simone nodded, and Lucia descended the rest of the stairs and followed the woman into the cellar.

★   ★   ★

The French woman was true to her word: Lucia was unharmed, in many ways. She thought the woman was a nurse, or once had been. She'd seemed to know what she was doing and everything had looked and smelled clean. That was something. It was probably the best she could have hoped for in the terrible circumstances. She supposed she had Simone to thank for that.

She struggled home on the train that afternoon with a flask of tea that Simone gave her and a small bag full of 'provisions'. Their parting was difficult. There was a hug, of sorts. Simone said she must telephone her if she started to get pain, if there was too much blood. There probably wouldn't be . . . but 'Madame G' would be able to help if there was.

Lucia sat on the train, a thick towel between her legs. She was glad she had remembered to

137

wear dark clothes. She felt nothing but a dull ache in her abdomen. The pain was not much worse than her regular monthly cramps. She was tired. She could feel the blood seeping from her, and she told herself it was her monthly — a bit late, a bit heavy, but her monthly. Nothing more. By the time her train pulled into her station, she had started to believe in the tale she had told herself.

She told Mum she was ill. She'd probably caught a bug in London. Yes, she'd had a nice day. They'd bought pink lipsticks and white stockings, and false eye-lashes and ivory satin bridesmaid shoes. It was all back at the flat in London. Simone was keeping everything close to her, to be organised. No, she hadn't seen Edward. He was at work, of course. No, she didn't need to wear the shoes in just yet. There was plenty of time. Yes, it was good of Simone to provide her with the flask of tea. There was nothing in the bag! Simone had popped sandwiches in there for her and Lucia had eaten them on the train.

'I need to go to bed now,' Lucia said and the effort of walking up the narrow, steep staircase was immense. Never had her small bed in her small, dark bedroom looked more inviting. She visited the bathroom to change her towel. There was an awful lot of blood. No wonder she felt so weak. She hid the bloodied towel under her bed to dispose of later. She would burn it on the fire when Mum was at the shops. That was how she and Mum always disposed of their 'private things'. She had another dozen or so towels,

138

bought for her by Simone. Besides those she had a few of her own hidden away in her knicker drawer. She had plenty of supplies. Simone had also bought her a new sanitary belt, a pretty white lacy one. Lucia had never seen anything so beautiful. Her old belt was worn and blood-stained and had turned a horrible grey-ish colour. She hoped she wouldn't leak onto the beautiful new one, or onto her clothes or her bed, but of course any suspicions could be dispelled as Mum would assume she was on her monthly, which she was, she reminded herself. There was really nothing to worry about.

She climbed into bed. The sheets were clean — cool, calm. They smelled of Mum. Lucia closed her eyes. She lay there for several minutes, not sleeping, not crying, not regretting. She thought about Edward and their secret — the secret she now half-shared with Simone. Life was complicated, and she was tired, and she turned to her pale yellow bedroom wall. She was vacant, she realised; emptied out. She had no feeling at all. It wasn't that bad. The worst was over. Soon, she slept.

Tuesday 29th June 1976

Dear Elizabeth
My mum and dad keep on arguing. My mum
wants a job and she has aplied for one at the
habadashary shop. She says it is right up her
street and I think she means it would suit her
which it will because she is good at making
things. She makes my dresses. I do'nt mind if
mummy wants to have a job but daddy is
cross and says its his place to earn the money
and keep us. Mummy tells him to stop being
old fashiunned and he says its not old
fashiunned its common sense. I want them to
stop arguing and I think my dad should just
give up because Mummy told me in secret
she is going to take the job REGARDLES.
I want to go and live with the Fossil sisters
because nothing like this ever happens to
them. The Fossil sisters are in Ballet Shoes,
the book I told you about before. Your name
has to begin with P to be a Fossil so I would
choose Pippa. By the way, look out for an
exciting parcel heading your way in a few
weeks, once I have saved enough pocket
money. I cant say more about it now apart
from it might be a very nice book that I think
you will love.
I will close now,
From your couson in England,
Tina xxxx

19

JANUARY 2014

Tina picked a space in the near-empty car park and shuffled the car, back and forth, back and forth; she couldn't manoeuvre when she was nervous. She was an appalling driver, she decided, cursing herself. Finally, she parked to her satisfaction and checked her face and hair in her vanity mirror. Perhaps she should have applied more make-up? She touched up her powder. She snapped shut her handbag, got out of the car and locked it. She turned to face the building, took three deep breaths, and walked towards the door.

Denise the receptionist looked much the same, Tina was pleased to see. Her nails were still bright pink, her face well made-up, her short brown hair neat. It was reassuring. And she remembered Tina.

After a brief chat, Tina took a seat in the waiting area and Denise bustled off to make coffee.

There was nobody else waiting. This was good. Tina didn't like being nosed at and wondered about. This place was discreet and quiet. Denise brought the coffee and handed it to Tina with a warm smile. 'Kate won't keep you,' she said. 'She's just reading over your notes again. She's running a tad behind this morning.'

'Kate?'

'Ah, you saw Virginia last time didn't you? She left a couple of months ago. I'm sure I told you when you rang for your appointment?'

'Oh. I must have forgotten.'

She hadn't forgotten, she just hadn't been listening as usual. Was the departure of Virginia a good thing or a bad thing? Probably it was good, Tina decided as she sipped the coffee. It might be better to talk to somebody new. The coffee was better than she remembered. Good coffee was always a comfort, so she settled back in her chair. She took from her bag *Mrs Dalloway* by Virginia Woolf — Kath's reading group choice — and tried to read. It was an odd book, quite beautiful in places, but opaque. *Concentrate, concentrate!*

She didn't want to have to start all over again, either with the book or with the counselling. Being asked all those horrid questions that she couldn't answer. In many ways it would be easier to try to carry on where she'd left off. But she couldn't remember where that was, or what she and Virginia had talked about. All she could remember was discomfort and pain. She wished she was at the Haynes's house, as she would normally be on a Thursday morning, tidying away Poppy's toys, hoovering the stairs. She had cleaned their house yesterday instead, by prior arrangement. She hadn't told them why.

Denise sat at her desk and worked, her bright pink nails flashing like jumping beans on her keyboard. The fish tank in the corner hummed and clicked; *it must be the pump that makes the noise,* Tina thought, and she didn't want to look at the little bright blue fish, trapped in the tank, swimming around aimlessly in the artificial world. They could never ever get out. The door to the left of the reception desk opened a crack, something was said, and the door was left ajar.

'Christina?' said Denise. 'Christina? Would you like to go through? Kate's ready for you now.'

Nausea. Heartbeats. Sweat. Flight. Sob. No. She smiled weakly at Denise, who beamed back as though she was saying, 'Go on, you can do this,' and perhaps that was exactly what she was saying, with her smile and the gentle nod of her head. She probably saw nervous people every day. Tina finished her coffee in three gulps, put the mug down next to the neat pile of *Country Living* magazines, tucked *Mrs Dalloway* back into her handbag, and got up from her chair and walked slowly towards the door marked KATE WISHAW. Tina reached out and took two deep breaths and pushed the door. She couldn't bring herself to look at Kate Wishaw just yet, the stranger to whom she was soon going to be pouring out her heart. She was aware of a figure sitting in one of the chairs, but Tina still couldn't look, so she turned towards the door and closed it, making sure it clicked shut; she wanted to be private, unheard. She took two more deep breaths and only then did she turn towards the room, to look at the woman who occupied it, who was rising from her chair, her mouth open in shock and surprise to mirror Tina's own feelings.

'Tina?!'

'Kath?!'

20

AUGUST 1964

The bridesmaid's dress could have been silk. It should have been silk. Somehow that would have made everything more bearable. At the first fitting, the day they had bought the material, the day Lucia had told Simone about her . . . predicament, Lucia had been terrified, self-conscious of her small bump, her fleshier-than-it-had-ever-been waist. Simone had been kind about it. 'You will diet, Lucia, no?' she'd said, nodding in a knowing fashion to the dressmaker. 'At the next fitting she will be super slim!' The dressmaker, herself rather dumpy, had smiled. 'Seams could be adjusted,' she'd said.

Now the wedding day was here and Lucia would have to smile for the camera. It wasn't easy to smile these days. On the morning of the wedding she listened to her Helen Shapiro records. She had grown to love them once more. In those dark days, weeks, after the trip to London, Lucia had come to rely on Helen's voice as her comfort, her companion, her confidante. There was something so strong about that voice, something invincible, and Helen was so young, and therefore courageous. Lucia wished they could be real friends, in real life, which was a stupid girlish thought, but there it was. They were the same age.

Lucia knew that today she would have to put on a brave face. She had seen nothing of Edward since . . . since. He was busy at work, or helping Simone with wedding preparations. He had visited Lane's End House only once since Christmas time, and Lucia had contrived to be 'out' on that day. But Lucia knew that today he would be unavoidable, and so would she.

Robert was back from New Zealand. Lucia was rather unmoved, unlike their mother, by his return. He'd always been nothing much to her, and vice versa. It was the same with Ambrose, who was a law unto himself, secretive and, Lucia suspected, quietly engaged in unlawful activities. He was a little strange. Not a traveller like Robert, more of a roamer. Often he'd disappear for days on end, then come home bearing a bad smell, and he'd be ravenous, with an odd look in his eyes. Mum and Dad didn't like it, but there wasn't much they were prepared to do or say. He was a grown man, after all, and he paid his keep when he was at home, which was more than Lucia did.

Mum was thrilled beyond measure that all her children would be together for the wedding. It was going to be lovely.

* * *

It was Edward and Simone's day and, of course, nobody really noticed Lucia, the nylon-besmirched bridesmaid, over made-up, hair piled up on her head in a beehive do. Lucia's hair was too short for the style and she knew she looked silly. She

145

spent most of the day switched off from all that was around her. Many of the guests wanted to hear all about Robert's New Zealand adventures. He was going back, he said to everyone who asked, for good. This was just a flying visit. When Robert and Lucia finally got around to talking at the reception, they exchanged a few meaningless wedding day pleasantries. Then Robert told Lucia off for not smiling for the photographs. It was bad form, he said. She was the bridesmaid and it was Edward's big day. She should buck her ideas up.

'I don't want to smile,' she said. 'I have a headache.'

Robert nodded. He looked at her in disdain. 'You're a selfish little cow, aren't you?' he said. 'You always have been.' He moved off to speak to somebody else. The tears came, too readily as they always did nowadays. She sought out her mother, and was comforted when she detected Anne's familiar scent of violets. She shed tears over her mother's pretty mauve jacket, which had been bought brand new for the occasion. The mauve of the mother did not look well alongside the peach of the daughter. It was a clash that Lucia tried to ignore, but couldn't avoid. It was just as well the photographs would be black and white, and people would only be able to guess the colours in years to come. Mum tutted and consoled, and gently rubbed her daughter's back. The nylon scratched and sparkled and clicked. Mum took out a handkerchief, and tried to wipe the streaks of black mascara from Lucia's thin cheeks. Lucia told her mother exactly what Robert had said. Mum murmured about young men and their wicked tongues; men and their ugly ways. 'Take no notice, there's a girl.'

Lucia stiffened when she felt Edward's gentle hand on her shoulder. Something ran through her, a bolt of dread and fire. Something else.

'Is everything all right?' he asked, raising his eyebrows at Mum.

'Oh yes, she's just had words with Robert.'

'He had words with me!' said Lucia, and she shrugged off Edward's hand.

'He's getting a bit drunk,' said Edward. 'Take no notice. Shall I have words with him?'

'No!' cried Lucia. 'There's no need for that. Enough words!'

Mum moved off to talk to somebody else. Lucia watched her go, willing her to stay. But Mum was gone, surrounded by a gaggle of guests offering up their congratulations. Lucia looked down at the floor. She needed to get to the ladies to clean up the mascara properly.

Edward had removed his jacket, and his smart white shirt looked nice on him. She didn't want to notice. But she couldn't help it.

'Thank you for being our bridesmaid,' said Edward. 'You look beautiful.'

They both reddened.

'Thank you,' she said. She looked at him then. He was still her brother, never mind what had happened between them. She wiped at her face.

'Lucia, I — '

'What?' Surely he wasn't going to —

'I'm sorry for what happened.'

He was. Oh. Oh no.

'It was abominable,' continued Edward. 'I don't know . . . I was drunk, I think, and a bit out of sorts. I . . . I don't know what happened. I don't drink any more. Not a drop.'

'You had champagne during the speeches earlier. I saw you.'

'I only held the glass and pretended. I'm stone-cold sober.'

'Oh.'

'I'm very happy with Simone. I'm crazy about her.'

'I know.'

'I hope you'll be crazy about somebody too one day.'

The image of Clive rode into her mind and out again; his handsome features slipping away from her, deformed and twisted. If it hadn't been for Clive, the thing that happened with Edward wouldn't have happened. Her disappointment that evening, her desperate walk home, the warm fire and the gentle Edward, drunk, and waiting for her . . .

She threw back her head. 'I think it would be better if we never mention . . . it . . . again. That night.'

'Yes,' said Edward. 'You're right. I'm so sorry. I'm more than sorry. I really am . . . words can't express it.'

'It's in the past,' said Lucia. 'It's over.'

'Yes, it is over,' said Edward. 'But it should never have happened. Truly.' He looked like he was going to cry. His lip wobbled.

'We all make mistakes,' she said, trying to comfort.

148

'Indeed.'

'So shall we agree that it's all dead and buried and carry on as if it never happened?'

'Yes. I think that's the only thing we can do.' Edward whipped out a white handkerchief and blew his nose. After that he looked more composed.

'Then that's what we'll do,' she said.

'Thank you, Lucia.'

★   ★   ★

Robert and Ambrose drank together, laughing at everyone and everything, for the whole world was apparently hilarious. William drank with them too, sipping at wine. No doubt he considered himself 'one of the boys'. Lucia watched her brothers from her vantage point of a stool at the bar; she sat alone, sipping demurely at a lemonade, and her brothers glanced back at her, sniggering.

'Path-et-ic!' she mouthed across to them all, glaring. They laughed all the louder. Later, she went home with Mum and Dad. She tore off the peach dress and threw it onto the bedroom floor, not caring what became of it. She kicked off the ivory satin shoes. She peeled off the false eyelashes, removed all traces of make-up, and let down her sticky hair. She brushed it ferociously, flakes of lacquer floating around her.

Much later her three unmarried brothers returned, laughing, then whispering. One of them tripped over the scraps bucket in the kitchen and they all loudly shushed each other.

She huddled in her bed, straining to listen. Later, when William was sick in the bathroom, she heard their mother creep from her bed to stay with him, comforting him, until Lucia heard him fall, in a moaning stupor, into his own bed. Even later the smell of toast wafted up the stairs, and she must have fallen asleep then, lulled at last by the muffled murmurs of Robert and Ambrose talking late into the night.

Saturday 16th July 1976

Dear Elizabeth
I hope you like the book I am sending you
and I hope you enjoy reading it too. It is one
of my favourites and I have read it twice this
year. Of course, it is Ballet Shoes!!! I saved
my pocket money and I went into town with
Uncle Edward and Tante Simone this
morning to buy it for you. Meg chose
clackers for herself but I don't like them
much. They are noisy. They are dangeros too
if they hit you on the back of your hand. One
time at school a boy's clackers smashed and
there was bits of sharp plastic everywhere.
His hand got cut and his face. I won't use
them and Meg says I'm a chicken. Uncle
Edward drove me and Meg and Tante
Simone into town in his car and he bought us
ice-creams because it is so hot here still.
Uncle Edward said we were good girls and
we deserved a treat. Meg thinks they took us
into town as an excuse to get away from
Aunty Lucia because neither of them like her.
It was fun to have a ride in their car and we
had the windows open and everything
smelled like petrol and hot seats and it was
nice. When we got back Tante Simone and
Aunty Lucia chatted in the garden. They were
quiet and talked for quite a long time then
Tante Simone played with Meg's clackers

and she looked strange and she made them go up over her hand and I was a bit frightned but it was OK they didn't smash and then Mummy came home from work and daddy came home from the pub and we all had tea at grannys house. Tante Simone gave me a big strong hug when it was time for her and Uncle Edward to go home. She whispered something to me in French I think but I don't know what she said. My mum started her job last week and me and Meg have to go to granny's house after school and wait for mummy or daddy to pick us up. Yesterday we broke up for the summer holidays and we will have to go to grannys house every day. This is just a note to put in with your book, I will post it tomorow morning first thing,
Love from Tina xxxxx

21

JANUARY 2014

Tina continued to stare at Kath, who had by now composed herself.

'Tina, of course!' Kath sat back down in her chair.

'I don't understand,' said Tina.

'You don't? Well, I'm a counsellor. I've been doing it for some time now. I'm sure I told you?'

'But your name . . . '

'I use Kate Wishaw professionally, I always have done. Wishaw's my maiden name. My husband always calls me Kate. To everyone else I'm Kath.'

'This is so . . . weird.'

'I had no idea it was you. You're Christina Fathers on my notes, you see. I thought you were Tina Thornton. You use Thornton on Facebook don't you? But I get it now. Tina — Christina.'

'Christina is too posh,' said Tina, remembering the playground taunts. She sat down in the chair alongside Kath's. There was still no desk, no couch, none of the clichéd trappings of 'therapy' that Tina had naïvely expected before her visits to Virginia last year. She knew what to expect now, of course. This place was calm and friendly, and she supposed it had been silly of her to have given up on it. But Meg had been persuasive, and Virginia hopeless.

'Such an unusual surname,' said Kath. 'Fathers. Christina Fathers.'

'I'm never Christina. Only officially.'

'Well, Tina Thornton, Christina Fathers, whatever your name is. What would you like to do?'

'What do you mean?'

'I need to arrange something else for you with a colleague. I can't be your counsellor as we're already friends, right? It would be too complicated, wouldn't you agree?'

'Oh. I . . . No, thank you. I'd like to . . . Are we really friends?'

'I think so.'

'That's good.'

'So I need to transfer you to somebody else.'

'But I'd like to work with you.'

'I'm more than happy to help. But not as your counsellor.'

'As friends then?'

'That's what friends are for, right?'

'I suppose so.'

'There we are. Shall we have a coffee to celebrate? We have cream.'

'I know.'

Tina grinned and shook her head while Kath bustled off to make the coffee. This was all so . . . serendipitous. This was the sort of thing that only happened in books, encountering each other like this, not recognising each other's names. It was all so strange.

After a couple of minutes Kath came back in bearing a tray with two mugs and a plate of chocolate digestives. Tina took her mug, held it

154

for a few moments, then placed it on the coffee table. She took off her coat. She was hot, bothered, excited. She did recall Kath saying she had a part-time job that she loved. And hadn't she recently told her she was a counsellor? Probably she had, but Tina hadn't been listening. She was the most switched-off person she knew. Maybe it was time to switch on again. Or just switch on for the first time.

'Tina Fathers,' Kath said, 'you fascinate me.'

'Really?' Tina pulled herself into the here and now. *Concentrate*, she told herself *Listen. Listen to Kath*.

'Really. I've read through your notes that my predecessor . . . Virginia . . . made . . . '

'Oh. Those. Say no more.'

'Actually, I think there is rather a lot to say. Don't you?'

'Probably.'

Kath contemplated Tina for a few moments. Tina picked up her mug and sipped her coffee. Kath sipped hers. Then she put her mug down.

'Look, I can't counsel you professionally but now that you're here . . . do you mind if I ask a question?' said Kath. 'Because it's unclear from your notes.'

'OK.'

'Are you sure? I don't want to put you under pressure. But sometimes it can really help if you maybe struggle with certain . . . facts to just answer a simple question off the cuff. It can be easier than you think, too. There's no pre-warning and you can just answer it. It might clear the decks. You're not my client but

. . . you're my friend and I do want to help you. And anything you say in these four walls stays in these four walls, obviously. I think you need a lot of help. I thought that about you the night we met.'

Tina liked this unsurprising directness. Virginia, she recalled, had tiptoed around her, not really getting anywhere. Kath — Kate — was not a pussyfooter. This directness was what she needed, Tina thought, and yes, this was it — let her ask, let her ask her question.

'I'm sure,' said Tina. 'Please.'

Kath/Kate (Tina wasn't sure which) nodded slowly, glanced at the notes again, looked hard at Tina and ran her hands through her purple-ish hair. She leaned back, puffed out her cheeks. She threw the notes to one side, muttering about not needing those any more. She leaned forward and sighed, putting her hand on Tina's knee.

'How did she die, Tina?' said Kate. Tina's heart lurched. It was most definitely Kate the counsellor asking this question. Kath the friend wouldn't have dared, for all her directness. *Oh my god oh my god. What is she aski —*

She knew. Yes. Of course she did. All that stuff was in her notes. Probably it was peppered with lots of question marks. Kate was on to her. Kath was on to her. Just like Virginia had been on to her. The question was impossible to answer, and it was cruel. But Tina understood why Kate had asked it and she could see the logic in it. Facts had to be established, even if the facts were wrong, even if they didn't fit, even if the whole thing was crazy, even if pretend facts were better

156

than the actual facts or no facts at all. Even if one person's fact was another person's fiction. Even if there was actually no such thing as 'facts', even if they were a myth created to help people make sense of the world; for this was a world in which facts didn't truly belong. There was no place for them — not in the heart, not when it was broken and smashed. *In actual fact*: Meg had liked to say that when she was young, putting her sister, and others, straight. Meg had been a very factual person.

Kath eased Tina's mug from her trembling hands and placed it on the table. She then took Tina's hands in hers. She was such a kind woman. Tina felt a sob rise in her chest. She didn't think she'd be able to keep it down. Everything was going to burst. Panic took over, as she ran away from a truth that others wanted for her, that she truly wanted for herself. The running away part was, she knew, never healthy, not in the end.

'Tina?' said Kath, almost in a whisper. 'How did Meg die?'

How did Meg die? Tina couldn't say. She'd never been able to say. Meg was dead, wasn't that enough? Why couldn't people leave her alone? Why did she have to talk about this? She felt she might slap Kath, hard and sharp across her wide, kind face. But it was a reasonable question, and for once she must give a reasonable answer. Where was the harm? She had got away with it for all these years. What good would it do to shy away from the truth now? All that business at Christmas with Lucia, falling off the steps, the way she'd had a flashback, or whatever it was — it was all in her head. And Meg's silly idea, the idea she wouldn't let go of . . . it was all nonsense, wishful thinking. She was the only one to blame. Nobody else. This she knew. Meg was wrong, quite wrong.

'I killed her,' said Tina.

22

JULY 1967

Lucia looked from her mother, to Pamela, to William, on whom she lingered, staring at him in hot disdain. She was aghast. This situation was typical, absolutely typical, of her younger brother's hapless state of being. He didn't think. But now he would have to think. Pamela looked back at Lucia in a brazen fashion, which Lucia didn't like. She didn't like anything about Pamela, who was pretty, not quite sixteen and pregnant with William's baby.

Ever since that business with Clive Stubbins and her bitter disappointment, Lucia had kept herself away from men, cloistered from the world, convincing herself and her parents that she was 'needed' at Lane's End House. She had cast herself in the role of her mother's helpmate, her keeper, and nothing had swayed her from it. She refused to get a job. She barely left the house. Her father supported her financially and it had become a habit, a way of life, and nobody spoke any more about Lucia finding employment, or standing on her own two feet, or being a layabout.

William refused to look at his sister, and she took that as a sign of submission. What a little coward he was. Mum had nothing to say, just sighing and shaking her head. It was almost as though she couldn't take it in, this news, that quite apart from anything else, she was going to be a grandmother at long last. Mum had longed for grandchildren for years. But now she seemed not to hear the news, not to grasp it. 'I don't know what your father is going to say,' was all she could contribute. Tom was at work and the teenaged couple had decided that this was the best time to broach the subject with William's mother and sister.

'You will have to get married, as soon as you're able to,' said Lucia.

'It's too late for that,' said Pamela. 'Look at me. I'm showing too much already. The earliest we can marry is the end of August anyway. By then I'll be enormous. I'm not going to look fat in my wedding photographs.'

'Photographs?'

'A wedding's a wedding isn't it?' said Pamela.

'Not always,' said Lucia, looking to her mother for support and receiving none. 'Look, if you won't agree to marry in August you'll have to go away, Pamela, and have the baby and when you come back nobody will be any the wiser.'

'They might wonder about the baby I bring back with me!' Pamela glared at Lucia.

William frowned, as if perplexed by a crossword puzzle, and looked at the floor. Mum retreated from the arena atmosphere of the dining room and crept into the kitchen to make tea. The three young people sat on in silence, Pamela and William on the high-backed sofa, holding hands. Lucia couldn't look at them. She trembled, but managed to control it by tapping

160

her delicate fingers on the table. She felt something rise up in her, something desperate and crawling. Mum brought the tea through. In silence, she poured out four cups and handed them around. She did not produce any biscuits.

'So you intend 'keeping' the baby then?' said Lucia, once everybody had taken their first polite sips of tea. She thought she saw Pamela waver.

'Yes,' said Pamela, looking at William for support. He refused to meet her gaze.

'Bigger fool you, Pamela Rose,' said Lucia. 'You know, I presume, what that will mean for you?'

'I should think so,' said Pamela, and she glared again at Lucia. 'You seem to be the ringleader,' she added.

'I'm just trying to help,' said Lucia. Now she had to fight tears. She swallowed, cleared her throat, held her cup up to her face. Something was upon her, something cold and creeping, not to be acknowledged.

'We don't need your help,' said Pamela.

'So what's your plan?' said Lucia.

'Bill? Tell her the plan, please.'

William looked nervously at his sister and his mother.

'Tell her, Bill,' urged Pamela.

'We're going to have the baby,' muttered William, looking at Mum. 'Then once Pamela is recovered and all thin and that, we're going to get married.'

'Ha!' said Lucia. 'How very modern.' She put down her tea cup, the threatened tears now under control. Bitterness was always preferable to sadness.

'What's it got to do with you anyway?' said Pamela. 'We can manage our own affairs. You should look to yourself sometimes.'

'What on earth do you mean?'

'Nothing,' said Pamela. 'Just leave us alone. We are old enough to take care of ourselves.'

'Old enough? You can't even get married yet. It's . . . it's indecent as well as . . . as well as illegal. And where exactly do you propose living with this new baby? And who is going to pay for everything?' Pamela and William glanced at each other. Their silence suggested they had not fully thought through the finer points of their plan. Pamela appeared to pull at a thread on her pretty green and blue frock. She frowned. She poked William.

'I've got a job now,' said William, 'and I'll pay.'

'And we'll stay at my mum's house until we can get one of our own,' said Pamela.

'And is your mother in agreement?' asked Lucia, guessing the answer and revelling in her moment of superiority. Pamela Rose's mother was a snob. She was well known for it, and she was going to have a fit when she got wind of her daughter's fall from grace. And who would blame her for being furious and fearful? Her fifteen-year-old daughter, expecting a child by the young and hapless brother of Ambrose Thornton? That alone would surely be enough to worry any mother.

At least Ambrose was gone; nobody knew where. Lucia had been right in her suspicions that he was a criminal and he had been convicted of theft two years ago. He had been jailed for a few weeks, that was all, but had never come home after his release. They had 'lost touch' with him. The Thornton family were mildly disgraced, for it had been public knowledge, and the story had made the local newspaper. Many of Mum's friends had stopped calling. She no longer attended the Women's Institute meetings in the village. She now pined for two of her sons, and it showed in her drawn, pale face; in her lack of interest in anything. 'Well?' said Lucia.

Pamela and William again glanced at each other, uneasy, fidgety. Lucia smirked.

'Mum and Dad don't . . . they don't know yet,' conceded Pamela, her teenaged bravado failing her at last. She burst into tears. Mum got up to console her. This was too much. Lucia left the room.

★   ★   ★

The plans were made. It was far too late to 'see to' the pregnancy, as Mum said. One afternoon she confided in Lucia that she was secretly glad. This was going to be her first grandchild. It was starting to sink in and she was beginning to feel excited about it, despite everything. Whenever it was spoken of, Lucia looked away, pretending to have something in her eye, or she left the room, or felt the need to shovel coal onto the fire. Her memories were not only awake again, they were loud and crashing around, knocking into her mind's furniture, spilling things, refusing to be still or silenced. The drabness and darkness of the corridor in that London house; the ultra-bright light of the 'consulting' room. The smell of . . . what? Antiseptic? A smell she would not forget. The clinical equipment, the cold metal instrument between her legs, inside her, the warm water (she thought it was water), the soft words as the French woman tried to explain what she was doing, the grey ceiling she had stared at throughout. Simone's smart pale-blue skirt and jacket, Simone rising anxiously from the chair with the dull patchwork cushion when Lucia hobbled back up the cellar stairs; the indent on the cushion where Simone had been sitting, waiting . . .

Lucia helped to arrange a hasty wedding for her brother and his girlfriend for the earliest possible date, which was during the first week in September. William and Pamela were late August-borns. They were still children, as Mum lamented. But still, too much was being arranged for them, over their heads, without their consent. Pamela's mother, as Lucia had foreseen, was heartbroken and disgusted, and fearful of her daughter's by now unavoidable connection with the Thornton family. Nevertheless, Mrs Rose concurred with Lucia's arrangements, and indeed joined her in making them. It clearly pained Mrs Rose to have dealings with any of the Thorntons, but Lucia availed herself, and behaved like a willing and capable ally. The avoidance of scandal was uppermost in both their minds. Marriage for the young couple was the only answer. Pamela was adamant that she would not give up her baby, despite the pleadings of her mother, her father, and Lucia. The girl would not give in, and her parents were not evil, so a dress was hastily bought and altered, the paperwork was completed, and the wedding took place on a sunny, warm Tuesday afternoon. Mr Rose and Tom were witnesses. They were polite, and there were no photographs, as Lucia had predicted. There was no reception to speak of, just tea and sandwiches at the Rose household. The young couple were packed off on the train for their 'honeymoon' (paid for by both fathers) somewhere in the north, and they returned a fortnight later. Pamela ballooned during their time away and tongues inevitably wagged on their return. But Pamela and her parents held their heads high, for the young couple, whatever their sins before, were now a married and therefore respectable couple, and the gossip was short-lived.

William returned to work after the honeymoon. The couple, as Pamela had planned, set up home in her bedroom and put their names down on the housing list. Despite all of this, or perhaps because of it, they were happy together, laughing often and enjoying the process of choosing a name for their forthcoming baby. Pamela was particular about names, William less so. She wondered about Marghuerite for a girl?

Sunday 1st August 1976

Dear Elizabeth
I haven't heard from you so I'm just checking if you received the book I sent you? I hope it has'nt got lost in the post. I was careful to wrap it properley in enough paper and string. I sent it by airmail which cost most of my pocket money I had been saving but I wanted you to get it quickly. Please let me know if you have or have not received it because I am worried. I am probably being inpatient though. I excpect you are enjoying reading it and have'nt had time to write to thank me. That will be it. I bought these new notelets with my pocket money, the kitten is the cutest picture so that's the one I have chosen for you. I do'nt like the shiny pink background much and Meg says it makes her feel a bit sick it is so horrible but the kitten is sweet. My mum is still at her job. Aunty Lucia said she thought she would give it up. It would be too much for her she said but she has'nt given it up and she told me and Meg that she loves going out to work. One day she will take us to work with her so we can see what she does. This is going to be a long letter because I'm a bit bored. I took a blankit and a pillow into our den and I read all morning. I read a book called A Stitch in Time by Penelope Lively that I got from the

book club at school. Do you have a book club? We get a magazine to take home and we get our mums and dads or our aunts to fill in the order once we dicided what book we want and we take it back into school and the school orders all the books and they get sent a few weeks later. It is so exciting and one of the small ammount of things I like at school. The book is handed to you with the order form your aunt filled in stuck to it with a lastic band so Miss Tyson knows who ordered which book. Anyway I started to read mine today and its very good a ghost story set at the seaside and a girl called Maria hears a dog barking although there is no dog and a swing swinging although there is no swing and I want to finish it soon but I had to stop reading for our lunch. Lunch was marmite sandwichs and an apple and a plum from the garden. Aunty Lucia let us eat in our den. The den is nice and cool. I think you said once you have orange trees in your garden? I wondered about that and before school broke up I asked my teacher why we have'nt got orange trees and she said that we can't grow oranges in England because it is too cold. But it is hot here, hot and dry and we are running out of water. I cant believe we could'nt grow oranges. But Granny told me its not this hot every summer. The plums are nice, very sweet, but the apples are a bit sour. Meg wants me to go down to the brook with her now with our jam jars we like to catch sticklebacks and minnows and the water is see through and theres not much of it left because its drying up. She is going to climb the big oak tree but I do'nt climb trees because I did it once and even though I didnt get very far up it I allmost fell down and I felt sick and dizzy and my knees felt like they would colapse.

Must go lots of love from Tina in England xxxxx

23

JANUARY 2014

'I killed her.' Had she really said it? Tina swayed in her seat and thought she was going to be sick. But she recovered and forced herself to look at Kath. She clung onto Kath's hands; they were strong and warm, and Tina knew she was going to cry. She let go of Kath then, and rummaged in her handbag for a tissue. Before she could find one, Kath silently handed over a box, and Tina took three, loosely scrunching them up and using them to cover her face, to hide her tears. But it was hopeless. There was no hiding. The tears would come.

'I'm sorry,' said Kath. She showed no signs of shock or disgust.

'Sorry?' muttered Tina, and she blew her nose. She made an effort to stop crying. It was time to talk. It was time to face up to the truth.

'Are you OK to carry on? Let me know when you're ready or if you'd rather not talk at all.'

'I'm ready,' said Tina and she wondered, what was she ready for?

'So . . . ?' Kath's face was open and friendly; she was clearly the sort of person you could say anything to. Kath was Kate the counsellor, after all, and it was a comfort. Kath was a professional. If only Tina could begin to listen to voices, actual real voices belonging to actual real people.

Tina took a deep breath, and another one. This was it. She had to open up, and here was her chance to do that, to tell it like it was. What was said in these four walls stayed in these four walls, Kath/Kate had said. Nobody would ever know. Nobody else was here. She could say what she liked, and that was the point, wasn't it?

'My sister, my twin sister Meg . . . who I loved so much . . . she died . . . she died? . . . she left me on . . . so long ago . . . the twenty-fifth of August in 1976. It was a Wednesday and there was a big thunderstorm in the afternoon. Meg's death was my fault . . . all my fault . . . but our Aunt Lucia was . . . she . . . I think . . . Oh! Why did you have to go? Meg says . . . I don't know . . . Oh, I don't know! I feel funny . . . '

Tina swirled, the world swirled with her, and she was only vaguely aware of Kath reaching out to try to catch her. Tina felt herself slip from her chair and her bottom thud onto the floor. Somewhere, from a long way away, she heard once again that mocking laugh that followed her everywhere.

Tina came out of her faint after a few moments and Kath helped her to sit in the chair. Tina cried some more, and found she couldn't stop for a long time. But she stopped in the end. She had to: as Kath said, there were only so many tears to be shed. And sometimes the crying had to stop in order to let the talking begin, and it was her belief that it was the talking that healed. She seemed sure about this.

Tina and Kath each had another coffee with cream, with a generous spoonful of sugar in

Tina's, and they ate a couple of biscuits, and Tina heard herself say things she'd never spoken of before.

'Meg's death was inconceivable. I couldn't get my head around it. I saw her there, on the ground, dead. She looked so small and pale. She looked like one of my dolls. Yet she'd always seemed so big, to me. I thought she was invincible. But I knew she was dead, right there and then. Something just went out in her. I knew it. She was gone. And I was terrified. I froze, I think, something in me froze over and it still hasn't thawed. Does that make sense?'

'It makes perfect sense,' said Kath, reassuringly matter of fact. She listened to Tina speak about the death of her sister.

'I couldn't accept she was dead. I was so guilty and ashamed and I couldn't let her go. I refused to attend the funeral. I stayed at Lane's End House by myself — that was Lucia's house, the family home really, and I . . . well, I think I read my book. Or something. Anyway I didn't go and I would never visit her grave or anything like that.'

'Have you ever been to her grave?'

'Oh yes, I started going a few years back. Well, many years back I suppose, in my early twenties. I go all the time. Practically every week, apart from . . . apart from . . . if we argue. Then I stay away for a while. She's in the cemetery in town. I take her flowers and, it sounds silly, but I tell her things. We talk.'

'Ah, yes. That's quite common. I think it helps. I like to talk with my brother.'

'Yes, but . . .'

'But?'

'Nothing. It doesn't matter. I feel so tired.'

'Of course.'

'Can we do this again? There's still so much to talk about.'

'You bet we can. But not here. How about the diner again? Or we can meet for coffee? Or I could come and visit you in your exquisite home.'

'How do you know it's exquisite?' said Tina.

'Because you don't have kids. And your clothes smell nice.'

Tina rose from the chair and put on her coat. But she was sweating, filmy all over her body. She would have a long shower as soon as she got home. Crying made her extra hot and bothered these days. Perhaps it was her age. Forty-six. Really? Forty-six? Inside, in her thoughts, she still felt like her eight-year-old self, helpless and scared and grieving, but refusing to grieve — fighting it, refusing to believe. She slung her handbag over her shoulder. She turned to Kath. It was time to grow up now.

'I'll always feel guilty,' said Tina.

'We'll see,' said Kath.

★ ★ ★

Keaton was as surprised as Tina that Kath was Kate. Or Kate was Kath. She sounded like an excellent therapist.

'Counsellor,' said Tina, firmly. 'I'm not nuts. She said so. My counsellor.'

172

'Not in fact your counsellor,' corrected Keaton. 'Thank goodness for that. It's going to save us a small fortune.'

'Keaton!'

'I'm only kidding. You know I'd pay whatever was needed if it meant you getting better. We'd re-mortgage this house, anything.'

'Do you think I should get a counsellor? Kath's my friend and she said she'd help. That's all.'

'Just see how it goes. She'll recommend somebody if she thinks you need it, won't she?'

'Yes.'

'There you are then.'

But later, after Keaton had gone to sleep and Tina was alone in the dark of the bedroom, Meg came to her and said, 'You are you know, you are nuts, and I told you this would happen, I told you they would get to you, persuade you, make you change your mind and turn away from me. You're all I have, Tina, you are all I have. Please don't leave me. I'm cold and lonely and you are my only friend.'

That much was true, Tina conceded.

'But please go away now,' Tina said. 'It happened. It's over. We can't change these things.'

'I don't agree,' said Meg with a toss of her hair; then Tina thought, *No, she hasn't just tossed her hair because she doesn't exist. I didn't see that, I can't hear her or smell her. I can't touch her. She died in 1976. A long time ago. Meg is dead. And I should know because I killed her. And today I made progress; I made the*

173

progress I've needed to make for thirty-eight years . . . and Meg, you just have to accept that you are dead and I am a new woman and I'm not nuts. Not any more. Starting now.

'Bollocks to your new woman bullshit,' said Meg. 'You're a chicken, cluck cluck. A scaredy-cat. And stop quoting that Kath/Kate woman. I hate her.'

Tina could tell where this was going so she crept from the bed and slowly made her way downstairs. She felt Meg follow her. Yet there were no footsteps, no sounds of her quick breathing. There was nothing, nothing at all and Tina knew that truly she was alone in the house save for the sleeping Keaton.

'Meg,' said Tina as she entered the kitchen and closed the door quietly, 'you have to go now. I'm exorcising you.'

'Ha! You're what?'

'I mean it!'

'There's only one way you can 'exorcise' me, I promise you.'

'What is the way?'

Tina was breathless, her breathing shallow and laboured, her heart thumping. Wasn't she supposed to be over all this now? Hadn't she made a significant breakthrough only this morning? Wasn't all this stuff in her mind? Wasn't she simply psychotic? Wasn't Meg dead?

'Don't you listen to anything I tell you?' said Meg. 'I want revenge.'

Meg seemed to swoop — she lunged, her anger roaring around the kitchen, a swirling vortex with Tina at its centre. Tina panicked,

174

looked wildly around her, she was going to be swallowed, swallowed up in her sister's vicious fury.

'Revenge?' whispered Tina. 'On me?'

'Revenge on you?' said Meg. The room was still again; Meg was quiet, invisible.

'I've tried, Meg, I've tried to put things right. I visit you. I'm the only one who didn't give up.'

'I know that, you cretin.'

'So why do you want revenge? Do you want me to die too, is that it? To join you properly?' Tina sobbed, and looked around for Meg who was all around but not seen: hiding, hiding everywhere and nowhere. 'I'm sorry, I'm so sorry. But I can't go on like this any more. Meg, do you hear me? I can't!'

'I don't want you to die,' said Meg, there at the table, sitting down, her long, light brown hair waving around her gently freckled face. She smiled, not unkindly. She was so pretty. 'Why on earth would I want that?'

'What do you want then?' said Tina. 'Tell me!'

'We discussed this before, don't you recall? On my birthday? Just get on with it, please, would you?' She looked serene, patient, not at all Meg-like. 'I'm tired of waiting.'

'What is it you want me to do? For God's sake just tell me!'

'I'd rather hoped I wouldn't ever need to spell it out. I was hoping you would know already or at least work it out for yourself. You are a little twit, Tina. You always were.'

'Please don't call me names.'

'Fine. I'm sorry. Let's start again. Are you

going to get a grip?'

'Yes. I am. This time, I am.' But get a grip on what? She didn't know. She just wanted to keep Meg calm, quiet. She just wanted to go back to bed.

'Good. So when are you going to do it?'

'Do what, Meg?!'

'You know what!' Meg seemed to gather herself. She finally hissed, 'Lucia.'

'What about her?'

'Stop being thick. I really do have to spell this out don't I? Listen carefully. When are you going to pull yourself together and kill that bitch?'

24

AUGUST 1976

Edward had not once forgotten his wedding anniversary, and this year was no exception. He and Simone had been wed for twelve years, and for most of that time, things had been good. Edward had his translation work and Simone, once it became apparent there would be no children, asked for her old job back, and got it. Their 'trying for a baby' had been carried out without a great deal of conviction on either side, and when after a year of 'trying' there was still no pregnancy, the 'trying' part ceased and still no baby came. Simone was contented enough with her *adorables jumelles*, she always claimed. But in recent years Edward had become less convinced of this. They didn't see too much of Meg and Tina, but when they did visit, Simone spoiled the girls, giving sweets and dolls and colouring-in books and brand new packs of felt-tipped pens. Also, books. Simone took great pleasure in choosing those for the little girls, although Edward suspected Meg didn't read her books as enthusiastically as Tina read hers. The twins loved their Tante Simone as much as she loved them. Simone would have made a wonderful mother and perhaps they should have looked into the medical side of things. It was clear that at least one of them was not able to conceive a child. Often, he suspected it wasn't him. It was a vague feeling, nothing more. But it was too late now; they had long ago ceased to discuss the possibility of having their own child. So, the nieces it was, and there were four of them now. They always remembered Robert's girls at Christmas and on their birthdays.

Edward and Simone enjoyed Robert's annual Christmas card and letter and photographs. In the correspondence, on both sides, there was always talk of a visit. One day, they both hoped, Edward and Robert would meet again. Lucia didn't know Edward was in regular, if infrequent, touch with Robert. She would be jealous, just as she was jealous of Simone. Lucia was always uncomfortable in Simone's presence. She was uncomfortable around Edward too, which was understandable. Of course, he had not forgotten what had happened between them. He wished he could forget. He wished Lucia could forget too. Sometimes he caught her staring at him with such longing, such a haunted look about her. It always reminded him of that dreadful New Year's Eve, those dire moments when he and Lucia had abandoned themselves to the unspeakable, the unrepeatable. So many years had passed, surely now it could be regarded as water under the bridge? They had been so young, so innocent; Lucia had been, at any rate. What on earth had he been thinking? He'd been drunk. Dad and Edward (and even William) had put a few away in the earlier part of the evening, after Ambrose and Lucia had left for the dance at the hall. But surely there had to be more to it than being drunk? Had he loved Lucia then? Loved her in the wrong way? Was he a pervert? He'd asked himself those questions constantly over the years. He thought he wasn't a pervert, but he didn't know what he was. The brief, shameful episode was, he knew, his life's one great mistake — his life's dark irremovable shadow — and it was all too awful to contemplate, so he tried hard not to.

Edward was sorry for his sister, despite everything. She'd had no sort of life for years, tucked away in that dwindling house with their aging parents. She had no job, no man, no friends. What did she have? She had nothing, and that was why Edward felt sorry for her, as well as frustrated by her. And another unanswerable question: was he to blame, at least in part, for her ways? Had their . . . their encounter . . . damaged her? He had to consider these questions alone. Never had he discussed the matter with anybody, and he never would. Such a conversation was impossible to imagine, impossible to consider.

'Her silly ways are self-imposed,' Simone reminded him whenever they discussed Lucia, which wasn't often. 'Do not forget that, Eddie. Why doesn't she get a job? Why doesn't she get an education? Something. These are her choices.'

Lucia had become accustomed to being kept by her hard-working father for all those years. Now Tom was dead, and these days Lucia was describing herself as 'depressed'. Edward and Simone were sceptical of this. She was clearly an unhappy woman. But depressed . . . ? In life,

Simone always said, we make our own happiness, or we sink. It was not harsh. It was simply true. Life was so much simpler than most people made of it. You just had to believe. Simone had been brought up as a Catholic but she was not devout, and she harboured no particular guilt. She simply believed in the essential goodness of her Almighty.

Edward was clock-watching. He'd arranged to leave the office an hour early this Friday afternoon, so he could go to the shops for flowers and wine. They always drank wine to celebrate their anniversary. Often it was something expensive: champagne, sometimes a nice claret. Edward, teetotal for the rest of the year, indulged himself on this special day. And the flowers were white lilies, always lilies, because Simone was an admirer of their large petals and expensive scent. Edward had noticed a recent change in his wife. She was distant from him. They had not been 'close' for two or three weeks. Edward wasn't sure why and today he was determined to spoil his wife and bring things back to normal for both of them. Rarely had they argued or lost touch with each other.

He said goodbye to his colleagues at four o'clock, and slinging his jacket over his shoulder he sauntered, whistling, along the August-dry high street, heading first for the florist, then to the wine merchant. He reached the cinema, which was screening a film called *Bugsy Malone*, and wondered if Simone would like to see it. They could go to their favourite little Italian restaurant afterwards.

180

As he passed the cinema, something familiar, a movement, a certain rustle of a certain dress, caught his eye. He stopped. He stared at the couple emerging from the large double doors, and everything became slow and laboured, muffled, like being under water. He couldn't breathe for a moment, as he watched his wife, in her best black taffeta frock and her best black shiny court shoes (old-fashioned he supposed, but classic) emerging from the cinema, smiling, laughing, arm in arm with a man. She did not see Edward. She did not glance in his direction. Edward knew that she saw nothing, only this man. They walked a few jaunty, confident steps, and then the man stopped, pulled Simone to him, and kissed her, their arms entwined, oblivious to all around them. It was love, or it was an impression of it. Edward felt surprise at first, more than anything, just simple surprise. Practical things, cheap little meaningless complaints, occurred to him. The phrase 'broad daylight' weaved through his mind. If only he'd walked past just half a minute earlier, he wouldn't have seen his wife with this man. And, he thought pettily, how indiscreet she was, in public — anybody could have spotted her. Just around the corner! The corner! Just around it. In broad daylight. The cinema. Our cinema.

Could he forget about it? Pretend he'd never seen them? It was an idea, but no, no, of course he could not. He began his walk home to the flat, the lilies and champagne heavy in his arms. And he thought, with regret, now that Simone had already seen *Bugsy Malone*, she probably

181

wouldn't want to see it again. All his plans drifted up, up and away, and trying to prevent his thoughts and sanity from untethering themselves and going in the same tortured direction, he kept his eyes to the ground and strode towards home.

★ ★ ★

Meg took her turn at hopscotch without enthusiasm. She was bored. She tried to hop too fast to get her turn over and done with and stumbled, falling onto her knees and getting grit and dirt on her already grubby trousers, which were a murky mustard yellow. They were Meg's favourites and she wore them as often as she was allowed. They had been patched twice already on each knee by an exasperated Aunty Lucia.

Tina was missing their mother, although she hadn't yet confided in Meg about this. She guessed that Meg missed her too. It was strange not having her around during the day. Tina took her go at hopscotch, and just as she finished her turn a familiar red Mini flew around the bend at the top of the lane.

'That's Uncle Edward's car!' cried Tina and she carefully placed the hopscotch stone at her feet. She and Meg stood, watching the car as it careened down the lane, faster than usual, *more weirdly*, Tina thought. She couldn't think of the right word. Was it clumsy? The girls stepped backwards as the car came to an abrupt and untidy halt outside the gate, right over their hopscotch grid. The tyres made a small screech.

Uncle Edward stayed sitting inside the car for a long time. Tina and Meg stared in at him. He was crying. Aunty Lucia came to the front door, wiping her hands on her apron, and stood silent and still at the top of the steps, waiting.

Uncle Edward finally opened the car door and climbed out. He tried to smile at the girls, but he crumpled into more sobbing instead, and the girls drew back in horror; they had never seen their uncle so grim and so sad. He managed a ghastly smile, then walked through the gate, letting it clang shut behind him, and stumbled as he walked towards the steps leading up to the front door. The girls followed him at a safe distance. Uncle Edward threw himself up the steps and reached out for his sister, who reached out towards him. He sobbed on her shoulder. She tried to hold him, but it was clearly difficult for her, the girls could see. She looked stiff and uncomfortable.

'She's gone, Lucia!' cried Uncle Edward. 'She's left me. My Simone, gone.'

The girls looked at each other in alarm. Tante Simone, gone? It made no sense. Where had she gone? They understood now their uncle's tears. Tina looked up at Aunty Lucia and was shocked to see a small tight smile as her brother sobbed on her shoulder.

★ ★ ★

Tina and Meg gazed silently at each other after Uncle Edward disappeared into the house with their Aunty Lucia. The front door was closed

183

firmly, shutting the girls out. They were fearful for their uncle; he was trembling and he had disgusting yellow snot running down over his mouth and chin. They had never seen him like this. And why was he here? Once, they had overheard Uncle Edward and Tante Simone talk about Aunty Lucia and it had not been complimentary, as Tina had carefully said at the time. Aunty Lucia was the last person anybody should turn to for comfort, and both girls knew this by instinct as well as by experience. They crept up to the open dining room window and listened to the adults, whose voices became strangely foreign and mingled. It was hard to hear everything, and the girls were motionless as they strained to listen and remain undetected.

She's run off with another man, they heard. *I always thought her a careless person.* I saw her leaving the cinema with him on Friday afternoon . . . *Are you sure?* I confronted her later at home and she admitted it without even batting an eyelid. Cool as you like. *That's shocking* . . . She was going to tell me anyway she said. She still loves me, whatever she means by that . . . *Well, she is French, isn't she* . . . Half-French . . . *I could have told you it would all come to nothing* . . . I didn't need to hear that . . . *I'm sorry but I must speak as I find* . . . She said she was glad we never had a child . . . *I . . . I don't know what to say.* I suspected she might have wanted a family but was putting on a brave face all these years. *Well, a face anyway* . . . It's over so would it be all right for me to stay? *Of course* . . . She says she feels betrayed . . . I don't

know why. Why would she say that? I've never
. . . *Of course you haven't* . . . I can't bear to set
foot in that flat ever again. She left on Friday
night and it's been hell being there all weekend
. . . *You should have come before now.* I
couldn't think what to do . . . I'll let her wind
things up . . . *Very sensible.* Fuck that bastard!
(The girls opened their eyes and mouths wide at
each other — never had they heard Uncle
Edward swear.) *Hush your language.* I'm sorry.
Oh, she said so many things. She's furious with
me and she said she was frightened of me, can
you believe that? Frightened! *What on earth can
she mean?* And she met this chap at work she
told me and he is nice she said, just nice and not
complicated. *I see* . . . Am I complicated? *No,
Edward.* Is Mum having a nap? *Yes, she usually
naps in the afternoon.* Best if we don't tell her
everything. She loved Simone . . . (Uncle Edward
crying again) Simone loved her, I thought. How
could she, Lucia? *Well, I never trusted her and
she's been very unfair to you* . . . I trusted her
. . . *But do you think* . . . No, no chance, she's
gone for good. I don't think she'll ever come
back. *I see* . . . Thank you, Loose Ear. I'll go up
to see Mum in a bit . . .

And Meg sneezed — a loud, shrill, unmistak-
able sound — and it was too late to run, too late
to hide, as the pale, anxious face of Aunty Lucia
loomed out of the window.

Monday 16th August 1976

Dear Elizabeth
I have things to tell you about. Our Uncle
Edward has left his wife, actually, I think
that's wrong, she has left him. It is sad
because me and Meg liked her so much. Her
name is Tante (which is French for Aunt)
Simone and she has gone for good which
really should be for bad because theres
nothing good about it. Meg and me
overheard Uncle Edward and Aunt Lucia
talking and Meg sneezed and it wasn't her
fault but even so it got us into trouble
because Aunty Lucia caught us eevesdrop-
ping and she said 'Stay right where you are
you little madams!' and she looked scarey
and very cross and out she came and she
spanked us both, and made me cry and my
hand is still sore and she said we were nosy,
and we were trooble, and we were bad, bad
girls and no better than Uncle Ambrose with
his wickid ways. She said lots of other things
and really it is she who is bad because by the
end even Meg was crying and Meg doesn't
cry much. Lucia (I am not calling her Aunty
anymore and neither is Meg, we have made
up our minds) said we were evil little weerd
twins and how she wished we had never come
along and how our mother should of listened
to her and she was glad Tante Simone left

186

because she spoilt us and tried to turn us into pretty dolls which we most certanly are not. She was spitful. She said we didn't deserve anything that we got and she took Ballet Shoes and The Diddakoi and A Stitch in Time. She started to rip them up and she threw them into the fireplace and she set them alight and I was crying a lot and Meg said she wasn't going to put anything of hers on the fire and Lucia said she would do as she liked. Meg ran off and found her clackers and hid them in the shed round the side of the house. Our Uncle Edward asked ~~Aunty~~ Lucia to calm down and leave us poor girls alone and then SHE ran outside crying like we had thrown HER books on the fire and Uncle Edward ended up following her outside and comforting HER even though he is the one who is sad and me and Meg. Tomorrow he has promised to take me to the shops to replace my books. I hate her. I wish she was dead. One day she will be, Meg told me and we hugged.

From your sad cousin Tina x

Tuesday 17th August 1976

Dear Elizabeth
I know I only wrote to you yesterday but I will put both letters in the same envelope. I want to write to you again tonight because I have some good news for once, hooray!! My mum was cross about my books and she had an argumant with ~~Aunty~~ Lucia which I didn't like I don't like argumants and shouting but the happy thing is our Uncle Edward took me and Meg shopping today like he promised and he brought me new copies of my books that Lucia burned and was that really yesterday she burned them because it already feels like a long time ago. He also brought me some brand new books I haven't read before. One of them is a Famous Five book, it is called Five go to Mystery Moor. I have already read Five go to Smugglers Top and I like Anne the best but Meg who actually quite likes The Famous Five says Anne is nothing and George is the best because she does things and is never scarred. I'm not sure that's true but I didn't argue with Meg because we are very good friends again and I don't want to spoil it. Uncle Edward also brought her a cowboy suit which she is wearing right now as I write these words and she looks like a cowgirl not a cowboy she is Calamity Jane but she loves it and he got us

ice creams and said we shouldn't put up with Aunty Lucia's nonsense. He told us she was a spoilt little girl. He said she is not always nice. Uncle Edward has promised to try to help us and he is going to have a word with Lucia we hope he will tell her off but she doesn't like telling offs but Uncle Edward says she deserves one sometimes just like everybody else and she is mean to us but also kind because she does look after us most days and she makes us food even if its not nice food it is dry and she does our washing and other stuff so we have to be good little girls and remember all of that. Uncle Edward says we should try to help more around the house so in a few days we are going to help Granny and Aunty Lucia with jam making. We are making plum jam with the plums that grow in Granny's garden. I haven't made jam before but I am looking forward to it although we will be hot because you have to boil the frut Uncle Edward told me but he says Meg and I should put on our aprons and help out like good girls then maybe Lucia will see the better side of us.

That is all for now,

Love from Tina xxxxxxxxxx

25

JANUARY 2014

Keaton woke up before his alarm went off and rolled over, reaching out for his wife. He felt ecstatic, and early morning was the best time to feel ecstatic. This was energy and it was new, and he wanted to share it with Tina. But she wasn't in bed. She was sitting huddled in a blanket by the wide open bedroom window.

Keaton sat up. 'Tina?'

She didn't turn around. She didn't seem to hear.

'Tina? What are you doing?'

'Thinking,' said Tina quietly, still staring out of the open window. The morning was murky and foggy.

'Well, could you do your thinking with the window closed please?'

Keaton threw back the duvet and sprung from bed. He was a morning person. Awake when he was awake, like a child.

'I thought I was going to be all right,' said Tina, and she turned towards Keaton. She had been crying.

'You are going to be all right,' he replied, making for the shower.

'No, I'm not. I'm so not, Keaton!'

'What on earth's the matter?'

He turned and came to the window then, and

190

closed it. He drew Tina towards the bed and sat her on it, and kneeled in front of her.

'Meg,' gasped Tina.

'Oh, for heaven's sake!'

'Don't be like that. Please.'

'Don't be like what? Tina, Meg is dead. Right? You know it, I know it, everybody knows it. You admitted it to Kath or Kate or whatever her name is and most importantly to yourself only yesterday, right?'

'In one sense she's dead.'

'In the sense that she's dead, or she's 'dead'? You're either dead or you're alive. There is only one dead. You can't be both.'

'But you can. You really can be both. She can. She's not truly dead. She told me that once . . .'

Keaton stood. 'I'm going to have my shower, then I'm going to make us coffee and toast and then I'm off to work, but tonight we can talk. We'll talk for as long as you want. I'm happy to talk to you forever about this if it means you get over it.'

'I don't want to talk. I need to do.'

'Do what?'

'You'll see. You'll see. Meg will help me, I know she will. Actually it's her idea. She always has the ideas.'

'Oh, Jesus Christ. Tina, just . . . shut up about it, can't you? I'm so worried . . . No. I'm frightened for you. Damn it, Tina!'

'But you have nothing to be frightened of.'

'Oh really?'

'Your life is so pure and so easy,' said Tina, almost singing, almost chanting. She was clearly a long way away, somewhere Keaton could not go. 'You have no worries and nobody to mourn and no troubles of any kind.'

'What?' Keaton shouted, furious at last, broken at last. He withdrew from Tina, took two steps backwards, and glared at her.

'You're so lucky,' said Tina, looking up at him and trying to smile.

'Lucky? Me? Living with a . . . It's you who has no idea, Tina, you. Now, I'm going to have a shower and then I'm off to work. Forget breakfast. I'll grab some on the way. Tonight, if you want, if you're going to talk sense, we will talk about this. Otherwise . . . Tina, do try to pull yourself together. We can't . . . I can't keep on like this. Our life, it's so . . . no. Your life is so unhinged. You spend so much time in that weird place in your head and as for your constant bloody cleaning — this house, other people's houses, why? Why the hell? Why do you do that? What's it all about, really? It's high time you stopped cleaning houses and dropped this whole bloody charade and cleaned up your life. Clean up your mind, that's what's so soiled and untidy! That's what needs decluttering! Can't you see? You're psychotic. More than that, you're . . . you're not all there. You're a fucking mess!' He glared at her, panting. She looked back at him, blank. Just blank. He turned away from her, her gormless gaze, and made for the shower. He slammed the door shut.

Tina knew what he meant. To be fair, he had a point. He truly did. She listened to her husband shower, then she watched him get dressed. She remained seated on the edge of the bed. Keaton did not try to speak any further to her. He finished dressing. He left for work after kissing her quickly on her head. She did not return the kiss. She heard him open the front door and close it behind him. *Come back, come back,* were the words she could only think and not say.

Later, mechanically, Tina made herself shower, dress, eat toast and drink coffee. After her lonely breakfast, she tidied the kitchen and made the king-size bed that she and Keaton had shared every night for the last eighteen years. Hard to believe they had been married for that long and had been a couple for even longer. It was inconceivable that so much time had passed. It was her fault there was so little to show for it. No children. Not one. But there could still be a child for her and Keaton. It wasn't too late, not yet. The change had not quite come upon her, not in its entirety. She had only skipped the one period, that one time, and now they were almost regular again. She was fortunate, even if the cycle was drawing out a little, becoming less noticeable, much less painful. It was not too late to fulfil Keaton's dream of becoming a father and in truth, she owed it to him.

In December, her doctor had been keen to explain the issues with pregnancy for the older woman. Tina had listened politely, then eventually, she had managed to get her doctor to concede that it was possible for her to become pregnant and give birth to a healthy baby. Her doctor was a nice woman really and was trying to help, doing her job, and she had printed off a leaflet for her, and urged her to take her time and think about it. Tina thought about it for a day, then made an appointment to have her coil removed. She'd bled; it had been uncomfortable. But only for a day or two.

Keaton would make a wonderful father, she knew. He had never been anything but patient and kind, if not fully understanding. How could he understand her when she didn't understand herself? The fantasy she had spun around her life was unfathomable. Often she felt she was a mere butterfly, small and helpless, unable to struggle free of her chrysalis, caught up in the silk and frass of her imagination. Her life was a mockery of something, she felt sure. But of what? Was it grief? Did she just not know how to handle it? Was it guilt? Guilt that her sister was dead and she was not? Survivor's guilt perhaps? Or the guilt of the wrongdoer, because she had done wrong. She'd read about child murderers, of course, furtively borrowing books from various libraries; looking articles up on the internet and deleting them from the search history. Mary Bell. Pauline Parker. Juliet Hulme. She'd watched *Heavenly Creatures* alone, in fear and fascination. Was there another name to add to the infamous list? Christina Thornton? Children were capable of horrible acts, just like adults. If only she could see clearly, stand apart from the things that had happened on *that day* and watch; be a silent observer among the leaves, listening, listening, her eyes and ears attuned to all that was said, all that was done. There was a sequence; there always was. This happened, that happened — one led to the other. Logic was ever present. But there were no watchers, no witnesses, just participants — Lucia and her nieces. Meg, dead, and Tina, shocked and frightened into a lifetime of silence, an inner reverie of blame.

'Tina? What have you done?' Those were the words. The pale, accusing face, eyes wide and haunted, looking up at her, the rain drip-dropping onto the leaves, the clouds heavy at last, opening up. The only words until everything sprang into action, until the rain began to hammer down properly for the first time in weeks; until Lucia ran off, shrieking and calling for Uncle Edward, for Granny, anybody, leaving Tina alone in the tree looking down at her sister, coffin-still on the ground, willing her to move, open her eyes, stand up. And Meg did open her eyes and stand up. Meg looked up at her and waved — weirdly that was all she had done, just waved, smiling up at her. And then she was gone, but Tina felt she hadn't gone far, and then the men had come running, farm hands summoned by Lucia's wails, and eventually Uncle Edward had come too and he'd gently touched the dead Meg — the one still lying on the ground — turning her head towards him, his shirt wet with big spattered raindrops. And then the ambulance men and firemen had come across the fields and Tina had sat, wet and forgotten for a while in the rustle of the green canopy, where she was alone, truly alone for the first time, knowing that her life had changed irreparably, and forever. And the words, musical in their monotonous refrain: What have you done, Tina? Tina, what have you done?

★ ★ ★

Keaton slammed his office door behind him and took off his coat. He put his deli-bought lunch in the fridge. He'd skipped breakfast. He placed his bag carefully under the desk and turned on his PC. So this was it, another day. Another day of work. Another day with a mad wife made madder by becoming less mad. Or something like that. He'd thought yesterday had seen a breakthrough. But today there was no break-through, just more of the same. Today, the long-dead Meg was back, alive and kicking. Damn her! So he was going mad too. Was he becoming as crazy as his wife? No, actually, nobody was as crazy as her. Those that were, were locked up somewhere, and one never encountered them.

Keaton tried to stem this tide of irrationality and nastiness, but it was hard to do so. He was being uncharitable. But he'd lived with this for years; he'd known before he'd married Tina that she fantasized about her dead sister and imagined her to be alive, if not well; he knew Tina visited her sister's grave weekly, and he'd been able to establish what he'd long suspected, that Tina blamed herself for Meg's death. That Lucia woman was involved too, somehow. She had some kind of hold over Tina, Keaton was convinced, but it was impossible to get Tina to talk properly about it, to get her to understand

196

she had been a little girl and even if it had somehow been her 'fault', she was not to blame. She had not been old enough to blame.

Keaton's office door opened and Sharanne entered, proffering Keaton's customary cup of morning coffee. Sharanne looked spring-like and fresh.

'A penny for them?' she said, a favourite phrase of hers that had annoyed him on several occasions, but today did not. Keaton took the mug from her. She positioned her hands on her hips. Keaton carefully placed his cup on his desk. Sharanne was wearing a pretty shade of pink lipstick. It was frosty, shimmery. It suited her.

He wanted to kiss her. There was no doubt. Something opened up in him. In the silence they regarded each other, Sharanne's breathing becoming quick and shallow. Keaton stood up. He walked around his desk. Sharanne stared at him, her eyes wide. He had two options. He could go to the door, open it, and politely usher his assistant from the room, and then the temptation would be gone, and probably forever, because he would go, leave this job and get another. Something had to give. His whole life was in the balance, and he knew it.

His other option was to take this last step towards his assistant, put his hands in her hair and pull her towards him. This is what he did. He reached the crossroads and took the most enticing turn, knowing it was the wrong one, knowing it was unfair on two women, one of whom he loved as much as ever, despite everything. Sharanne's lips were not frosty, they were moist and grasping. There was little pre-amble. The sex was reckless and clichéd and dreamy. It was Perrinesque, like lots of things in his life. Even as he indulged himself and felt his body convulse and Sharanne's hands greedy on him, he knew it was hopeless — a huge mistake. He wondered, somewhere in his muddled mind, how they must look — silly, of course. And anybody could have knocked on his office door and entered, but that was half the charm of it. It was all rather shocking and nauseating. But it was uncomplicated. Sharanne was uncomplicated. Except it wasn't. She wasn't. These were actually the most complicated moments of Keaton's life. And it was his own fault, because he had a choice. Sharanne's body was firm and compact. Her vagina didn't feel like Tina's vagina. Tina's body was soft and gracious and giving. Sharanne's was hard and ungenerous — taking, taking, taking. Sharanne was the same age as Tina, but how different they were in every way. Keaton considered stopping. He ought to stop, he realised; he ought to recover his senses, and apologise. But it would be stupid, he would look childish, and it was too late, so he hurried. He blotted his wife from his mind and heart and gave himself up to the lust of the lost for a few frenzied minutes — giving, giving, giving — lost in Sharanne's firm flesh, her clawing hands, her new rhythms. Quite soon, it was over. Possibly Sharanne was disappointed. Probably it was a good thing if Sharanne was disappointed. Afterwards Keaton trembled and he could not face her as she pulled her appearance back into shape and fiddled with her hair. Her cheeks were now as pink as the lipstick which had gone from her lips. He wondered where it had gone and he could taste it. What had he done? How was this helping? He hastily tidied himself, tucking his shirt back in, doing up his trousers. He longed for a mirror. He had been faithful to Tina throughout all the time he had known her. Now that spell had been broken and very likely his marriage was broken too. He just didn't do this sort of thing. And yet, he did, clearly, because he just had. Self-loathing seeped through him like an infection he knew he would not be able to fight off

Sharanne, tidy at last, and not obviously disappointed at all, smiled at him, and moved to kiss him — he now sat primly behind his desk — but he turned away. The kissing was over. He couldn't. He was being a pig, even a prig, but he couldn't kiss her.

'I'm sorry,' he said, for want of saying something — anything. The whole encounter had been wordless, harsh, hard, not at all his sort of thing.

She left his office and closed the door, not looking at him. Keaton sat alone and lonely, and leaned across his desk, lowering his head onto his arms. He felt like he might cry. He ought to cry, but this day, and it was still early, was already beyond him, out of reach and irretrievable. He wished he could begin it again — go back to bed and wake — and not find Tina sitting in the foggy morning air at the open window. What a moment that had been, a sudden fall and crash onto hard ground. He was scared. He was hurt. He was a helpless flailing creature. He couldn't help Tina, he knew that now. She was impenetrable.

26

AUGUST 1976

Tina wept for her books, her poor lost books, the remains charred and ragged, curling wisps of paper and words. Some fluttering, anchorless pieces had made their forlorn way up the chimney and had floated down into the garden; strange unintelligible messages from on high. Meg was furious, and she was sympathetic; seething, muttering, 'She's a bitch!' Tina wasn't shocked any more by that word. She allowed herself to be comforted by it. Tina wrote a letter. Later, Meg said she was bored and begged Tina to play hopscotch again. They asked Uncle Edward, very politely, if he could move his car. He apologised, and moved it. He seemed at a loss to know what to do with himself. The girls resumed their game and pretended not to notice their uncle's unhappiness. He sat in the garden watching the girls play. He drank a cup of tea. Granny ventured out to sit with him, and she cried and held his hand. He didn't seem to mind, but Meg whispered to Tina that she didn't like old people's hands; they were always cold. Lucia, hard of face and unrepentant, made fish fingers and chips and baked beans for the girls' tea, and allowed them to eat in the garden on the tartan picnic rug. Tina ate slowly, the food stale and dry, it seemed to her. Meg picked at hers for a while, and when nobody was looking crept into the den in the laurels and buried the food. Hadn't their dad told them that Lucia had tried to poison him once? Meg was making a stand, she said, against Lucia and she would begin with her rotten food. They also had orange squash to drink, too weak, as Lucia always made it. They were pleased to see their dad when he arrived after work. But where was Mum? She was usually the one to pick them up and take them home, holding their hands and swinging them back and forth energetically all the way home. Sometimes she sang them funny mischievous, made-up songs. The best ones were about Lucia.

Lucia told William it was good of him to finish early. 'Thank you,' she said. 'I hope you didn't mind my ringing you at work. I didn't know what else to do.'

William spoke to Edward in the garden and Tina heard their father say he was sorry. Uncle Edward acquiesced with a small sigh; a nod of his head. The girls felt bad for him but didn't know what they could do to make things better. Dad didn't seem to know either, so he chivvied his daughters up and said it was time to go home. Tina and Meg said nothing about Lucia ripping and burning Tina's books. They had decided to wait and tell their mum about it instead. She would do something. The twins said goodbye to their granny and to Uncle Edward, deftly avoiding the inclusion of Lucia in their farewells. She stood at the top of the steps and said nothing. She didn't wave when William's car pulled away.

★ ★ ★

They told their mum in the morning, over breakfast, what Lucia had done to Tina's books. Meg did most of the telling, because Tina felt too upset to talk about it. Mum was predictably furious. Why hadn't they told her yesterday? Tina wasn't sure why they hadn't, but the rambling shame of the bullied, which she surely felt and Meg understood, had of course prevented her. She'd begged Meg to say nothing. But this morning, Meg had given in and told. After her initial anger, Mum became stony-faced, quiet. Once they had eaten their toast and drank their milk, she told the girls to hurry and brush their teeth and comb their hair. She was going to have it out with Lucia. By God, was she.

Meg couldn't wait. Tina could. When they arrived at Lane's End House, Meg ran across the grass to the front door and banged the door knocker — once, twice, thrice. Tina followed her mum across the lawn, wanting to hide, trying to hang back. Lucia opened the front door.

'You can enter via the kitchen, you know,' she said, wiping her hands on her apron and sighing. 'Girls, take off your shoes. They're wet with dew'

'First things first, lady!' cried Mum. Meg retreated down the steps, and stood off to one side with Tina. But of course, Meg wasn't cringing. She was grinning, anticipating the confrontation that was surely to come. Tina gripped her sister's hand.

'Apologise to my daughter!' demanded Mum.

'I beg your pardon?' said Lucia.

203

'You heard me. Or do you have a Loose Ear?'

Meg sniggered. Tina covered her mouth with her free hand. Oh no, no, no . . .

'You do not call me by that name,' said Lucia, and she could barely be heard, her fury small and quiet. She crossed her arms, pulling herself up tall. 'Do you understand?'

'No, I don't,' said Mum, and she was . . . what? Tina thought the word might be *brazen*. 'Why all the fuss? It's just a stupid name. But you understand this: apologise to my daughter and replace her books.'

'What?!' Lucia looked genuinely surprised.

Mum went up one step. She looked strong. 'Do not 'what' me, lady. Take your skinny arse into town today and replace my girl's books.'

'I shall do no such thing. And mind your language, Pamela Rose. Who on earth do you think you are?'

'I'm Pamela Thornton. Your sister-in-law. Mother to your nieces.'

'You call yourself a mother? You're no mother. You're never at home! I do all the mothering of these — '

The slap was sharp and unexpected. Now Meg had her hand over her mouth too, eyes wide in intrigue and horror. A barefooted Uncle Edward appeared behind Lucia. He pulled her gently to one side as she stroked her face and started to weep. Tina felt bad for her, at last. It must have hurt. Mum had smacked her backside once, and Tina could still recall the smart of it and that had been with clothes on.

'Pamela, that's quite enough,' said Uncle

204

Edward in a quiet voice. 'I'll take the girls shopping and buy the books today. I've already promised.'

'It's hardly your place to, Edward,' said Mum. She was calmer now.

'Nevertheless, I'll take them. I told Tina yesterday that I would. Girls, say goodbye to your mum now, she needs to get to work. Off you go, Pamela. Please.'

'But — '

'No matter. I'll buy them. I promise. Go to work. We'll pop in to see you later if you like?'

Mum kissed Tina and Meg goodbye. Meg was giggling again and Mum gave her a playful pinch on her arm. She left to run up the lane to catch her bus. Uncle Edward and Lucia went back into the house. Tina looked at Meg. Meg shrugged and smiled, a wicked gleam about her.

★ ★ ★

So this was the routine at Lane's End House now (but perhaps without the doorstep row and the almighty slap). How different from his time there, his youth. Nothing was permanent, obviously, but this morning he knew that for the first time, he truly understood what that meant. Mum struggled down the stairs, roused from her sleep by the doorstep commotion. Edward reassured her there was nothing going on. Pamela had words with Lucia, that was all. We all know Pamela can get a little fiery. Lucia disappeared into the kitchen, and soon Edward smelled eggs and bacon. That was permanent.

He returned to the small bedroom, finished dressing, made up the bed, and peered out of the large but oddly dark window. There was a dwindling mist on the field behind the house. The cows were busily grazing. The sun was launching itself into the day. He opened the curtains wide, as far as they could go.

Sunday 22nd August 1976

Dear Elizabeth
Another letter! Sorry. I like writing things down. It makes them seem real. Yesterday I stayed on my own most of the time and I read more than half of Ballet Shoes. I want to read it again one more time before I start my new Famous Five book. I decided to colour in some of the pictures in the book which is naughty but I like colouring and Meg does too and she helped me. She read a bit on some of the pages we coloured and she said Petrova sounds all right. ~~Aunty~~ Lucia has a pink mark on her cheek still where my mum slapped her when they had their argumant the other day. Mum told us she is a bit sorry for slapping Lucia but she deserved it she says. Mum said she should really have held her temper but Lucia has a bad effect on her. Mum said she would pay Edward back for the books but he said no need for that. Mum told me Lucia should pay but she has no money of her own because she is lazy and hasn't worked for many years. I don't think she's lazy she works all the time but I hate her for burning my books. I don't know what we would do without Uncle Edward being here. He makes everything better. It was his birthday and my dad's birthday on Thursday Lucia made a

cake. Meg didn't want any of it so I had her slice.
Write soon,
Love from Tina xx

27

JANUARY 2014

Keaton entered the front door and slowly closed it behind him. The house was quiet and empty. Normally, Tina would be in the kitchen preparing their evening meal or would have the meal ready and waiting on the stove, and be curled up on the sofa with a book or watching television. Today she was doing none of these things. She wasn't there.

Had she left him? Had he been too harsh this morning? Should he have been kinder before he'd left for work? The answer was yes, he should have been kinder, but it was far too late now, and how long ago all that was. He'd avoided her all day, deciding not to call or text. He'd tried to avoid Sharanne all day too, but that had been more difficult.

A terrible thought occurred to him as he searched the house. What if Sharanne had told Tina what had happened that morning? Surely she would not have done so, but people could be hard to read. He was a pretty good observer of his fellow human beings and one thing he had noticed was that sometimes people did the unexpected thing. Even quite predictable people like Sharanne. And there was a streak in her he didn't like, and never had, something untrustworthy. What a fool he was.

There was no sign of any bags having been packed; everything was neat and tidy as usual. Tina's toothbrush was in the bathroom. He was being illogical and paranoid, he told himself. Of course Sharanne hadn't rung Tina. What a ridiculous notion. Tina's winter boots were not in the hall, nor her coat. He knew where she would be. Panic over, he supposed, although living with his neurotic, desperate wife was to live in a permanent state of panic. He made for the front door.

*　★　★

The cemetery was cold. The day had remained clammy and foggy, oddly disappointing for the time of year because although it was still January, it was its last day. February was nigh and that filled Tina with hope. February was the month where winter could be banished, when all around, life could break free. Snowdrops and crocuses were already poking through the hard ground. They looked small and bullied as though January was stamping on them, forcing them back into the earth. Tina tended her sister's grave, as she had done for the past twenty-five years. She snipped at the grass although it wasn't yet growing and tidied away the dead poinsettia she'd left on Christmas Eve.

Tina sat back on her haunches and arranged a new bunch of pink carnations in the urn, taking care to set them to advantage. Her sister's grave was one of the prettiest and most well-kept in the cemetery. Tina was proud of it. After her work, she looked around. Her favourite wooden bench — dedicated to 'Norma, beloved wife and mother' — was empty today. Sometimes the lady with the green coat was sitting on the next bench along, sometimes not, and today she was not. The woman had been visiting the cemetery for a few weeks, Tina thought, but they had never spoken. The woman didn't seem to visit a grave. She just liked to sit on the bench to read and contemplate, or so it seemed. Sometimes the woman brought lunch with her. Tina knew she was missing somebody. She could tell the woman was lonely. The cemetery was quiet, the sounds of traffic out on the main road distant and dull; it was a good place for solitude. Nobody bothered you here. Birds sang all year round, and in the summer bees and other insects thrummed the long afternoons away. Tina made for Norma's bench and sat down, even though today was not the day for sitting around out of doors; something the insects had obviously grasped, as had the green-coated woman.

Tina pulled on her mittens, rewrapped her thick self-knitted scarf around her neck and did nothing for several minutes, apart from sit. Meg was 'off' with her today, clearly. Tina had denied Meg's existence yesterday. Last night Meg had been weird — demanding. Yet Tina couldn't really blame her for being peeved. She wasn't here. Tina was.

And Keaton was too. He was walking up the slope towards her. He never came, but today he was here, making his determined way along the path towards this upper, quiet end of the cemetery. He looked cold and out of place. Tina watched as his breath billowed around him. His coat looked heavy, and Tina knew that underneath the coat his body would be snug and warm. She stood up as he approached her. It was just as well Meg wasn't around today. Meg hated Keaton. Keaton hated Meg, in a sense.

The husband and wife's eyes met and in that moment they both felt a huge surge of relief.

* * *

She doesn't know; that was Keaton's immediate thought as their eyes met. She has no idea. She was there to tend her sister's grave. All was well. And tomorrow he would hand in his notice. He would find another job and once he'd left, he would never see Sharanne Kite again. How stupid he had been today. Tina looked small and lost and as he drew nearer he could hear her breath coming in short, quick bursts and gasps. He wondered if he should have come. He wondered if Meg was 'here'. Tina looked strange; pained and pale. And cold. He reached her, opened his coat, pulled her to him and wrapped her in it, kissing her head.

They stood for some time, wordless. And Keaton could see why she came here, how she managed to 'communicate' with Meg. There was a sense of peace here. This was a place of reconciliation, and he felt it now. He hadn't realised it before, those few times he'd come alone to his sister-in-law's grave, without Tina's knowledge. He'd wanted to feel what Tina felt, to see what Tina saw, to hear what she heard. Of course, he'd felt nothing, only sadness. The death of a child was inexpressibly tragic, even if it had occurred thirty-eight years ago. Time meant nothing.

And death was one thing. Refusing to accept death was another. Blaming yourself for a death, another matter still.

'How did you know where to find me?' asked Tina eventually, her voice muffled as she snuggled inside Keaton's coat.

'I know where your sister's grave is, you idiot.'

'Oh.'

'And I guessed you'd be here.'

'I am here.'

'Is Meg — is she here too?'

'Not today.'

'I see.'

'Take me home, please?'

'Gladly. It's bloody freezing!'

'Keaton?' Tina drew away and watched as Keaton did up his coat.

'Yes?'

'Whatever happens . . . will you forgive me?' She stooped and picked up her things.

Keaton took the things from her to carry to the car. He was glad he wouldn't have to walk all the way back to their house on the other side of town. But it had been worth the long, cold trudge up here, and he was glad he'd come. He'd do anything for Tina, he realised anew. He suppressed a sob. His skin prickled.

'I won't ever have to forgive you,' he said. 'You've done nothing wrong.'

28

AUGUST 1976

Tina was a bookworm, no doubt about that. Meg less so, but she was a good and patient girl, waiting while Tina chose her new books. After the bookshop they were going to the toyshop, for Meg to pick something, just because. She deserved a treat. Edward wanted to talk to the girls. They needed to know he was on their side. He'd been shocked by his sister's actions yesterday, the vitriol towards her nieces, and the actual burning of books — Tina's books, her prized possessions. Tina was a bright child, and books were her great ally in this world, as they were his, and it had been unforgiveable of Lucia. He'd talk to her too, he resolved. And all of this stopped him from dwelling too much on his own life; his own loss and his wife's undreamed-of betrayal. It was a melodramatic word, betrayal, but he couldn't think of a better one.

He'd phoned work and asked for a few days' leave, after he'd explained the situation. His boss was a good man, and a week or two, more if he needed it, had been granted with only a few questions asked. Everybody loved a bit of intrigue, Edward knew. He didn't tell his boss that he doubted he'd carry on living in London. He didn't say he'd probably give up the job. He needed time to think, time to consider.

214

So today he had time to devote to his little nieces, and time to try to discuss things with them. He wanted to make things better.

Edward treated Tina to three or four other books besides the replacements. Then the party made its way to the toyshop. Meg was decisive and picked out a cowboy suit within a minute. Wouldn't she rather have a tea set? No. It had to be the suit, complete with a plastic gun and holster. They popped into the haberdashers to see Pamela, who, Edward was relieved to see, was calm and serene once more. She was busy with a customer, so it was a flying visit. She excused herself from her customer, who smiled indulgently at the little girls as Pamela rushed over to them. She told Tina she could pick out her favourite material and she'd 'run up' a frock for her. But there was no time to choose material today. Another time, she promised. The girls waved goodbye to her as they left the shop. They were excited and hot, so Edward bought them and himself ice-creams and they sat on the frazzled grass in the park, the morning's purchases in cluttered heaps beside them. Tina had a 99 with a flake. Meg had a Zoom. There was silence as they hurriedly ate their ice-creams. The sun was high and hot and Tina's melted quickly. She was mindful of her clothes getting dirty and was dismayed when a blob fell onto her pretty yellow frock. 'Lucia will be cross,' she said. She always nagged at them to keep their clothes clean.

'That's not all she nags about, is it?' Edward said, slurping his own 99. In truth the ice-cream made him feel sick, but he didn't let that show. He took a large white hanky from his trouser pocket and passed it to Tina.

'No,' said Meg. 'In actual fact she nags us about lots of things.'

'Does she . . . is she . . . is she always fair to you girls?' asked Edward, carefully. If Simone was here she'd know exactly what to say. She was, she had been, so sensitive with them.

'No!' they chorused, glancing at each other. They had that twin thing between them, something Simone had often observed. They managed to communicate just by look, although sometimes they didn't even need a look. It could be unnerving or it could be charming. Today it was neither. Edward just wanted to help them.

'You know, girls, you really should tell your mum and dad if things get too much.'

They looked at each other. Meg, barely perceptibly, shook her head.

'Dad has enough on his plate,' said Tina. She was parroting her aunt, Edward felt sure. 'And Mummy's got her job now. She's too busy.'

'Even so, you don't have to put up with nonsense,' said Edward.

'We'll get our own back. One day!' cried Meg. She'd finished her Zoom. She looked hot and flustered and cross.

'Well, let's hope it never comes to that,' said Edward. His ice-cream was truly revolting, but it was too late now and there were no bins close enough. It was such a hot day and all three were uncomfortable lounging on the grass. It should have been green and soft and lush and cool, not this barren prickly brown. What a horrendous summer this was turning out to be. He finished his ice-cream quickly. 'If you can't tell your mum and dad, you must tell me,' he said.

'Do you live with Aun — Lucia now?' asked Meg.

'I think so. For now,' said Edward. And it sounded awful, and weak, and pathetic. Living with his mother, his sister . . . his wife gone off with another man. That made him a cuckold. His life had come to this. But the girls didn't seem to mind, for they smiled broadly at each other.

He spoke some more to Meg and Tina, drawing them out. He tried to advise them, but he wondered how much advice eight-year-old kids really took notice of? They didn't yet live in the adult world, and that was just as well, and long may it continue. But the girls would grow up, he knew, and soon, and there was nothing anybody could do about that.

Wednesday 25th August 1976

Dear Elizabeth

Another letter soon after my last one but I have more to tell. Meg still thinks Lucia is putting poison in our food and she won't eat any of the things that Lucia makes any more. I don't think there is any poison and I think Meg is being silly but she won't listen. This morning she ate some of her breakfast because Uncle Edward made it and it was eggs and bacon which you can't really poison, she said. But she wouldn't drink the orange juice because Lucia made it. Here we have powder juice, it comes in a packet and you mix it with water from the tap and it tastes nice. But it must be nicer to have real fresh orange juice that I have never had. This afternoon we are picking plums and making the jam I told you about in my last letter. Granny told me she has made plum jam in August ever since she has lived in this house which is a very long time. I am going to post this to you before we pick the plums. Meg says she will not be eating the jam but I reminded her we are helping to make it so we will know if it is poisened or not. I am looking forword to it as I have never done it before and I like cooking specially cakes and you use jam in cakes so this is going to be fun too. We haven't been allowed to help before

because the pans and the jam get very hot so I feel grown up today a bit.
It is still hot but last night I thought I heard thunder.
Love from Tina in England x

29

JANUARY 2014

They arrived home from the cemetery and Keaton cooked a simple dinner. After eating, he ran a bath for Tina, full of her favourite soak, and brought her a cup of coffee. He put down the lid on the toilet and sat, exhausted, but wanting to talk to his wife, to make her understand that he was on her side, despite appearances that morning. It had been a long day, draining and sad.

'What is it you want, Tina?' he asked, leaning forward, legs crossed.

'You know what I want. Lots of things. I want Meg.'

'But that can never be.'

'I know. I do know. Don't worry. I'm not entirely mad. It's just . . . I know this will sound stupid . . . She may have left this world but she hasn't left me. Her heart beats in my heart. It's like we're in tandem. She can't let me go.'

'Or, you can't let her go. You keep giving her . . . consciousness. And words and actions.'

'He lies in the laurels, he runs on the grass . . . '

'What's that?'

'Oh, just a poem. Robert Louis Stevenson. I used to read it a lot. It used to scare me.'

'Don't be scared any more.' Keaton leaned

forward and turned on the tap, topping up the warm water. He'd already made a hot water bottle and placed it under their duvet, wrapping around it a pair of Tina's pyjamas.

'I know now why I . . . why I can't . . . why she won't let me go.'

'OK Tell me.'

'I have to kill Lucia.'

Keaton looked at his wife. She looked back and she didn't flinch.

'That's a bit melodramatic, isn't it?' he said, after thinking through his options. There were many things he could have said.

'Yes, I suppose so.'

'You want to go to jail?'

'No.'

'As I thought. Be realistic, darling. Listen, why don't we offer to have Edward move in with us? We've all the space. We could convert a bedroom into a living room for him so he's got his own flat, more or less. We could do something with the garage, even. Let's get him away from that awful house.'

'He won't leave. I know he won't.'

'He might if we offer.'

'And leave Lucia all on her own?'

'I think she's quite capable. And since when do you care? You were just talking about killing the woman.'

'You haven't asked me why.'

'Why?'

'I don't know why you haven't.'

'Be serious.'

'We th — I think she was the one that killed

221

Meg. Probably. It wasn't all down to me.'

Keaton turned on the tap again although the bath was high and hot and didn't need topping up. But he wanted to do something. At least she wasn't blaming herself this time.

'What makes you think that?' he said.

'Remember when I fell off the steps in the kitchen at Christmas time? At Lane's End?'

'Of course I remember'

'I had a flashback, I think. To the day Meg died. I realised . . . it wasn't me. I don't think it was me. Lucia blamed me. But it was her. I'm sure of it. Her doing. I think I've blamed myself all these years but maybe I've been wrong. I don't know.'

'What happened that day, darling? You've never really explained . . . I know there was an accident . . . but . . .'

'It was horrible. The worst day of my life.'

'Tell me. I do want to understand.'

'I don't know where to begin.'

'Start at the beginning.'

'The beginning? If only I knew where that was.'

'Can't you try?'

222

30

AUGUST 1976

Lucia was worried about Marghuerite. She was growing into a wild, disrespectful child. Wilful, rude and disobedient, leading little Christina astray. If only Pamela would take her head out of the clouds and bring up her own daughters. It really wasn't fair on anybody, this ridiculous job of hers. Pamela was being selfish, there was no doubt about that, at least not in Lucia's mind. Didn't the woman want to be a proper mother? Why didn't William put his foot down? Lucia was tired, running around after those girls day in, day out, counting down the days until school would start up again in September. Mum wasn't much use these days, although she did try, with her insistence on baking, even hanging out laundry from time to time, in her haphazard fashion. Long gone were the days of her neatly hung washing line: clothes on a Monday, linens on a Tuesday. Now they had a washing machine (bought for his mother by Edward) and it was mostly Lucia who loaded it, any day of the week, any time of the day, once the pile was big enough. She found herself washing rather too many of the girls' things. Marghuerite especially made no effort to keep her clothes clean. She was rough, forever climbing trees, scrabbling around in this summer's interminable dry dirt.

223

She was a tomboy. And how difficult it was to tell girls from boys these days; all young people wore their hair long, and dressed in the same shapeless T-shirts and sweaters. And jeans, which were heavy and took so long to dry. She wasn't the girls' damned skivvy!

And so it was that Lucia was not in the best of humours on this hot, late August morning. The long summer was tired of itself, and she was tired of it too; how she longed for a crisp, bright morning with autumn's shivery fingers in the air. What a relief that would be.

★   ★   ★

Edward sauntered into the kitchen, whistling. He didn't feel like whistling but it was his habit, his way of going on, and he wanted to talk to Lucia, and to do that he needed to put her at ease. The small transistor radio in the corner babbled its nonsense, bacon fizzled in the pan, the kettle boiled. His sister was motionless at the sink, looking out of the expansive window, staring across the fields. The day was already hazy and lazy. Lucia looked thinner than ever in her brown slacks, and the horizontal stripes on her tunic could never make her look fat. Edward joined her at the window. She had lines on her face and her skin was pinched and dry, and surprisingly pale, considering the summer they were enduring. She looked old before her time. She needed a holiday. Had she ever had one? He couldn't recall. Perhaps, once he'd found a new job, he should offer to take her and Mum away somewhere. The Lakes. Scotland? France? No, not France. A song came on the radio, which was an improvement on the moronic ramblings of the DJ. Edward thought the song was by the Swedish group called Abba. Simone liked Abba. Lucia continued to stare out of the window.

'What are your plans for the day?' he asked, turning his attention to the bacon, flipping it over. He poured oil into the other frying pan for eggs.

'We're jam making,' said Lucia in her brittle voice, as dry and parched as the summer. 'The girls and I are going to pick the plums, and they're going to learn something useful.'

'Ah, yes, of course. I'm sure they'll help out. They're good girls, Loose Ear, if you give them a chance.'

'Are you saying I don't?' she asked, watching her brother as he inexpertly cracked eggs into the pan. The fat wasn't hot enough yet and the eggs swam around, effacing themselves gradually and slowly — too slowly. He was going to ruin them. One of the yolks had broken. He picked out a piece of shell. 'That was the new song frrroooorrmmm Abba! Abba with a backwards B, of course. That's cool isn't it? The song is 'Dancing Queen' and it's going to be a huge, huge hit; a classic to be sure. Mark my words . . . you heard it here first.'

'Heaven knows you work hard for them,' said Edward. 'But you — '

'What?'

'You could try to do it with a smile sometimes.'

'They're ungrateful little wretches. Especially Marghuerite. Nobody knows the trouble I go to, and now I can't even discipline them, can I? You bought those books for Christina.'

'Yes, I did. Burning a child's books . . . that wasn't a punishment, Lucia.'

'What was it then?'

'Well, if I'm honest, it was rather inhumane.'

'Spare me the melodrama.'

'All right. It was nasty.'

'I was nasty? What about Pamela?'

'She shouldn't have hit you. That was uncalled for. But yes, I'm afraid you were unkind. Those little girls deserve gentleness. They're your nieces for heaven's sake. They're wonderful little people.'

'Ha! And I'm Princess Margaret I suppose?'

'You're as bitter as her, it seems.' He knew as he spoke it was the wrong thing to say, utterly. Lucia stiffened.

'I know depression,' said Lucia, pouring the boiled water into the teapot. 'Yet I still manage to get up in the morning and get on with my life.'

'Do you?' The question gathered like a dark cloud, threatening heavy rain and lashing winds. But the mood between them remained as sulky as the morning air. 'It's still hot, hot, hot out there listeners! What a summer . . . we won't forget this one, right? There are just some things we never forget . . . and this dude won't forget his special night. It's 'December, 1963 (Oh, What a Night)' . . . ' and the DJ, clearly attempting to sound wholesome yet lascivious, merely sounded puny and cheap. But his words, and now the song, emanated around the kitchen. Everything seemed to hang in a dreadful hot suspense. Edward stared at the bacon and then busied himself turning it again, although it didn't yet need turning. Oh, what should he do? He thought the song was by The Four Seasons. A popular song, a rather good song, and another of Simone's favourites. Unbearable now. He started to sweat. He moved to turn the radio down, but Lucia got to it first and furiously pulled the plug from the socket. An embarrassed silence hung over the kitchen, broken only by the fizzling of the bacon and eggs.

'Do you have any plans for today?' asked Lucia eventually. She opened the kitchen window as wide as it would go, to let the awkward moments evaporate in the morning heat.

'I'm hoping to hear about a job. I applied for one on Monday.'

'Let's hope you get it,' she said. Her tone was unreadable, but he didn't like it.

'Thanks. We'll see. Just be kind to those girls, please,' said Edward, flipping the now spitting eggs. He'd turned up the heat. He, and the girls, liked hard yolks. 'Or one day it will come back to haunt you. Children don't forget easily. Bugger!' Splashed by oil, Edward continued to curse.

★   ★   ★

Later that morning Tina and Meg argued, over what Tina didn't really know. It might have been

Lucia's food and Meg's mad conviction that there was poison in it. Tina was tired of it. She wrote to her pen friend, and tentatively asked her sister if she'd walk to the post office with her to post the letter and buy some sweets. Tina had a few pence to spend. And Uncle Edward would give her the money for the stamp, if she asked him. They could get a Panda Pop. Meg was bored, and hungry and thirsty, yet she refused to accompany her sister. So Tina went off alone to the post office in the village, kicking up the ubiquitous dust as she went. Today was a strange day. There was something new coming, a change in the atmosphere. Tina could feel it pressing, looming, whispering. She walked as quickly as she could to the post office, clutching Elizabeth's letter.

★　★　★

Lucia thought it was becoming obsessive, this letter writing, and there seemed to be little waiting for replies. She understood Christina had been writing to this girl for several months now. Presumably it had been facilitated by Robert and Edward. That rankled. The American girl could scarcely be described as family. Robert obviously had no idea what family meant and for years he'd kept himself distant from all of them apart from Edward. She didn't understand why Christina chose to write to this Elizabeth, and Lucia thought the habit should be discouraged. But nobody else minded. Edward supplied money for postage, which was typical of him.

This morning he'd also given Christina money for sweets and treats. He spoiled those girls. Christina was so secretive, not allowing anybody to read her cousin's letters. Lucia had read some of them though, of course, rooting through the girls' things while they were out across the fields. She had found one or two recent letters, and they had seemed harmless enough, if peppered with Americanisms. Christina was a sweet girl, dragged off-centre by her sister, who was odd; naughty, defiant and unpunishable. And Edward now, sticking his oar in, telling her how to take care of those girls. He should tell Pamela, not her! Pamela was the one who did precious little for them, her own daughters. Lucia did everything and got complained at, complained about, even slapped for her trouble. Edward lecturing her . . . and buying all those books for Christina, undermining her authority. She was beginning to think he could go the way of Ambrose and Robert, for all she cared. Not that she relished that thought. In fact, she hated it. Oh, why couldn't things be different!

It was so hot, but as Lucia washed up the breakfast things, it looked as though clouds were building up in the distance, for the first time in weeks. It felt strange and ominous. Would it rain? At last? Would the rain come and break the atmosphere, change things, perhaps forever? Lucia felt a change was on the way. The clouds were gathering, their darkness as milky and muted as a Turner painting; a gentle breeze bathed Lucia's face as she hung out laundry. Later, she made her mother a cup of tea, and one for herself and Edward, whom she refused to look at as she wordlessly passed him his cup and saucer. She needed the stepladder from the shed, but she would not ask Edward to fish it out for her. She would do it herself after she'd finished her tea. Mum said she was too tired to pick plums so she'd sit and read her book for a while and help with the jam later. Had Lucia found the pans? Did she have enough sugar? And lemon juice? Lucia told her not to fuss, she had all she needed. Be careful on that ladder, chided Mum. Then — was it going to rain? It felt like rain. Wouldn't that be lovely? She'd almost forgotten what rain was like.

★ ★ ★

Lucia lugged the stepladder up to the top of the garden and positioned it alongside the tallest of the three plum trees. She heard Christina walking back from the post office, scuffling along the crusty lane beyond the hedge, talking to herself in her skittish, sing-songy voice. Christina was innocent and sweet, Lucia had to admit to herself. She was a lonely little girl, in many ways. Marghuerite really wasn't the ideal playmate for her.

Lucia considered as she picked the ripe, soft plums, what may have happened to her by now if she hadn't had to take care of her mother all these years, and now the twins. What could she have made of herself? She was thirty years old and her life was empty and barren. She allowed herself to imagine how different everything may

230

have been if Sheila had not fallen pregnant with Clive's baby all those years ago. She and Clive would have dated, she was sure of that. They would have danced at the New Year's Eve dance. He probably would have walked her home, helping her through the snow. Perhaps he might have come into the house for a cup of tea, or even some rum, and met Edward. They may have married and then she would have had children of her own. Normal children. Healthy children. Proper children.

But somehow, she told herself, that idea did not appeal. Children were a nuisance: they took over a woman's life and made her fat. And, thank heavens, she'd never had to suffer the pains and indignities of childbirth. She'd overheard the horror stories.

A fresh vision of Clive as he'd looked years ago, handsome and suave, drifted into her mind and she allowed herself to stare at him, something she had not felt able to do at the record shop, refusing always to allow herself to appear gormless and silly. Perhaps that had been the problem, perhaps he hadn't realised how much she had — But what did it matter? It was all so long ago. She wondered what Clive looked like now . . . thinning hair, billowing stomach, lines deep and rutted on his once handsome face?

Her life was brighter now that Edward had returned home, notwithstanding his ticking off of her this morning. He seemed to have taken it upon himself, since his return, to police her life, her feelings. Yet Edward, despite everything, was

231

the one person whom she could honestly say she loved. If Marghuerite and Christina had been his daughters, she wouldn't have objected to taking care of them. Edward's daughters . . . a lovely thought. And the idea that had haunted her all these years. Had . . . it . . . been a daughter? The . . . the thing she had . . . but she would never know. There was no point in dwelling on it. Yet, perhaps it would have been all right? Had she acted in haste? Hardly. She had been well into the pregnancy by the time . . . but of course Simone had been to blame for that. Rushing her into it, everything arranged within a week of Lucia confiding in her. Wanting her to be thin for the wedding. Selfish. Frivolous. Simone had it coming. It was true. And to Lucia, it was fair, it was obvious. A few people counted, most people didn't. As she repositioned the ladder — the ground was uneven, clumpy — she felt a faint twinge of guilt. She had quite possibly wrecked her beloved brother's marriage. But Simone had never been good enough for Edward and she didn't like Simone, so it was all right. Lucia could not forget the look on Simone's face when she had spoken with her last month, on that July Saturday afternoon when the girls played with Meg's new clackers. The clack of those damned things! She would never forget that sound. Clack-clack-clack. Lucia could still see the shock and confusion on her sister-in-law's face. Had it been wrong? Should she have let those dark days simply slip away into obscurity? The past belonged in the past, didn't it?

Who could tell? Sometimes good things came

from the bad. The saving grace was that her plan had worked, and Edward was home and Simone was gone. All as it should be. Yes. Yes, she felt peace in her heart.

Christina came through the gate. It clanged shut behind her. 'Come on!' called Lucia. 'I need your help.'

But Christina ignored her and trotted up the steps and into the house. Two or three seconds later, Lucia heard her cry out. There were shouts, both girls' voices raised in anger. Lucia hoped Mum might see to them but the angry exchange continued, and Lucia sighed heavily and descended the stepladder. She put down the trug and made her wearisome way back down the garden towards the house. She stopped short of the steps as Christina, crying, ran from the house and almost fell down them. The distraught girl pushed past Lucia and through the gate.

'What on earth . . . ?' said Lucia, and she entered the house.

$$\star \quad \star \quad \star$$

How dare she? They were private; they were hers! Elizabeth had told her all sorts of secret things and now they weren't secret any more and she had told Elizabeth all sorts of secret things and now Meg would know the kinds of things they wrote to each other about.

'Who wants to read about stupid boring books?' Meg had said, her face angry and red. 'Who cares what you call your soppy doll!' and, 'You big scaredy cat!' and Meg had laughed at her, laughed, and not in a nice way. She was a baby, Meg had said, pointing at her. A big, fat baby. Tina had shrieked something back about jealousy.

Well, Tina would show her. She would. She knew what to do. She did! So she ran, ran hard. She didn't stop even though her sides hurt and she felt she might burst open, because she didn't run much and she didn't run often but she would run all the way there. She had to go there, all the way to the oak tree that Meg had long ago conquered and Tina had not.

★ ★ ★

'Marghuerite?' Lucia stalked into the lounge. 'What on earth is going on?'

'Nothing,' said Meg, red-faced, hiding something behind her back.

'Tina has just run off in tears so please don't tell me it's 'nothing'. Don't fib.'

'I read her letters. That's all.'

'Those letters are not for you to read.'

'But it's all right for you to read them, isn't it?'

Lucia coloured. How did this girl always know so much? 'I'm going to pick plums and I want you two girls to help me. We've a busy afternoon ahead. Please go and find your sister and apologise to her.'

'I will if you will.'

Lucia was too hot to feel disconcerted. 'Just find her, Marghuerite. Do not play games with me.'

★ ★ ★

And the most horrible thing about it was that Tina knew it was going to happen. Three, four, five steps up . . . five stages of grabbing and pulling and pushing, already trembling, breathless, and she knew she would not get back down, not on her own. And she knew, right there, she could see it played out before her, the sequence of events that she had put in train, unfolding in her mind's eye. Like a silent black and white film; flickering images she knew would haunt her forever more.

What had she been trying to prove? That she could climb the oak as well as Meg? Of course she couldn't! And that hadn't needed proving. Now she was five, six feet up and the only way was further up. She had to make it to the big branch that Meg liked to sidle out onto — the branch she loved to sit on, swinging her thin legs, nonchalant. Tina was not nonchalant; she was dizzy already and her knees were oddly floating around outside her legs.

She climbed again and again, pushing with her knee-less legs, reaching up with her trembling hands — pushing, hauling — and finally she was there; she had reached the big branch. But she didn't wriggle out across it; she crouched and clung onto the trunk, whimpering, crying. What had she done? What on earth had she done?

★ ★ ★

She saw Meg running across the first field. It was cut, and when Tina had pounded through it the stubble had pricked cruelly at her bare fleshy legs. But Meg had jeans on, of course, and she was nothing if not fearless; Tina watched her sister pelt across the stubble field, free and wild. Often Meg seemed to feel no pain. Tina saw her reach the bramble hedge and shoot through the gap that she and Tina liked to think of as their own, but in truth had been forged many years ago by their uncles and their father. Meg ran effortlessly and soon she was halfway across the second field.

'No! No!' called Tina. 'Go back! Leave me alone! It's not safe!'

But Meg ran on towards her. And Tina — caught in the grip of one of those strange, glittering moments in life where impending events are revealed; where you know beforehand with the clarity of a bright-running stream what will happen — cried helpless tears and closed her eyes, but could only see the future more clearly.

★ ★ ★

Tina looked down aghast at Meg as she stood below her, panting.

'What are you doing up there?' said Meg.

'I wanted to climb it to be like you,' said Tina and cried some more, adjusting herself so she could cling ever tighter to the trunk. 'To show you!'

'You're such an idiot,' said Meg. She closed her eyes, and smacked her forehead with the palm of her hand.

'I can't move. I'm trying not to be sick.'

'Shall I get Uncle Edward?'

'Yes, please. But nobody else. Don't bring Au — Lucia.'

'What if she comes anyway? She'll want to. You know what she's like.'

'You can't bring her. Promise me.'

'Why?'

'Just because. Bring Uncle Edward.'

'Will you be all right while I run back? Shan't I just climb up and help you down?'

'No! Don't come up here, Meg, please. You mustn't. Promise me.'

'Why not?'

'Just trust me for once in your life. I know better than you this time.'

'All right. If you say so. I'll run as fast as I can.'

'I'll wait for you,' said Tina.

'I know.'

★   ★   ★

'What do you mean, she's stuck up the oak tree?' said Lucia, cross and hot, picking plums on the wobbly stepladder, half stung by a sleepy wasp just moments before.

'She climbed it to show me she could do it and now she can't get down.'

'Oh, for heaven's sake, you ridiculous girls will be the death of me,' said Lucia, wiping her face with her sleeve.

'Where's Uncle Edward?' said Meg.

'He just left to go into town to see about a job.

237

Somebody telephoned him.'

'Tina wants Uncle Edward to help her down.'

'Well, she'll have to make do with me.'

'You're not to come,' said Meg. With a weary sigh, Lucia climbed down from the stepladder.

'Come along!' she said.

* * *

And there they came. Just as she had foreseen and she knew now, yes, she knew, her vision was not as she'd hoped, wild and meaningless; it was real and it would happen. It was already happening, the two figures hurrying towards her across the field and neither of them Uncle Edward because Uncle Edward was not at home, as she had known he would not be. And how small Meg looked and Tina shuddered and slowly forced herself to look down at her feet, beneath her feet, to search for the way down, but she couldn't see the way down, she could only see the brook, shallow and clear, almost unflowing, dried out and desiccated by the never-ending summer.

* * *

Lucia and Meg reached the tree. Tina was snivelling. Lucia was not in the mood for this. She'd had just about enough of these nieces of hers and it was high time their damned silly mother lived up to her responsibilities. Why wasn't she here? Why didn't she rescue her own damned daughter from this stupid damned tree?

238

Tina was a long way up. Higher than Lucia was prepared to go. She had never climbed a tree in her life and she wasn't going to start now. There was little she could do, as she'd thought. Meg would just have to go up and help Tina down. Lucia would be sick. The stepladder had been bad enough.

'No!' cried Tina. 'No, Meg, you're not to!'

'I reckon I can. You're not as high as you think you are. If I climb up to meet you I can guide you down.'

'It won't work . . . ' said Tina, but her voice was lost. She realised the sky was turning much darker. It was going to rain. It hadn't rained for a long time. Meg was climbing the tree. She was shimmying up, effortless, a sprite. Lucia stood below, looking up, frowning.

'Go on up, Meg. Take no notice of your silly sister. It's not that bad.'

Meg was in reaching distance within a minute. 'See!' she said.

Everything that happened next felt as though it had been rehearsed, over and over, the lines well learned, the props in position, the business attended to. Meg was almost level with Tina, standing on the branch below, the gnarled one that curled around the trunk.

'If you lean down,' she said, 'I can hold your hands and you can step down and I'll be here.'

'I'm sorry we argued,' said Tina.

'Did we? I can't remember.'

'I can't move.'

'You can. You have to trust me. Lean forward a bit, reach out your hands.'

Then, Lucia spoke: 'The branch, Marghuerite. Reach up, you can reach . . . '

And Meg, for a second, looked strong and invincible and she reached out and grasped the branch and held out her other hand for Tina, and Tina thought, I'm being silly. Meg is right. I can do this. She leaned forward. Her stomach lurched. She looked into her sister's hazel eyes — she couldn't look away — and yes, said Meg, yes, and she reached up, up, up, and at that moment Meg proffered both her hands, and they touched for one moment. 'Come on, you idiot!' said Meg and then Tina recalled her vision, the certainty of it, and she gasped, screamed, startling Meg, who was tiptoeing on the gnarled branch, reaching up to grasp the chubby hands that couldn't quite reach hers; and Meg lost her balance and with a small sharp cry she fell, fell, fell to earth and landed at her aunt's feet with a thud; a thud so final and — crack! — the sky split open and at last the thunder came, the rain spattering onto the leaves that shook and whispered in the gathering breeze.

Lucia fell to her knees. She shook Meg, crying out, 'Marghuerite! Marghuerite?!' And the brook was suddenly alive and rushing with raindrops and the leaves shaking harder in the grey breeze. And there was no movement from Meg — no noise, nothing — and Lucia looked up into the trees, and Tina clung once again to the ancient trunk, and they looked at each other — a beat, another — then Lucia seemed decided and delivered the most rehearsed line of them all: 'Tina? What have you done?'

Monday 13th September 1976

Dear Elizabeth
I don't know how to write this letter to you.
So much has happened and so much will
happen and I don't know how to begin to tell
you about things. On the day I wrote my last
letter my sister Meg had an accident. It was
my fault. She hurt herself badly. She can't do
anything now. She can only talk to me so she
does that all the time. Nobody else knows
and it's a secret and I'm only telling you
because I know you will keep it. Everybody
says Meg died but I know she didn't because
she can't die because she's my sister and I
love her and she won't leave me she
promised. There was a funerel but everybody
was fooled. I didn't go I refused only dead
people have funerals. Meg and me stayed at
Granny's house and we played in the garden
and after that I took my book into our den
and I read for a while. I might of gone to
sleep, I'm not sure, but when I woke up Meg
was lying next to me, looking at me. Lots of
people cried at the funeral, my Uncle Edward
told me. We felt bad for Uncle Edward
because he is so sad but Meg and me laugh
about it because we don't believe in it and we
know it isn't real but everybody else thinks it
is. If only they could see what I see. I haven't
gone back to school yet because I am still too

upset but I'm not upset really I let them think I am so I don't have to go to school which as you know I hate more than anything. I will have to go back to school soon though. Our headmaster was at the funeral and Lucia said even he cried. I cant imagine that. Our mum colapsed and my Dad and Uncle Edward had to carry her home. I'll write again soon. Have you finished Ballet Shoes yet? I hope you love it as much as I do then we can talk about it. You know we have had a long hot summer over here? It's over now. It rained a lot the day Meg had her accident and it thundered, and lightning lit up the tree it felt like I was in the negative of a photograph and it was scary. It has rained quite a lot since, which is good everybody says, thank goodness the weather broke, they say, but I miss the summer and the long days that me and Meg spent together and it's all over now because things will never be quite the same again. Meg isn't alive but she isn't dead either. Its difficult to explain.

Love from Tina (and Meg) xx

31

FEBRUARY 2014

Keaton went to work as he had done for the last three days. He had tried hard to appear normal, both at home and in the office. The sad story of Meg's death was dreadful, of course, and he was glad Tina had told him about it at last. He wasn't sure if he believed all of it, but all weekend he had tried to be kind and understanding. However, Tina was distant; he couldn't get through to her in the way he wanted. And he was so tired with it, with her stark refusal to fully accept her sister's death. And Keaton was a man. His desktop encounter with Sharanne on that Friday morning had awakened something in him, a recklessness he hadn't realised was his. And all weekend he had not been able to stop thinking about Sharanne, despite his guilt and best efforts. It wasn't love; with Tina he had love, of the most complicated kind — Sharanne was his relief. She was lust, nothing more. And so Keaton gave in to temptation again and again, and yet again. He took part in secret, sordid, satisfying sex in his office on Monday, Tuesday (twice) and Wednesday. They had locked the door, unlike that first, unexpected time. It was as though in the dark quietness of his office Tina no longer existed. Tina didn't matter. Nothing in the entire world existed or mattered. He gave

243

himself up to his deepest, wildest temptations and Tina was entirely absent. In frightening moments, he even thought of leaving her. It was energising to turn to another who didn't live in a dream world, who was — that hateful word — normal.

But today, Thursday, was a sensible day and he was going to be sensible. He'd awoken this morning with the certain knowledge that the 'affair', if their sordid encounters could be dignified by the term, must come to an end. He contemplated the nature of guilt: Tina's, so misplaced and wrong, and his, real and justified. Tina had been a blameless child. Keaton was anything but.

He handed in his notice. He had not discussed it with Tina. She would want to know the reason, naturally. He could not tell her the reason. He would bide his time and think one up, a good one. He would use his office computer to search the internet for a new job. Tina would be bemused to begin with, then she would be anxious, then she would grow suspicious, Keaton was sure. There was no reason for him to suddenly give up and walk out on a job he enjoyed. He was going to work four weeks' notice; time aplenty, he thought, to find something new, and to ply his wife with his false reasons. He would have to lie this time, there was no other course for him. He'd rarely lied.

Sharanne did not take his resignation well. He told her their liaison had been a ghastly mistake. She said she knew and she agreed. It was wrong. It was madness. It could never happen again, he said. He could never see her again, once he had gone. It would be better if she never tried to contact him once he had left. He would never try to contact her. Sharanne cried, apologising repeatedly, begging him not to leave because actually she felt bad about it — it was wrong, and she saw that, she agreed, and couldn't they just forget it had ever happened and carry on as before? Or shouldn't she be the one to leave? No, Keaton said, I'm going, not you. It wouldn't be fair otherwise.

'I'm senior so I must take responsibility for my actions,' said Keaton, and he knew he sounded pompous but it couldn't be helped. He fiddled with his favourite stapler. He decided he would take it when he left. If the firm could spare him, and apparently they could, they could spare a stapler.

'But you don't need to take responsibility for my actions,' said Sharanne, and she burst into tears once again. Keaton fought the urge to comfort her. What a mess. But he had nobody to blame but himself.

32

SEPTEMBER 1976

Tina had not yet returned to school and Pamela had missed four weeks of work. It was high time they both went back, Tina heard her mum say one Monday morning towards the end of September. It was a bright day, the mellow autumnal sunshine slanting through Tina's window.

'Get her out of bed, could you, Bill? Make her some breakfast?' It was hard, Pamela continued, but they all had to try. Things had to be as normal as possible for Tina. It was she that mattered now. Dad must have been surprised, like Tina, but he did as he was told, and he poked his head into Tina's bedroom and told her to get ready for school. Pamela got up and dressed for work. She didn't eat any breakfast. She was thin and pale. She didn't look like Mum at all. She had fear in her eyes. Tina slowly ate a burned slice of toast. She reluctantly drank her milk, which was not quite as fresh as she liked.

'Chop, chop, madam!' said Mum. Her tone of voice was pretend, but it was all right. She ordered Tina to brush her teeth and have a wash. Dad went off to work. When it was time for Tina to leave, Mum gave her a squeeze, then stood at the front door and waved to her. 'I'll be here when you get home!' she called. 'I'm only going to work for a couple of hours.'

So Tina found herself walking around to the village school clutching her brown satchel and wearing her dark blue dress with the white puffed sleeves. She wore a pair of white socks that were not as white as they once had been. Her shoes were her brown ones she hadn't worn all summer. They were tight, but she didn't want to say anything. Her mum had forgotten to polish them so they looked scruffy. Her dad had tried to plait her hair but he wasn't good at doing it. Meg walked to school with her, saying nothing. But Tina felt herself abandoned at the gates. Children stared at her as she entered the playground. She headed for her classroom. She wasn't going to play outside with all the other kids. She wanted to find her drawer and her place at the table and sit down and wait. One or two of the nicer girls smiled at her as she walked past them. She tried to smile back.

Tina entered the classroom alone to find her teacher preparing for her day. She was putting pots of pencils and crayons and exercise books out on the tables, and she looked surprised to see Tina. She introduced herself as Miss Christianson. Tina thought her very nice — pretty and young — prettier and younger even than Miss Tyson.

'I'm so glad,' Miss Christianson said, 'that you will be in my class this year. We're going to have a lot of fun and do some interesting topics.'

Miss Christianson didn't mention Meg, and Tina wondered if she even knew what had happened to her. She must know, Tina decided.

The head teacher had gone to the funeral and surely he would have told all the other teachers?

When the other children came in, it was noisy and Tina cringed. It had been such a long time since she'd been in a classroom. A girl she had never liked sat next to her. The register was called and Tina forgot to say, 'Yes, Miss Christianson,' who didn't mind; but some of the children laughed.

Soon the class were put to work on their Monday morning 'news'. Miss Christianson said she was hoping to see some good work, and wanted to hear what everybody had been up to over the weekend. She was looking forward to seeing some nice, colourful pictures.

'But, Tina, you can write about your summer holiday if you'd like, seeing as you . . . weren't here at the start of term. If . . . if you want to.' Miss Christianson's face burned red. So, she did know. If anybody was stuck, she said to the whole class, they were to put up their hand and she would call them up to her desk one at a time. Quiet talking was allowed. Tina sat and thought for a long while. She wasn't 'stuck' but she needed time to think. Miss Christianson didn't know, not really. Nobody did. So Tina would tell her. She began work on her news.

★ ★ ★

It was Thursday afternoon and time to go home; just one more day to be endured at school. It had been a strange week, and a lonely one. Miss Christianson had tried to talk to her about Meg.

248

She had taken a long, hard look at Tina's 'news' every morning: each day Tina had drawn a picture of herself and her sister — playing in the garden, playing with Meg's clackers, reading books together. Underneath she had written, 'Meg played with her clackers' or, 'I read Ballet Shoes to Meg'. Miss Christianson was kind and concerned, Tina could tell, but Tina didn't want to talk to her about Meg or anything else.

Tina ran from her classroom at a quarter past three and walked home with her sister. Meg didn't have to go to school any more so naturally she kept away. Tina was cross about this — it wasn't fair! — but Tina knew she would have done the same, so it was all right, really. It was 'one of those things', as grown-ups liked to say. Yet it was strange being so alone. The twins had always gone to school together, apart from those rare occasions when one or the other had been ill. Meg had been too ill for school once with mumps and Tina hadn't caught it despite her and her mum's best efforts, and Tina had gone to school alone every day for a week and a half She had endured loneliness and questions, endless queries about the whereabouts and well-being of her loud, confident sister. Meg was not exactly popular, but everybody knew who she was and she was more than capable of taking care of herself. Tina was the exact opposite — a weakling, unnoticed.

Tina also remembered the long summer days when she and Meg had skived off school and hidden themselves down by the brook, spending the days paddling, trying to catch the shimmery minnows in their bare hands, eventually giving up and lying in the grass and watching the clouds drift by; light and burdenless days, those had been the best times they had ever shared. Sometimes Meg had climbed the oak tree, leaving Tina on the ground, and they had talked about all sorts of things and the things they'd talked about had made sense. Tina couldn't grasp that those days were over and it was a relief to hear the familiar voice reassuring her as she walked home.

'Those days are not over, you idiot. I'm still here and don't forget it. You can't get rid of me that easily.' And Tina couldn't; Meg was always 'there', hovering around the edges of Tina's days, like a vision. Like a ghost, but not a frightening one.

Friday 22nd October 1976

Dear Elizabeth
I'm sorry I didn't write back until now.
Thank you for your letter. When your dad
rang Uncle Edward he was pleased to hear
from him it was good he said to speak but the
curcumstances were sad why did it have to be
like that its always the sad things that bring
people together Uncle Edward said. My mum
has gone. She left a few weeks ago and I'm
waiting for her to come back soon. She told
me she needed a rest and she has gone to the
seaside. My dad is upset and I am a bit upset
but not too bad because she promised me she
would come home. I was allowed more time
away from school and I went back on
Monday. My dad doesn't know what to do
and he is not COPING very well which is a
word grownups love to use when somebody is
drinking too much alcahol which makes them
stink and not act like a grown up at all. I am
staying at Lane's End House for most of the
time. Lucia makes my lunches for school
which is better because at school the dinners
are revolting, which means they are horrible.
Once it was lamb with mint sauce and I
couldn't chew it or swallow it and I thought
I was going to be sick. Lucia is putting treats
in my lunch box. Today I had lunchoen meat
sandwiches (with the crusts cut off) a KitKat,

Horror Bags, which are my favourite crisps, and a Satsuma and a packet of Pacers which are a nice minty flavour not a horrible minty flavour like the mint sauce and they look a bit like Opal Fruits. I have wanted to remind her to make a lunch box for Meg but Meg said I mustn't and besides she doesn't need to eat any more and she doesn't trust Lucia's food anyway as well I know. I said what choice do I have she said none. Just check the sandwiches first she says so I do. Today the sandwiches looked all right and they smelt all right so I ate them. My granny is very sad at the moment and cant stop crying about Meg and my mum and what will William do poor William poor Tina and its all gone wrong in our family what a trajic lot we are and unlucky too Lucia says and I think she might be right about that. Lucia says my mum was selfish she had a daughter to bring up and comfurt and she should have pulled herself together and stayed put. I said I didn't mind because I want my mum to be happy and she needs to be by the sea with her friends. Lucia kissed my head which is not something she has ever done before. It felt nice. I'm glad you read Ballet Shoes and you enjoyed it and I've never been to London either but like you I'd love to go there one day to the Victoria and Albert museum wouldn't it be funny we might bump into the Fossil sisters imagine that. But I suppose in real life they would be old women by now but we can pretend. I'm glad you have picked Penelope for your Fossil

name, it's nice and long like Elizabeth. My
Fossil name is still Pippa.
Love from Tina x
(PS, don't worry about me)

33

FEBRUARY 2014

'You could start at the beginning,' said Kath.

'The beginning . . . ' Tina's voice vanished into the warm air of the bustling café. She and Kath were enjoying afternoon tea (but they were having coffee with their cakes and sandwiches). Outside the rain lashed at the windows and a wind buffeted and howled, but Tina felt safe and enclosed.

'It's hard to know where the beginning is sometimes isn't it?' said Kath.

'Funny that's what Keaton said. OK I don't think it was me that killed Meg,' said Tina. It still sounded like sacrilege. 'I once thought it was . . . I've always thought it was my fault. But not any more.'

'I see. Actually, I don't see.' Kath cut her haunch of coffee cake into manageable bite-size pieces, so Tina did the same to hers. She was feeling rather full already, having already eaten three or four tiny sandwiches, and a small scone. She was on her second cup of coffee, and caffeine emboldened her.

'On the day my sister died, we were going to be picking plums with Lucia to make jam that afternoon, the day the rain started after the long hot summer. Do you remember that hot summer?'

'1976?' said Kath.

'Yes.'

'I do. My dad was rather too fond of his dahlias. He used to sneak out in the night with his hose to water them.'

'Really?'

'Really. Hmm. This cake is divine . . . Naughty of him, wasn't it?' said Kath. 'I'm amazed nobody twigged. Although they might have done, I don't remember. I was only six. I had sunburn, I remember that. God, I was so sore . . . I read through Virginia's notes again after you left the clinic last week, I must confess. I hope you don't mind? Go on.'

'I was frightened of heights you see, terrified. We had an argument. Meg annoyed me . . . '

'Yes?' Kath was clearly confused, much like Keaton had been. But at least Kath was paying attention between bites of cake.

'I had a pen pal. My cousin Elizabeth, who lived in America, actually she still lives there . . . Anyway, I was quite secretive about the letters and Meg was jealous. She was a bit like a boy in so many ways. She never wanted to show her feelings, especially if she thought the feelings were weaknesses.'

'I understand.'

'She got hold of Elizabeth's letters and read them. I caught her. She was quite . . . scathing, I suppose . . . and I was upset. I ran off I wanted to prove something to her. She thought me pathetic, she said, playing with stupid dolls and reading boring books.'

'So what happened next? Can you tell me?'

Kath poured more coffee for herself. A customer entered the café along with a blast of cold, wet air. The door closed and the raging afternoon was banished once more.

Tina took a mouthful of coffee. She swallowed it and felt the warm comforting richness seep down towards her stomach. Coffee was her drug, no doubt. 'I ran away. I ran to the large oak tree that Meg always loved to climb. I'd never climbed it, not high up. Meg was right, I remember thinking, I am pathetic. So I climbed it. I was terrified and I was grazed and bruised, but I got as high as I dared. I got vertigo. I was stuck and I couldn't move. Anyway, Meg came looking for me and I told her to go and get Uncle Edward because I knew he'd know what to do. But she came back with Lucia. Lucia sent Meg up the tree to help me down. Meg . . . fell. Because of me . . . maybe. I'm not sure. I didn't push her. I know I didn't. But I've always thought I was to blame. I startled her and she lost her footing and . . . well . . . she . . . she died as a result of the fall. Internal injuries, I think it was, that caused her to . . . to die. She bled inside. She hit her head hard too. She landed in the wrong way they said afterwards, the medical people. They said it was unfortunate and on another day or in another fall she probably would have survived. But all that came later. At the time we were shocked I think, Lucia and me. I remember she shook Meg and called her name and then we just stared at each other and it seemed to last forever . . . it was raining. The rain was really loud. It was like it had never

256

rained, you know? It was just seconds, I'm sure, but time stood still. Then she asked me, what had I done? In a horrible whisper.'

'Oh, no,' said Kath and she leaned across the table and took Tina's hand.

'Oh, yes. But it wasn't me, was it? I should never have gone up the tree of course, but I was cross with Meg. She belittled me. I was only a girl . . . The fault was Lucia's, wasn't it? She shouldn't have put that responsibility onto Meg.'

'Quite possibly.'

'She was — is — a horrible woman. Not long before *that day* she burned my favourite books. It was a punishment, in her mind.'

'She burned your books?'

'She did. That tells you all you need to know about her.'

'I see.'

'But that's it, really. There's nothing more to say. Lucia pretended to blame me and frightened me into silence. She said she would never tell if I didn't.'

'Was nothing done? Were there no investigations into Meg's death?'

'I think the police asked Lucia about it but nothing much happened. It was just accepted that it was an accident with nobody to blame.'

'Tina,' said Kath gently, 'could that in fact have been the case?'

Tina looked frankly at Kath's wide face; her common sense expression. 'Am I mistaken, do you mean?'

'Yes.'

'I don't know. I don't think so.'

'Did Lucia force Meg into climbing up to help you or was Meg hell bent on climbing up anyway? She sounds like she might have gone up no matter what. She was good at climbing trees, you said.'

'A bit of both, I think. Lucia certainly didn't discourage it and she should have done. I don't know. It was a long time ago . . . my memory may have distorted things. I'm a complete nutter after all. Don't trust anything I say.'

'Nonsense. But it's fair to say that Meg's not your only loss, isn't it? You had a difficult childhood?'

'Mum you mean? Poor old Mum. But you know, and this is how I really feel, it was nothing compared to losing Meg. Nothing at all.'

'Did she . . . have you seen her since?'

'No. I think she just had to get away and start a new life. I looked her up on the internet once. She's a successful businesswoman, or she was. She's possibly retired by now. She was quite big in fashion.' Tina sipped her coffee. She took a tiny jam tart from the cake stand and popped it into her mouth in one go. The pastry was light, the jam thick and golden.

'Did you ever try to make contact?'

'No, never. I don't want to, not now. Too much time has passed. I don't need to see her. She left and she had her reasons, but it was wrong of her, wasn't it?'

'Possibly' said Kath. 'It's hard to say. It was wrong from your point of view. I think you needed her.'

Tina nodded slowly.

'So, what do you want to do?' Kath popped her last piece of coffee cake into her mouth. Her lipstick was remarkably intact, a deep plum colour that complemented the purpleish hair, the snug-fitting black dress, the blue coat. Kath had style, Tina realised wistfully.

'About what?' said Tina.

'About all this. The way you feel about Meg and her death?'

'It's quite simple. I want revenge. Meg was murdered wasn't she?'

'I'd hesitate to say murder . . . and of course there's no way of proving anything now. Your sister fell out of a tree. It was an accident, by the sounds of it. But one that could have been avoided?'

'It would have been all right if Uncle Edward had come back with Meg. He would have got me down. He would have brought a ladder. Something.'

'Have you ever discussed it with him?'

'No!'

'So it's a taboo subject in your family?'

'Yes. Very much so. Dead and buried, so to speak.'

'It's hard to see a way for you to get closure. I'm really sorry about using that term. Revenge . . . it's a tempting thought, but it's not the answer. But you do need closure, Tina.'

'I know.'

'What would it mean for you, do you think?'

Tina took a deep breath, and another. She looked squarely at Kath. 'I want to kill Lucia.'

'Oh, love, I'm sure you do.'

'No. I mean I really . . . it doesn't matter'. Tina shrugged. She looked at the rain coursing down the windows, and studied the woman at the bus stop across the road as the poor thing struggled in vain with a tossed about, inside-out umbrella. *I mean, I want to kill her. For real. Blood and violence. I want to watch her die. I want to watch her die in agony.* Tina knew with certainty that Kath would be horrified, would not understand these thoughts, these ideas. Nobody would understand, only Meg. Tina smiled at Kath. Kath smiled back. Tina didn't want to deceive her, but that couldn't be helped.

34

SEPTEMBER 1976

When Tina and Meg arrived home from school on that sunny Thursday afternoon, they found the front door wide open. Tina could hear voices from deep inside the house, loud but muffled. Mum and Dad. They were arguing.

The girls stood by the front door and listened until a door slammed, and their mother hurried along the small, cramped hall, carrying a suitcase. She stopped when she saw Tina.

Mum stepped out into the sunlight and the sun shone on her pretty brown hair. 'Tina . . .' said Mum and she burst into tears and flung her arms around her daughter.

Tina said nothing. She didn't know what to say. She could see Mum was leaving; going somewhere, she knew not where. She couldn't guess. She would have to wait to be told.

She didn't have to wait long. Pamela dried her tears and offered Tina the handkerchief. Tina shook her head. 'Tina. I'm going away for a few days. I'm . . . your dad and me . . . we're finding it hard to get along. We're both missing Meg . . . and we're so young . . . so stupidly young, or we were. Perhaps that's it? We were too young you see . . . I'm sorry, darling, if none of this makes sense to you. I'll send for you, I promise. I'm going to the seaside. Won't that be nice?

Mummy's going to stay with her friend who lives by the sea. You can see it from her bedroom, she told me that. I'm going to have a nice rest and then I'll feel all better again. Tina, I need just a few days to sort myself out, and I need to find a new job and then you can come to me. Is that all right?'

Tina may have nodded, she may have not. An ugly brown car pulled up at the kerb and Mum said she had to go. She hugged Tina again, and made for the car. She called, 'Soon, Tina. I promise!' and got into the car and the car drove away. Mum turned and waved. Tina raised her hand and waved back. Then the car was gone. Tina wondered who the man driving it was.

She slowly ventured into the house and along the hallway to the kitchen. From behind the door she could hear sobs, swearing, more sobs. She didn't want to open the door. She stood alone for a few minutes, listening. Meg said hadn't she better go and find Uncle Edward? And Tina felt like crying herself then because she knew Uncle Edward would not be the one she found.

Tina turned from the kitchen door and left the house. She thought she'd better close the front door behind her, or thieves would come into their home and help themselves to all their things and her dad might not even notice. The girls began their slow walk down to Lane's End House, knowing who waited for them there.

Sunday 7th November 1976

Dear Elizabeth

Thank you for my birthday card. I had four cards including yours. I had a new book. Miss Christianson gave it to me. She's my teacher. It's called The Painted Garden and its a little bit about the Fossil sisters again. I read a lot of it on my birthday. Meg said I was ignoring her too much but I told her I needed to be alone. Daddy is unhappy because of Meg and Mummy, and he can't look after me at all at the moment so I live at Lane's End House now all the time with Granny, Lucia and Uncle Edward, who I hope doesn't move out because he is so nice, Granny is too but she is quite old now. Lucia is actually being very nice too, helping me with things and teaching me to sew. We're going to make a new clippy mat. She seems happier now that Meg is not here which I do not like she should be sad but sometimes I think she is putting on a brave face. She must feel bad about what happened and the police talking to her about it and she covered up for me so I have to be nice to her. Of course she thinks Meg is dead but I know different as I told you before and anyway Lucia is bossy and it was probably her not me I would never try to make my sister fall. I just wanted to get down from that tree and I wanted Uncle Edward to help me.

263

I think I might have pushed her but I am not sure. I didn't mean to push her. I don't know what to believe any more it is all so confusing. At least I still have Meg and of course my new book The Painted Garden which is really really good. Some of it takes place in America! In Hollywood. If you like I will send a copy to you? I am glad my birthday is over as I am 9 years old now and that means I am growing up. Granny says I must learn to look to the future and she will help me to do that. Uncle Edward says it was hard for him to start a new life after Tante Simone left but he has his new job which he likes and he's getting on with it and I must too, he says. School is all right at the moment. There is a new girl who has moved into the village her name is Kimberly which I think is a lovely name it is modern and she is nice and pretty with yellow straight hair with flicks, she is very fashionable, sometimes she wears a bright red tank top which I love and I shall ask Granny to knit one for me. Kimberly likes me. Miss Christianson has moved Sharon Kite who kept being mean to the other side of the classroom and now Kimberly sits in her place. She is American like you! Her father is a pilot in the United States Air Force. He is tall. Her mum is nice and she is fashionable too she wears jeans and pretty scarfs in her hair and she drives a big white car and I have been to their house for tea after school. They have a special machine in their kitchen which does the washing up it makes a lovely swooshing noise and they have heaters in all the bedrooms. We had tacos to eat for our tea. I didn't know what they were but I liked them. Then we had a big slice of cake which had pink and white marshmallows on it. Her baby brother stole one of the marshmallows before we were allowed to eat the cake but nobody minded in fact they laughed so I did too.

I have to go, Meg and me will walk up to the post office and post this in a minute then I'm going to help sort out some scraps for the clippy mat. It is also called a rag rug, Aunty Lucia told me. Meg says it's boring and why do I want to sit with that B.I.T.C.H. when I could be with her playing. But there are days when I don't want to play.

Love from Tina xxx

PS, please send your letters to Lane's End House from now on, I will put the address on the envelope. PPS, did you know we have been writing letters for a whole year now? Such a long time and I hope there will be many more years.

35

FEBRUARY 2014

Keaton had found a new job to go to, which was a huge relief. He would start mid-March. For the last couple of weeks he and Sharanne had been formal and distant. Any awkwardness between them they steadfastly ignored. They were boss and assistant once again, nothing more. It was simple and it was right and Keaton already felt assuaged after the dark days of their brief and misguided fling. He now felt a new thrill of confidence, a surety in his and Tina's future. He'd made up his story: he was bored in his current job, it was stale and dry; he wanted to try something new and it was all part of his plan for them as a couple — their new start. He would suggest, in time, that they move house, perhaps even move to a new area and start a truly different life. His new job didn't have to be his forever job. He was resigned now to never being a father. And it was all right. He would never discuss babies with Tina again, he decided. There was no point. Although she had said she wanted a child, he didn't believe her. And, his trump card — they would take that exotic holiday. At lunchtime he popped to the travel agent and picked up a pile of brochures with photographs of impossibly blue skies and snow white beaches.

She sat on the bench and pulled her green coat closer around her. She didn't want to be recognised, not just yet, and to date she thought she hadn't been. Tina carried a bunch of pink carnations, as she so often did, to put on Meg's grave. Tina looked as she'd ever looked: a quiet, lonely figure. Tina, dear little Tina, who was now a grown woman.

Simone's guilt knew no bounds. Simone knew the birthdays and the death days. Simone watched. But she did not approach. She couldn't, not yet. She felt that she had let those girls down. She had let her husband down and she shouldn't have. She had foolishly, vainly listened to the poison-tongued sister and had allowed her marriage to fail; she had withdrawn herself from the man she loved and those delightful little girls and therefore from everything that had been good in her life. And Meg — Marghuerite — dead for all these years, reduced to a pretty grave, an elegant name writ in stone. When Simone had decided to look for her grave, she had found it, high up in a quiet corner of the cemetery, pretty and fresh. She had brought flowers on that first visit but there were already fresh pink carnations on the grave, and Simone had rightfully guessed who had placed them there. She took her own flowers home with her. Perhaps, Simone often thought, if she'd been around, if she had been there that day, Meg might still be alive. Simone knew it was illogical — if she and Edward had not gone their separate ways, they both would have been at work on that dreadful Wednesday. Neither of them would have been there. The mythical taunt of what-ifs had no place in this tale. The outcome would have been no different had she and Edward still been together. Edward had contacted her of course, through her work, to let her know Meg had died. But she hadn't attended the funeral. She couldn't bear to stand alongside her husband, her sister-in-law. She had sent no flowers. She should have done. She'd simply allowed herself to fade away, away from her old life and into her new one, and had forced herself to forget.

Today, Tina tidied the grave as she usually did, snipping at the grass with the scissors she always brought with her. She brushed off the grave-stone, rendering it truly pristine. She cried, a little. But there was no speaking today. It wasn't often that there was no speaking. Simone usually heard Tina talking to herself, conversations of an involved and intimate nature, weird one-sided arguments. Often she heard, 'Meg!' Sometimes there was shouting, arguing, and Tina would look furtively around, close her eyes and hum loudly, tunelessly. She was a tortured person, Simone knew. Ah, those poor girls.

Simone was aware of the passing years and had made a decision. She had mulled it over, formulated her plan, procrastinated.

She knew that Edward lived at Lane's End House and had done so since their separation. They had never divorced. Over the years, Simone had received two offers of marriage and had refused them both; she had been involved with 'unsatisfactory' men and had eventually shunned all romantic relationships. She lived simply, quietly, sometimes in France, sometimes in London. A couple of years in rural Somerset, post-retirement, had given her time to think, and she had found her thoughts returning, again and again, to her husband and his family. And now, after all these years, she had decided to attempt this reconciliation with him. She prayed it would not be too late. She had long feared Edward's non-forgiveness. She thought there was no other woman. The only residents of Lane's End House on the electoral role were Edward Thornton and Lucia Thornton.

Simone decided she would call at the house; she would push past the odious Lucia who no doubt would open the door and stand like a sentry, barring her way. But she would not let Lucia bar her, not this time, not now. Life was precious and life was short and time was slipping away as it was apt to do, and Simone had made up her mind.

She watched Tina walk away from the grave. No, there had been no talking this time. Just tidying and flower-arranging, nothing more. Simone felt a sense of relief although she wasn't entirely sure why.

* * *

Tina arrived home. She made herself a cup of hot chocolate with her customary large swirl of cream and lots of chocolate sprinkles. She felt that she had achieved something, going to the grave and not speaking to Meg. Meg had tried to speak to her, of course. But Tina had ignored her. It was the only way. Meg thought she could govern Tina's life but she was wrong — she could not. Tina was going to kill her aunt, she really was, and she knew that once that woman was dead, Meg would also be dead, because she would be 'at rest' whatever that meant, and Tina's life could begin. Tina was sure of this. She and Keaton could have their much longed for child. Tina felt she would make a good mother; surely it was a matter of instinct and imagination? Babies were remarkable and joyous. Keaton's talk of jail . . . that was silly and melodramatic. She would never be sent to jail. Wouldn't she just be sent somewhere 'secure', somewhere where she could get 'better' for a while, a few months? She was mentally unstable, wasn't she? Not dangerous. She found herself laughing out loud, shaking her head. She had to free herself of her past and her family, and accept that things happened that were not her fault. She had to start living. Visits to Meg's grave could be normal visits, not shouting sessions. Just a bit of dignified, quiet weeping, maybe, on her birthday, or the sort of conversations you can have with dead people where you know they are dead and they're not really listening, and above all, they don't respond. Meg would be dead, properly dead, once and for all, like Granny and Grampy. Visits to their graves were much simpler affairs. Tina was shocked to feel this way. All these years she'd wanted Meg to be alive and had fantasised that she was. But now she wished her dead.

Properly dead. Was it a betrayal? Or was it just the desire to be normal? Tina didn't know. She could only feel. Something had to change. Something had to be righted.

Tonight she would make a nice dinner for herself and Keaton. She would tell him she really did want to start a family; make him understand she was serious and she meant it, even if it was just one child. She would tell him she'd had her coil removed in December. Tomorrow she would think over her plans. She had some ideas. She would not tell Keaton. She would not tell Kath. They would call her melodramatic and Kath would try to talk her out of it, Meg was right about that. Keaton would tell her to drop it. But she would not drop it, not now.

Friday 10th December 1976

Dear Elizabeth
I have sent you a present for Christmas which I hope you will enjoy. I hope it will get there in time. Lucia told me to have it posted by surfiss but the lady at the post office said it wouldn't get to you for months so Lucia let me post it by air mail and she paid. Uncle Edward gives me pocket money but I spent that on the book. It is another one of my favourites. The School at the Chalet is a great story with good characters and Joey is my favourite. I think that is because she is meant to be everybody's favourite and the writer of the story wants you to like her. It is set in a boarding school in a country called Austria. There are mountains and lakes, a bit like in Heidi but that's in Switzerland which is next door to Austria. I would like to go to boarding school because the girls are all freindly there. In case you don't know, it's a school where you go and live, you stay there in big rooms called dorms with lots of other girls. Your mum and dad if you have them send you parcels and letters from home. Meg says she would hate to go to a boarding school but I don't agree and we argue about it. She is still very bossy. This year I will spend Christmas at Granny's house. My dad said he will be there too. At school we are

doing a play for Christmas and I am in it. A big girl in the seniors is Snow White and I am one of the animals she meets in the woodland glade. I am a deer. I hate school more than ever. It's too noisy. My best friend Kimberly is now Sharon Kite's friend. Kimberly hardly talks to me now and she laughs at me. I was going to give her Ballet Shoes for a Christmas present but I don't think I will bother. I have another friend called Karen who brought me some sweets all for me today. She lives next to our school and she goes home for her dinner and when she came back she had a bag of Black Jacks and Fruit Salads and a tube of Parma Violets. She is a nice girl. I will give Ballet Shoes to her.

Happy Christmas from your English cousin Tina xxx

36

MARCH 2014

It was Keaton's last day at work. Last week he had told Tina that he was leaving. He'd expected surprise, lots of questions, but Tina had barely responded. She'd nodded and said yes and no in the right places, and that was that. She hadn't been listening, of course. She was locked away in her own private world again. But it wasn't necessarily a bad thing, for once. During the same conversation she'd told him she really wanted a child. He still hadn't believed her, but he in his turn had smiled and nodded in the right places and let her prattle on. He knew there would be no child, coil or no coil. It just wasn't going to happen for them. He couldn't allow himself to hope. Tina was delusional. He'd mentioned the holiday and produced the brochures. Tina had glanced at them.

He was clearing his desk. The stapler he felt so attached to he'd already placed carefully at the bottom of his bag. He searched through the rest of the stationery. There were a couple of pens he liked. He had a few things to tidy up, files to pass on to his colleagues. But really his work here was done, and it was a relief. Soon there would be a new start, and his mistakes would be firmly behind him, those few regretful days he'd given in to his ridiculous 'urges'. Really, now, he felt nothing for Sharanne and he never had done. Temptation was a strange emotion. It was untrue. He'd never give in to it again, he knew, and that at least brought him a sense of bitter well-being.

Sharanne brought in his morning coffee for the last time. She looked sad. More than that — withdrawn, pale. It must be hard for her, Keaton conceded. She had feelings for him and he had taken advantage of her, he knew, and now he was leaving and their paths would not cross again. He would make sure of that. It sounded harsh, but it was the only way if he was to preserve his marriage.

'Thank you,' said Keaton and he took the coffee and held it in both hands. Sharanne held hers in both hands too. They regarded each other for a moment, and both attempted weak, ironic smiles.

'Keaton?'

'Yes?'

'I'm going to miss you.' Sharanne started to sob and she flung down her coffee. It spilled over the rim of the mug, all over the mercifully clear desk, and she went to the window, hunched and weeping.

'Oh dear,' said Keaton, and dabbed at his desk with tissues for a few moments before he joined her at the window. He would once have tapped her back or placed his hand briefly on her shoulder, or something else supportive but not intimate. Today he did neither. He just stood alongside her, waiting. She made an effort to stop crying. She wiped her eyes and turned to Keaton.

'I'm pregnant,' she said.

275

Keaton had fainted once as a teenager watching a dissection of a sheep's heart in a biology lesson. He'd never been sure why he'd fainted because he wasn't averse to blood. Maybe the ripping apart of a creature's heart had been the problem. He felt himself sway and put his hand to the wall to steady himself.

'Oh,' was all he could manage.

'Oh?'

'I don't know what else . . . Is it —'

'You're not about to ask if the baby is yours, are you?'

'No. Of course not. I . . . I can promise you that.'

'I'm sorry. You're a good man.'

'What on earth are we to do?'

She had no answer. She cried again and this time she leaned her head on Keaton's shoulder. He let her. He stroked her hair. He smiled to himself, despite feeling the pain and the pressure of the ever-increasing mess he was surrounding himself with. A baby. His baby. His much longed for baby. He was going to be a father at last. Ideas and thoughts flung themselves across his mind; he could not make sense of them, apart from one.

'You won't abort will you?' he said. He didn't care if it sounded blunt and selfish, and it did.

'No.'

'Really?'

'Really.'

'Oh! I can't tell you . . . thank you. That's all I can say. Thank you.'

'How was your last day? I'm so glad you have a week off. Let's hope the weather's fine and we can have some days out. Why don't we organise that holiday of yours? I've been looking through the brochures. Keaton? Are you listening?'

Tina was being unusually and deliberately garrulous, and she was taken aback by her husband's lack of response. He only smiled vaguely in her direction and it was as though his eyes were focusing inward, looking intently at something deep inside. Had they swapped roles, just for a moment? Something was amiss. 'Are you all right?' she asked him, moving to him and rubbing his chest. 'I've started on Bolognese. We have red or white wine. Which do you fancy?'

'You decide,' he said, and Tina thought for a moment or two. 'We'll have red, shall we?'

'Whichever you like. Do you mind if I hop in the shower first? I want to wash the day away. You know the feeling.'

'Of course I don't mind. I'll get on with tea and open the wine. Is that all right?'

Keaton nodded and made for the stairs. It was clearly not all right. Tina turned to the stove. Keaton hauled himself up the stairs, and she could hear his slow progress. She had expected him to bounce in the door, all smiles and stories about his last day. Hadn't they got him with shaving cream? No. There were no signs of any pranks. No signs of fun. He hadn't been drinking. Something was wrong.

The shower was hot and he allowed it to
pummel his body. He had a good body. He'd
never overeaten. He wasn't a gym type, but he
loved long walks and short ones, and in his
younger days he'd cycled a lot. His body wasn't
in bad shape for a man well into his forties,
approaching fifty. And his body had finally
spawned a child. It was the most amazing thing
and it would be the most amazing part of him,
and in the high summer meadow of his mind he
was elated. He felt strong. He felt tall. He felt
majestic. He was going to be a father. That
afternoon, Sharanne, amid further tears, had
calmed down enough to reassure him again and
again, that she would be keeping this baby no
matter what. He could or could not play a part.
It was entirely up to him. She would make no
demands. Keaton had explained to her what the
pregnancy meant to him, how it made him feel,
something he found surprisingly difficult to
express. But she seemed to get it. He knew the
child would need to remain a secret, at least for
now, if not forever. He had no intention of
leaving Tina. Sharanne got that too. She wasn't
asking him to leave, she said. But . . . her door
would always be open if he ever . . . changed his
mind. She said she loved him, and he hushed her
and said that kind of talk would get them
nowhere because he was married and that was
that. And he was truly sorry and what an awful
mess this all was but still, but still — he was
enthralled. He was thrilled.

It all moved so fast. He'd nipped out that afternoon and obtained a cheap mobile phone and given Sharanne the number. It was her phone, he told her; their phone. Nobody else would know about it or have the number. She should text whenever she needed to and he'd get to it as soon as he could. He'd keep the phone in his desk at his new job.

What else could he do? For now the phone was in the inner pocket of his bag. Tina never, ever went through his bag. His wife's trust in him was complete and he burst into tears in the shower and sobbed silently for his wife, their life, the new life in Sharanne's womb. He tried to work out how any of this could ever have happened. Things like this didn't happen to people like him and Tina; they were both too sensible, too mature, too devoted. And he'd wanted a child with his wife, conceived in love and tenderness, not in ridiculous, ill-judged moments — on a desk, on a floor, against a wall. This child had a shameful conception, if ever there was such a thing. He stopped crying, turned off the shower, stepped out and dried himself. He put on his black trunks, his most comfortable pair of jeans, his favourite black t-shirt and he stood, alone and quiet in front of the mirror. He took a long hard look at himself. His life was going to be nigh on impossible. Everything had changed and now he would have to go downstairs and spend the rest of the evening with Tina and pretend, act, feign — what? He wasn't sure. The good husband? She had missed the March reading group, claiming she hadn't had time to read *Fahrenheit 451*. He didn't believe that. He'd seen the book lying around on the sofa, on the coffee table, in the kitchen . . . It was a slim book, and not a difficult read as he remembered. She was just too preoccupied to read it, which was not the same as being too busy.

He was embarrassed by his wife — her strange ways, her odd ideas, the endless melodrama. He didn't believe for one moment that she was serious about her intention to kill Lucia. She'd seemed serious when she'd mentioned it, but it was hard to tell with Tina. She was easily led, by a dead little girl. He shuddered. He checked the secret mobile phone. Nothing. Yet.

He took four deep breaths, slipped into his most laconic smile and went downstairs and hugged his wife.

★ ★ ★

There was desperation in his body, a tenseness that had not been there before. He was a good husband and an undemanding but giving lover, and usually in bed they were comfortable and open with each other. Any tenseness had been in her, up until now. She was embarrassed by her weight, usually. But tonight it was all in him, and she said nothing and afterwards they cuddled until he fell asleep, which didn't take long. He was exhausted. Something must have happened at work, something he hadn't mentioned, something important. For the first time she doubted her husband. He was a long way away from her. Perhaps he'd changed his mind at the last minute about leaving his job. His reasons were . . . ponderous, at least. She wondered if he had in fact been dismissed. If so, for what? He was as straight as a die and she couldn't think of a reason for any dismissal, not one. Could it have anything to do with his assistant? No. Of course not. Still, she was glad he was leaving. He'd got stuck in a bit of a rut and his absorption in his own issues stopped him from talking too much about hers. She wasn't in the mood to be nagged at. It was a relief not to be questioned too much.

She supposed it might be her fault, with all this Meg stuff, all these years he had borne with her, humouring her when she spoke of Meg in the present tense, realising, she thought, from an early stage of their relationship how she felt about her lost twin. Rarely had he criticised her. Often he'd tried talking to her, wanting to understand. But she had never really allowed herself to be drawn out.

She could not sleep. She rose from the bed and tiptoed downstairs and found Meg sitting at the kitchen table, grinning at her.

'Oh, God,' said Tina. 'Who let you in?'

'That's a fine way to talk to your twin. All right, sis?'

'Not really.'

'Is Keaton up to something or what?'

'How would you know? You've never met him.'

'Ha, clever. Something's going on. All those glossy holiday brochures he brought back the other day. And why's he leaving his job? I thought he was supposed to love working there?

He's sorry for something, I'm telling you.'

'Nothing is going on. Only that I've made a decision.'

'Tell me! Tell me! What decision? You're going to chuck Keaton at long last?!'

'No. Why on earth would I do that? For once and for all, Keaton is the best thing that ever happened to me. Please get that into your thick head.'

'All right, keep your hair on. What is it then?'

'All right. I'm going to kill Lucia. Will that do?'

Meg cried and cried. Never had Tina witnessed such a release of relief in any living person or dead, and Meg dissolved in her own tears and Tina stood alone and shaking in the kitchen, the hum of the fridge the only noise, the only comfort.

37

MARCH 2014

Simone paid the driver and stepped from the taxi. The car drove off with an impatient squeal of its tyres and she turned towards Lane's End House. It looked much the same as it always had. Perhaps the hedges were more overgrown than they once had been. Perhaps the trees were a little taller. Perhaps there was more abundant ivy coiling over and about the house. She put her hand on the gate and took a deep breath, then another. The gate was still cold and weathered to the touch. She pushed it open and closed it softly behind her. She didn't want to draw attention to herself too soon. She had half expected to see her sweet little nieces playing hopscotch in the lane or skulking around the fruit trees at the top of the garden or running across the lawn to meet her. She had been popular with the girls. Of course those days were long gone, but for one of them, she hoped, it was not too late. She wanted to be her Tante Simone again. She hoped, for her and Edward also, it was not too late.

She took the steps leading up to the front door in her graceful stride, and was dismayed, but not surprised, to see the old knocker still hanging there. It had always made such an awful noise throughout the house. Its shuddering whump could shake the dead. But there was no bell, no other means of summoning the inhabitants. She raised the tarnished knocker, closed her eyes, counted to three, and let it swing back.

She waited, calm and measured. So long in the planning, this moment no longer held any terror for her. The nerves were spent. She felt nothing but determination and righteousness.

Wednesday 12th January 1977

Dear Elizabeth
I hope you had a good Christmas. Mine was all right. I had a set of Secret Seven books from Lucia which I don't really like. Meg likes them best so I'm letting her read them. On Christmas Day I was hoping my mum would visit and bring me a present but she didn't. Dad gave me a card with some money in it. He gave me £5. He also gave me some felt tips and a colouring book but I'm too old for colouring books. Mum sent me a card too and it was exactly the same one that my dad gave me! Isn't that funny? It says Merry Christmas to a Dear Daughter on it. Mum also sent me a letter and a £5 note. In her letter she told me she has a new job and is looking for a flat. Then she wants me to go and live with her but I don't know about that. I haven't told anybody all the things she wrote. I've put the letter on the fire because I know Aunty Lucia reads other people's letters and I don't want her to read what my mum said to me. Granny gave me a doll she cries real tears. I don't really like it. I don't like dolls that much any more. Uncle Edward gave me book tokens for £3 which I am looking forward to spending and he gave me a selection box with some of my favourite sweets in. It had a packet of Spangles! They

are just as nice as Tooty Frooties. Before we broke up from school for the Christmas holidays we had a party and we played games and watched cartoons in the hall we watched Tom and Jerry on a projector it was really good fun and we had crisps and nuts and cheese and sausages and jelly. Father Christmas came with a sack with presents for every kid. I had a book called The Secret Garden which I haven't read yet but will soon. I am back at school now after the holidays and so we haven't had a chance to go shopping yet with my book tokens. School is better this term because Sharon Kite has been expelled. Three days before we broke up for Christmas she dunked my nice friend Karen's head in one of the outdoor toilets and she flushed it and Karen is nice she brought me the sweets I told you about and it was really mean of Sharon and Karen's mum and dad complaned to the school and Sharon has gone. She missed the Christmas party which serves her right. Do you remember the American girl I told you about, Kimberly? She was Sharon's friend for a while but now she is my friend again and I am going to her house for tacos tomorrow night. They were very tasty last time. She told me she didn't like Sharon after all and I'm a much better friend. I didn't want to go back to school after Christmas but on my first day back Uncle Edward told me to be brave and to try to acept that there is something to live for. It is a new year he said and we both have to look forwords. He was sad and so was I but he smiled at me and cuddled me and I felt a bit better. Meg wispered I should cuddle him back so I did.

We haven't had any snow this year but it is cold. I hope we have snow next Christmas.

Love from Tina x

38

MARCH 2014

'Tina? It's Kath. I wanted to ring you before our next meet-up. We can't really talk at reading group. We missed you at the last one again by the way.'

'I'm sorry. I just . . . you know. Didn't fancy it.' She hadn't read *Fahrenheit 451* and had been chided by an irritable Keaton about it. Too bad. It was only a book. A jolly good one, Keaton told her. But still, just a book.

'What the hell, nobody minds,' said Kath. 'I told you that before. It was an entertaining meeting though. Angry Man got really angry and Tess told him off so he walked out, but not before he told Tess to fuck off! She ended up in tears, the poor thing . . . She calmed down though, and he's banned from the group. It was the chap who smells of pickles. By the way, have you read the bloody April book yet?'

'No. I haven't had the time.' She had in fact had plenty of time. The week between Keaton finishing his old job and starting his new one had been quiet, uneventful. They had done little in that time and talked little. Keaton had been distracted, wanting time alone. He'd been tired and listless. They'd had one day out, to a safari park. An odd choice as neither of them liked safari parks, and they had both been bored and cold.

'Don't bother with it, it's no good. Someone's idea of an April Fool, I'd say! I got halfway through and gave up on it. Anyway, I was wondering, how are you fixed for a drink tonight? Would you like to go back to the diner? Shall we have some nosh?'

'That sounds good.'

'Shall we say seven-ish?'

'Yes. Keaton won't mind. He started his new job today.'

'Oh?'

'Developments,' said Tina.

'I'm all for those. I'll see you later. Don't be late.'

★ ★ ★

Keaton arrived home from work at six to find his wife getting ready to go out. She was wearing the orange top with the floaty sleeves. Their bedroom smelled of body spray. She asked him about his day, his new job. It was all right, he said. Nothing special but he'd get into it, he'd do his best. If it didn't work out he'd find another. He was glad she was spending time with Kath again. She was a good sort. She was somebody to be trusted. You should believe in her, Tina, you should listen to the things she says. She knows what she's talking about. He would make his own tea. It was no problem. She should go. and enjoy herself.

★ ★ ★

Sharanne had sent Keaton a grand total of twenty-seven texts in the ten days that she'd had the secret mobile phone number. I feel sick, she texted at first. This swiftly became: I feel beyond sick. Soon it was: I want to die. Then it was: What shall I do, I can't do this. This is horrible. Why do I feel so bad? I can't eat. I'm too old for this. This should not have happened! I haven't gone to work for the last four days. I can't get out of the house. The front door has a nasty smell. It's vile. Only in sleep do I get relief and it's getting worse. Help me. Please. I need help. It's so unfair.

He found her texts strangely poetic, which was most unlike Sharanne. Until: I'm in hospital.

Keaton sent back consoling messages that he knew didn't help at all. He knew he ought to go and see her, but the intimacy of visiting her in hospital felt wrong. They weren't a couple. They weren't lovers. They weren't even friends, for God's sake. She would no doubt look dreadful and be wearing night attire and it would be wrong to see her like that, in her intimate clothes. He looked up morning sickness and progressed to *Hyperemesis Gravidarum* and was horrified by what he learned. Some women, he read, were drawn to terminating their pregnancy because the nausea was so unbearable. He shuddered. Poor Charlotte Brontë had possibly died of it, he discovered. He started to feel sick himself, but decided he must go. He must visit this woman who was bearing his child, and offer his presence, if nothing else. It was only right.

39

MARCH 2014

Lucia came to the door. Simone heard her grappling with the lock. She heard her mutter. Simone had expected nothing else although she had hoped Edward would get to the door first, open it and dissolve into delight at the sight of her. It was a dream, a fantasy; she couldn't wait to see his face. But now the door was about to be opened, she was momentarily terrified. She hadn't expected to feel terror. Yet she was determined not to show her feelings, and set her lips into what she hoped was a determined line, tilting her head back a few degrees. The door opened.

Lucia was as prim as ever: buttoned up, and still far too thin. Her hair was grey. Her face was as pinched up as it ever had been. It was a cruel face, Simone decided, and it was on the right person. For a second or two Lucia showed no sign of recognition. Then her face crumpled into dismay.

'What the hell are you doing here?' she said, staring down at Simone. Lucia's eyes were full of fear and that gave Simone strength. This time Lucia would not win.

'Hello, Lucia. How are you? Don't worry, I'm not here to see you. I'd like to see my husband, if you please.'

291

'Your husband?'

'That's right.'

'You most certainly cannot.'

'Lucia, I don't have time to dilly-dally here on the doorstep with you. Edward?!'

'Shh! He's asleep.'

'Then I shall wake him.'

Simone stepped up onto the threshold. She reached Lucia's level and the two women attempted to stare each other down, the hostility rising from them like tropical steam, their breath coming quick and shallow. Simone felt sick. She felt hot. She had known she would have to get past Lucia first. She understood that she would have to deal with her during the encounter; the reunion, as she hoped it would be. She needed every last wisp of her courage. Lucia might do anything, say anything. She was a dangerous person.

'I'm not asleep,' said Edward quietly and both women turned to him as he stood, frail but firm, at the foot of the steep narrow staircase.

'Edward? Oh, Edward!' Simone took two steps towards him, and shrugged off Lucia, who tried to bar her way, tried to pull her back.

'Get your hands off me!' cried Simone.

'My Simone?' said Edward. Lucia made an odd noise in her throat, like she was going to vomit, but the two people at the foot of the stairs ignored her and when Lucia burst into bitter tears, they took no notice and as she pushed between them and attempted to pound up the stairs as though she was seventeen years old again, they ignored her still. They ignored too the slam of her bedroom door. They gazed into each other's eyes, not wanting to break the spell and when Simone whispered, 'I'm sorry,' he shook his head. Then he led her into the dining room; he insisted she take his seat alongside the fire. He left her only to go into the kitchen to make tea. Two cups. One pot. Lucia was forgotten, she had no part to play, and *it is going to be all right*, thought Simone as she heard the kettle boiling, the clattering of cups and saucers.

* * *

He fussed around her, took her green coat and marvelled anew at how on earth she kept her clothes so nice, so clean. He remembered, of course, that she took a tiny spoon of sugar in her tea, and only a little milk. Her hair was grey, but styled so nicely, and it looked beautiful on her. She was growing old gracefully as he had known she would. He had thought for many years that he would never see her again. And now she was here, in his house, in his chair, sipping serenely at the tea he had made for her. It was a dream. He wondered if it was truly a dream; perhaps he was on the way out and hallucinating. Perhaps these moments were nothing but mind-trickery, his glorious death throes. But they weren't, because in truth he had never felt so alive. His hand shook as he held his cup to drink from it. He could not take his eyes from his wife and at first he didn't want to talk. It was enough just to look at her. She had not changed; in essence she was the same person, this lovely French woman, his wife. His wife. She was still sexy, and he was surprised that thought even came to him, but it did, and he wanted to sleep with her, and that was a surprise too, because that side of his life had vanished with her all those years ago. They sipped their tea and said little, smiling at each other, shy and happy. Talking would come later, they had both tacitly agreed. For now, looking was enough.

★ ★ ★

Lucia sat on her bed, stiff, upright, shocked. This arrival she had not foreseen, and she knew for certain that Simone had come back to tell Edward why she had left. At the very least, it would be mentioned. How could it not? She could hear no voices, but she knew they were drinking tea because she'd heard the kettle boil. How dare this silly French woman just flounce back into their home, hers and her brother's, as though she had every right to be there? She had no rights! She had, after all, chosen to leave Edward and break his heart. Lucia would not take responsibility for any of it. She had been younger then, a bit naïve. Perhaps she hadn't truly realised what she was saying or doing, the consequences of her actions not fully revealed to her until they had happened and by then it had been too late to put things right. She had felt the stirrings of guilt among her triumph when Edward had come home in tears that hot August day, many years ago. But she had pushed these feelings down deep inside herself and had ignored them.

It was over. Their life in this dark, cold house, their home nonetheless — it was finished. He would know and he would not forgive her. How could he? He would not see her point of view. She may have gone further than she had wanted or anticipated. She'd wanted to stir up their marriage, create a problem, but not actually end it. Or had she? They had been happy together, she and Edward, her dear brother Edward, all these intervening years. She had cooked for him, cleaned for him, nursed him through illnesses, helped him to pay bills, to open and close bank accounts. She'd made sure he'd claimed his pension when the time came, had shopped for him, made phone calls for him, made excuses for him. She had made herself indispensable, just like she had for Mum. She and Edward had lived together almost as a married couple since Mum had died, taking care of Tina between them, and it had been good and right, with little to upset them or interfere. They had been a family, of sorts, for all those years. They had been happy in their quiet and lonesome household. Any residual shame had been swept under the clippy mat. There had been an air of complaisant satisfaction all these years. The teenaged Tina had been such a quiet girl — no rebellion, no silliness. An easy girl to bring up, in the end. And in her deepest, wildest moments, Lucia had allowed herself to imagine that Tina was her daughter — their daughter. And she even believed it sometimes; was able to convince herself that it was true, and that all was well and all was right, as it should be. The household had reached a level of seething contentment that Lucia had grown to believe could never be destroyed. She sat motionless on her bed, not daring to move.

★ ★ ★

They drank their tea. Edward stoked up the fire, which grew into a welcoming, crackling thing, its flames dancing for joy, heating the eager faces and trembling knees seated before it. Once the tea was finished their politeness fell away and they were heads together, talking, talking, catching up. There was no room for sadness or regret, not here, not now, but there were earnest words and earnest laughter, and apologies, lots of apologies from each of them, hushed by the other. Simone claimed she had been 'restless'. Her workplace affair had been nothing, short-lived and silly, and how she regretted it! That was all. Edward was not entirely convinced, she could tell, but now was not the time to reveal the real reasons. Later, yes. That time would come. But for now, they drank more tea, smiled broadly at the wonder of the other's face, touched, held hands . . . The fire spat and roared, then subsided towards a gentle glow; the clock ticked and outside the fresh-falling rain pattered at the dirty windows.

Tuesday 3rd May 1977

Dear Elizabeth
I'm sorry not to have written for such a long time. I don't feel like writing letters much these days. If you like we can write just sometimes? I am busy keeping Meg company most of the time. She is lonely and wants me to be with her a lot. I don't mind. At school today it was our May Day. My best friend Kimberly was the May Queen. Miss Christianson decided it would be her because she is leaving England soon to go back to Michigan where she is from. Is that anywhere near California? I'm a bit sad that she is going back. She had on a blue shiny dress and had flowers all around her hair and she sat on a chair with flowers at her feet and the flowers smelt fresh and sweet and reminded me a bit of Granny's perfume. There were purple flowers that looked like bunches of grapes. There were orange and red and yellow flowers, a bit like giant daisies, and there were snap dragons. There was May Pole dancing but only for the older kids. I'm not old enough to do that yet but I will be next year. I was an attendant! I stood next to the May Queen and I wore a dress that was pretty but not a queen's dress it was pink and I had no flowers in my hair but I did hold a posy which I was allowed to bring home after.

Aunty Lucia came up to the school to watch the parade and the dancing and I didn't think she would but I'm glad she did. She stood behind the mums and didn't speak to anybody but she was there and she smiled at me and I felt proud. Meg was there too some of the time and she told me I looked stupid but of course she was jealous. I'll write again in a few weeks to let you know what I am up to,

Love from Tina x

40

MARCH 2014

This time Tina had tacos. Kath had a large burger and chips and they again shared a bottle of wine. They talked about the reading group; Tina promising to attend the April meeting. They talked about books they had enjoyed in their lives.

'*Ballet Shoes*,' said Tina. 'It was my big favourite as a kid. I've still got my old copy coloured-in pictures and all.'

Kath was more of a Roald Dahl fan. Tina wasn't surprised. Tina said she liked *Danny, the Champion of the World*, but she never had got into fantasy, she said; without irony. After a moment or two she realised what she'd said. Kath said nothing. She really was very wise and tactful.

But in the end the chat ceased and the talking began. 'Tina, I'd like to talk about your aunt? If that's all right? I've had an idea . . . I know it's sort of talking shop but I thought here . . . Well, we like it here, don't we? And we are friends, aren't we?'

'OK,' said Tina slowly, and took a sip of wine. She was hot and loose and full of energy. She felt good for once. The floaty orange top whispered against her skin. 'We're definitely friends,' she said. 'I don't talk about Meg to just anyone.'

'Quite so,' said Kath. She took a gulp of wine and smiled her big frank smile. She was an attractive woman. Her skin was good, clear and fresh-looking. Tina wondered which products she used. She wanted to ask, but felt that she couldn't. Things were becoming blurred. Tina wasn't sure if she was having dinner with Kath her friend or with Kate the counsellor, who wasn't supposed to be her counsellor.

'I know Meg's dead. Really I do. I've always known it. I just didn't want to know it. Does that help?'

'You tell me. Does it?'

'No.'

'My idea, if you want to hear about it, is closure. Sorry to bring it up again. You don't know what happened that day for sure, and you want revenge. You lost your sister in murky circumstances, your mother left home, your father drifted away. That's a lot of loss for any human being to live with, especially when it all happened to you at such a young age. I think it might help to have a meeting. With your aunt and your uncle and Keaton and me, and we'll try to sort things out.'

'Are you mad?'

'No.'

'Do you seriously think a . . . meeting would work?' said Tina. She was hot, panicked. No. No, no, no . . .

'My belief is that it's worth a try. There are things to be said, I think. Things you need to say. And maybe there are things you need to hear.'

'Yes, but — you don't know her.'

'I've met a lot of people in my line of work, Tina, and I can tell you, nothing or nobody surprises me. I've seen and heard it all.'

'Lucia won't. She wouldn't. She wouldn't do it. And what the hell would we talk about? There's nothing to be said. Nothing at all!'

'It's all ri — '

'No! It's not all right! I'm not doing it, OK? It's a crap idea.' And Tina found herself trembling, and Kath reached across the table and Tina thought she heard her say she was sorry, but she wasn't sure, and Tina began to cry.

'OK, Tina, it's OK . . . I truly am sorry.' Kath rubbed her arm.

Tina wiped her eyes with her napkin and took a few sips of wine. She glanced around to see if anybody had noticed her crying. It appeared as though they hadn't.

'No, I'm sorry,' said Tina, avoiding Kath's gaze. They had argued, almost. How Meg would approve, did approve. For she was always there, of course, in Tina's mind, her heart, her thoughts; waiting, waiting, waiting.

★   ★   ★

During dessert and after they had finally finished apologising to each other, Tina decided it was much better to say nothing further to anybody, anybody at all, about her plan to kill her aunt. She would no longer even discuss it with Meg. She'd exposed herself too much. It really did have to be a secret, from everybody. She would keep certain . . . ideas . . . completely to herself from now on. It was a waste of time trying to involve those who didn't understand. Keaton wanted the best for her and so did Kath, but neither of them were capable of understanding what was best. It wasn't their fault, far from it. They just didn't know the things she knew and hadn't seen the things she'd seen. She alone believed in her plan; she alone would keep her faith in it.

41

APRIL 2014

Edward awoke that drab morning with a new sense of purpose, the likes of which he had never experienced. Hatred weighed down on his heart like a slab, unforgiving, a boulder that would not be budged. Simone had visited him almost every day in the fortnight since her return, to sit and drink tea, and eat biscuits and talk. Lucia always left them to it, busying herself with laundry or dusting and even, once, a slow bitter walk up to the village shop.

The things that Simone had told him only yesterday, he could scarcely believe, and yet he knew them to be true. He felt like he had known these things all of his life. None of it shocked him. His life's hideous mistake, twisted, reformed, shaped into something new, something beyond condemnation, beyond punishment. He was at the mercy of lies. Evil had made a fool of him and it had destroyed his life, and Simone's. But it was not too late, he trusted it was not. He was going to avenge himself. Nothing would stop him, and mercy was banished from his heart, flattened and starved.

When Lucia made him his breakfast of eggs, bacon and toast, he thanked her and ate. Perhaps he even chatted to her. They possibly remarked on the greyness of the morning. They sat together at the dining table and looked out at the garden, which was wet with dew, green and growing and alive. This would be the last time they sat together and ate. He was going to be free at last, and so was Simone, and to hell with the consequences. He laughed, then checked himself, because it was no laughing matter. It was to hell he would be going, if there was such a place, which he doubted. And if it did exist, hell would be too good for some people. It was time to face up to the stark truths in his life. It was time to face up to the long-delayed consequence of his once foolish — unspeakable — actions. For too long he had escaped.

Of course, he had denied everything to Simone and she had believed him, he thought. She'd cried, apologised, lamented that she'd ever doubted him. He tried to convince himself that his parents would have forgiven him. It was shocking, this thing he was going to do to his sister. But it still had to be done. He could never forgive her.

Tuesday 6th December 1977

Dear Elizabeth
I'm sorry not to have written to you for such
a long time. Actually I think it's your turn to
write to me but I can't remember exactly. I
think I forgot your birthday in March and
you forgot mine too. I was ten on the first of
November. It was OK. Uncle Edward and
Lucia and Granny took me into town for tea
after school. We went to the Berni Inn. It was
nice. I had a Knickerbocker Glory for dessert
and I ate it all up.
Then my Granny died a couple of weeks ago.
It was really sad. My dad came back for the
funeral. He moved away a few months ago, to
a big city called Birmingham. Another family
live in our old house now. Uncle Ambrose
didn't come to the funeral and my mum
didn't either. It was the first funeral Meg and
I have been to and it was not very nice. There
weren't many people there which we were
glad about because we don't like it when
people stare. My dad looked different, thin
and hairy and taller which sounds silly
because grownups don't grow taller they just
get wider but not my dad. He talked a lot to
Uncle Edward and Aunty Lucia. I think they
were pleased to see him because we haven't
seen him since he moved away and I was glad
too and we talked quite a lot and I tried to

explain about Meg but he didn't get it. He has a new job and a girlfriend called Patti who is good for him, he said. I haven't met her yet. She lives in Birmingham too. My dad has cut down on his drinking by that he means alcohol. Cider and rum and stuff. Dad will come and visit me again. He promised. I think he will. But he didn't really feel like my dad. But it was nice. He told me to look out for something in the post at Christmas time. I'm sending you a Christmas card. I hope you have a happy Christmas,
Love from Tina x

42

APRIL 2014

It was an April morning, and it was warm and drab, the air damp, oppressive. An overcast Tuesday, not raining, and Tina could sense the sun behind the clouds, struggling to strike through. She wished the sun was shining. It would have made things better. Tina had decided she would just turn up at Lane's End House. She'd toyed with the idea of ringing, to let her aunt and uncle know she was going to visit. But it didn't seem the right thing to do. It would be unfair, somehow. Uncle Edward might look forward to seeing her as much as she would normally look forward to seeing him. It would be much better to turn up, raise the heavy tarnished door knocker and wait for Lucia to come to the door. There would be no anticipation. That was for the best. She'd told nobody about her plans for the day, not even Meg. She'd put her off the scent, allowing her to believe she was going cold on the idea of killing Lucia. It had taken a great deal of concentration. Tina had told her she was visiting her aunt and uncle because it was her duty, and she felt sorry for Uncle Edward, she said, and even for Aunt Lucia.

'Sorry? For Lucia? Tina, you're pathetic, allowing yourself to be persuaded by a fucking do-gooder of a counsellor or whatever she fucking calls herself. She's put lots of stupid fucking ideas in your head about forgiveness. It's all bullshit. Fucking bullshit!'

'No,' said Tina. 'It's for the best.'

'I don't believe in you any more,' said Meg. 'How the fuck have you been talked out of our plans just like that by a wishy-washy . . . shrink who doesn't know her fucking arse from her fucking elbow.'

And so it went on. Tina ignored her sister, who eventually left her alone. Tina thought that this time, she may not come back. She had been so angry, so disappointed. It could be the end. But Meg didn't know about the secret plan, and Tina did. How she had wanted to tell her sister to shut up and wait, to wait and see, but she'd let her rant, and it would serve her right afterwards, when Meg would have to utter those difficult words: I'm sorry.

★ ★ ★

Tina drove to Lane's End House. The clouds began to crack open. Tina swallowed constantly; she wiped sweat from her face. It prickled all over her body. She was hot so often these days, much too readily. She sweated, even on cooler days, worrying that her clothes would be dampened and stained. She was wearing more patterned things, tops with short or loose sleeves. Today she even had her hair back in a bun, off her neck, her face, caught up in a net. She wanted to keep as cool as possible. In the last week she'd felt a crushing fatigue. This she put down to her nerves, her troubled state, her endless planning. Soon it would all be over. She was convinced, once again, that she was menopausal, experiencing its unwelcome commencement — she thought she'd missed another period, although she wasn't keeping track these days. Another possibility had fleetingly occurred to her. But she couldn't entertain such an idea just yet. There would be time enough to think about all that later, she resolved, as she turned down the narrow, lonely road that led to Lane's End House.

It was good, this secret, this knowing something that Meg didn't know — something that nobody knew. For much of the short journey, she'd driven precariously. She was an erratic driver on the best of days. Today she was all over the road. She couldn't seem to steer correctly. She had to swerve once to avoid hitting a car, the driver of which blasted his horn at her and gestured furiously. She felt sick, an odd pervasive pressure all over her body, within and without.

She pulled the car to a clumsy halt outside the gate to Lane's End House. Before getting out, she carefully took the Swiss Army knife from her pocket and ran her fingers along the small blades. She'd procured it several days ago from Keaton's bedside cabinet, second drawer down. She'd played with it for hours, testing it out, and had accustomed herself to its feel and its uses. It would do. It would work. It was sharp. She might have preferred something a little longer, but this was the best she had at her disposal. Huge kitchen knives would have been too obvious, too difficult to hide, and probably too unwieldy to use. This she could only imagine. She had never stabbed anybody before.

She turned off the engine and sat in stillness and silence for a moment. She touched the blade again. She took one, two, three deep breaths and finally climbed from the car. This was it. All her life had led up to this moment, she could see that now, and whatever came after, would come.

She walked to the front door, climbed the steps and boldly, without hesitation, raised the knocker and rapped — once, twice, thrice. She backed down a step, and waited. *For you, Meg,* she thought. *Whatever you think of me, wherever you are, I love you and I'm going to do this.* She carefully grasped the small handle of the knife, and checked again that the blade was locked open.

Nobody came to the door. Edward and Lucia were always to be found at home. But of course, Tina did not pay impromptu visits. Could it be they'd popped out to do their food shopping? Had they gone to the doctor? They still had a car which they used solely for those purposes. The curtains were all drawn back, an upstairs window open. They were at home, surely? She would try the kitchen door, which was often unlocked. She hoped nothing was wrong. Had one of them been taken ill, rushed to hospital? Please, not dear Uncle Edward . . .

The car was in the shed. But there was no laundry flapping on the line in the back garden. The grass was too long — elderly people's grass.

Perhaps she and Keaton should visit more often, and get these chores done. Uncle Edward probably struggled with the mower. She paused to regard a brown cow in the field, standing right up next to the fence, looking at her inquisitively. Tina enjoyed the comfort of the kindly face, the huge brown eyes, the moist pink nostrils; she found herself mesmerised by the regal swish of the cow's tail as she brushed flies away. Then Tina recollected her mission, her reason for being here, and she felt that searing rush of excitement, the pump and flow of adrenalin, that unexpected thrill that comes out of nowhere, from nothing, like a fighter jet ripping into earshot, tearing the sky in two, and disappearing as quickly.

Yet she had not completely fooled herself — she knew what she was doing and she knew what the consequences would be. Her buoyant mood sunk in on itself. She fought tears. Now was not the time to give in to crying. Crying made you weak. How irrational she was being. Chores?! There would be no chores! There would be no comfort. No foreign holidays in blue idyllic places, no more cosy modern home and loving husband. And as for the other thing, if she was indeed . . . but she could not consider that.

She pushed open the gate to the walled backyard, and dragged herself up the steps to the kitchen door. She grasped the handle, twisted it, and pushed. The door opened. It made its peculiar noise: a grind, a lowly scrape that announced the arrival of visitors almost as surely as the front door knocker, or the clang of the front gate.

Tina entered the kitchen, where the smells of breakfast lingered.

'Uncle Edward?' she called. She opened the door to the dining room. The fire was alight, but almost out. She stood in the doorway and took in the long familiar smells of furniture polish, old books, old fruit. Window cleaner. She saw a thin film of dust on the television and bookshelves.

Tina heard a scream, a terrible strangled cry. She froze, her plans compounded. She felt a jolt run through her body and her mind, a sharp thunderclap of reality. In that moment, everything changed. She knew herself again. For the first time in years, she saw herself. What on earth was she — ?!

She made for the stairs, scrambling up them two at a time. The commotion came from Lucia's bedroom; grappling noises, strange grunts, Lucia's gasps of, 'No! Please! Stop! Forgive me!'

* * *

It felt odd and frightening and treacherous to tell the nurse at the desk that he was the father, even though it was true. He felt himself blush as he said the loaded words. They sounded almost holy. He was an imposter. Nevertheless, the nurse directed him to Sharanne's bed.

Sharanne was pale on her pillows, her eyes closed. She stirred and attempted a weak smile, and Keaton responded in kind. He didn't know what to say, so for a few moments they said nothing; Keaton found himself a chair and sat on it, positioning himself alongside the bed. He then got up to frisk the curtains shut.

She told him she couldn't keep anything down. Not even water. It had been a terrible couple of weeks, in and out of hospital, the sickness becoming worse and worse, day by day, but now she was having injections to stop the nausea. The injections hurt, like being stung by a wasp twice a day. In the arse of all places, so she had pretty much said goodbye to any dignity she might have had left. But anything was better than constantly being sick. She still felt sick though. She had lost a stone, which was ironic, wasn't it? She could only wear joggers and t-shirts; comfy stuff, nothing tight. Sometimes it was all she could do to crawl out of bed to use the toilet in the mornings. Smells were torture. All smells. She couldn't use deodorant, shower gel, soap. She couldn't wash up: for some reason washing-up liquid was abominable. She couldn't brush her teeth. She knew she smelled. The nurses were constantly encouraging her to try a shower. They said it would make her feel human again. Keaton said nothing, he just murmured along in what he hoped were the right tones, in the right places. She was hoping to go home as soon as she could. His support was limited and they both knew it.

'I've decided to terminate,' she said, almost as an aside. Yet there was a steeliness to her voice.

'But you promised . . . ' he tried.

'I know I did. But I was confused and I had no

idea then how bad I was going to feel. And I thought I loved you.'

'But you . . . promised me . . .'

'I shouldn't have done. I'm sorry, Keaton, I truly am, but I'm not keeping this baby. I discussed it with the doctor this morning. It's a formality, apparently. And I didn't want a baby anyway, deep down, not at my age. And this way we can both put the whole sorry episode behind us and get on with our own lives. We'll really never have to set eyes on each other ever again.'

When Keaton started to sob she turned from him. 'You'd better leave,' she said, curling up into a tight ball. 'You're upsetting me and I need to rest.'

43

APRIL 2014

It was easy really, and he was glad he'd thought of it. The windows were dirty, and he suggested, after breakfast, that they clean them. They could start upstairs, he said. She readily agreed. He left her in her room and went into his and waited, motionless, unsure how to proceed, breathing fast and erratically, sighing, swallowing. He felt sick. He'd never done anything like this before. Of course. He was a good man, wasn't he? Everybody had always told him so. He wanted to surprise Lucia; catch her off guard. He called through, 'Don't forget to open the window nice and wide, the old place could do with an airing!' and he heard the window open. All the windows at Lane's End House were big and they opened wide. Yet the house was dark and gloomy and cold. Edward silently slipped into her bedroom and watched his sister for a while. She looked small as she cleaned the window. The smell of window cleaner filled the room. Lucia didn't turn to him, didn't hear him. He took a step towards her. She reached up to the highest corners of the window. Her hands looked like the enfeebled claws of some ailing creature. She was thin. She was weak. This was cruel. But it wasn't wrong.

He heard a car. No. Oh, no. Who on

earth . . . ? They didn't have visitors; yet today, the worst time ever there had been for visitors, here they were. What kind of intervention was this? He would have to get on with it. *Just do it, old man*, he said to himself, and crept another step closer. His head swam; he was delirious with fury and regret and bitterness. Part of him looked down on himself from above, shocked at what he was about to do, but powerless to stop it. He felt strangely young again — strong. He reached the window. Lucia looked around at him. There must have been something dreadful in his face because she crumpled. She was terrified of him and in that moment he realised, of course, she always had been. His fault, and the punishment would be his, as much as it would be hers. The car below pulled up and after a few seconds he saw dear Tina emerge from it. Lucia looked around and saw her too, and glanced back at her brother, a look of haughty, smug triumph. He grabbed her then; he grunted, or roared, or something, an instinctive noise of determination, involuntary and crude, and he pulled her back from the window. He felt the huge rap of the front door knocker. He pushed his sister to the floor. He spat at her to be quiet. She tried to scream but he clamped his hand to her mouth. She struggled, but he was stronger than her, and they stayed like that until he peered over the window sill in time to see Tina disappear around the side of the house. The kitchen door was unlocked. He had very little time. He hauled his frail sister to her feet. She gasped, flailed her arms, tried to claw at him. He kept his hand to her mouth.

'Shut up! Shut your mouth! You despicable woman! You . . . bitch!' The voice was cruel and he was surprised that it was his voice, his words. This was really happening.

She clawed at his hands. 'Edward please — '

'You told her I raped you?!'

'You — agh! Please! You did.'

'No! No, Lucia! I did not. It was never that. Not that! It was wrong, every day of my life I've regretted it. Always. Can't you see? Don't you remember? It was something we both . . . it was mutual! You know it was!' They stared at each other. Broken, unspoken truths swimming between them. She knew. In her eyes he saw only a person he hated. Perhaps she saw the same in him. Her face was proud. He saw nothing sisterly or good. She was a traitor of the worst kind.

And he was no longer her brother. All the bonds were broken. He pushed her towards the open window. They fought, they grappled, they grunted. It seemed like hours but it was seconds, mere moments, and all his life's energies had gathered towards this, and in the struggle they knocked the lidless bottle of window cleaner onto the floor and Lucia slipped in the pink mess and her leg twisted. She cried out in pain. He took advantage and grabbed her around the waist, pushing her ever further through the wide open window. She resisted, still grappling, slipping, kicking; not crying or moaning any more, all her listless energy gathered in her struggle against this bizarre defenestration, this awful end to her life. And it was surprising to

317

him, her near silence. She was further out now and she gasped; he tightened his grip on her waist with one arm, his fingers clenching her meagre flesh, and with the palm of his other hand he pushed, pushed her so hard — and still she resisted. 'Please, no,' she said, a whisper, and: 'There was a baby.'

Edward stopped. He paused and breathed hard. 'What?'

'There was a child.'

'No.'

'We made a life between us . . . our baby.'

'No!'

'But I was persuaded to be rid of it. Ask Simone, she knows. She took me to see a woman — an abortionist, a back street abortionist. A French woman, of course. She flushed it out of me, scraped it all out of me . . . gone, just gone. Our baby. Didn't she tell you about that part? Your wife? She made me do it. She didn't want me to be fat in the wedding photographs. Selfish woman — friv —'

'You liar!' he roared. Sobs fell from him like huge raindrops, pregnant with dread.

He pushed and released his grip on her waist; they had reached tipping point and she cried out, 'No! Please! Stop! Forgive me!' and with a final push, she toppled. She shot forward, screamed, and a voice cried, 'Jesus Christ!' and something clattered to the floor and skittered across it and then . . . Then gentle arms, his niece's arms, eased him to one side, and Tina pulled Lucia in, in, in, back in, and his sister gasped and gagged and sobbed uncontrollably and sank to the floor beneath the window. Edward lowered himself onto Lucia's bed where he sat, stiff and terrified, staring at the knife Tina had dropped moments before. Remorse set in and he felt Tina's soft arms around him, rocking him, saying, 'It's all right, it's all right, Uncle Edward,' and now he trembled, trembled, trembled, and closed his eyes and prayed for his soul.

Wednesday 20th May 2015

Dear Elizabeth

I'm so glad that we have rekindled our correspondence after all these years. Facebook just doesn't count! Neither do all those Christmas cards. When I wrote to you I wasn't sure you'd want to write back. I'm so glad you did, and that you feel the same, and would like to resume our letter writing. You're right, it is a dying art.

Its great to hear all the news about your kids. What a successful bunch they are! You must be so proud. Please give my regards to your dad, who I still hope to meet one day. I find it incredible that you kept all my old letters! I'm afraid I can't say the same about yours. I think they may have been destroyed or thrown out by my aunt when Lane's End House was sold, or maybe it was years ago, as she was always one for a thorough spring clean.

Thank you for your invitation. Once Meggie is old enough to get something out of it, we shall visit. Uncle Edward says he would love to see his brother again. I'm sure I would enjoy looking through all my old letters to you! Although I'll be terribly embarrassed. They're full of girlish nonsense, no doubt.

You're right, I am incredibly fortunate to have Meggie. I didn't realise I was pregnant for the first two months or so! I thought it was too late for me to have a child . . . and now it probably is! But there's a natural order to things and there's no use in fighting it. Meggie will be an only child, but she is so loved I trust she will never feel lonely.

I don't know about God . . . but I do feel blessed, you're spot on there. And I hope, in the end, that I have done right. It certainly feels right. It is an amazing feeling to hold and feed my own baby, the baby I thought I didn't want and would never have.

You asked about Uncle Edward. Yes, it is wonderful to have him and Simone living here. And it's so good to have her back in my life, I can't tell you. I was amazed when Uncle Edward told me she was back. It turns out she'd been thinking about it for a long time. She'd often seen me in the cemetery when I visited Meg's grave. I never really noticed her at the time. I mean I saw a woman there quite frequently, but I didn't recognise her. People change so much.

After Lane's End House was sold, Edward used some of the money for the renovations on this place, and it's worked out so well for all of us. They have their own flat (apartment) which is the converted garage and an extension on the back with French windows into the garden. They have their own shower room and bedroom and kitchenette and living room. But they share our front door and Keaton and I can look out for them without being too overbearing. They are a fiercely independent pair, and next week

321

they're heading off on a Mediterranean cruise, the lucky things. Keaton and I are so envious. Again, when Meggie is older . . .

You asked about Lucia. She has cut herself off from all of us. In a way I don't blame her. They argued, you see, on that day I decided to visit, and later dear Uncle Edward told me he had just about had enough of her and that he once did something appallingly bad, and so did she. But he wouldn't tell me what it was he did (in fact he doesn't talk about any of it any more). He begged me to get him out of that house, away from her, so I had to. Lucia wouldn't speak to him once he'd left, and she still hasn't and you know, I don't think she ever will. Edward was fair with the money from the sale of the house; I don't suppose he had any option but to be fair, as the house belonged to both of them, but even so he was more than generous about it. She is living in a flat somewhere, we think, none of us are sure where it is. Not far away, I get the feeling, but it may as well be on the other side of the planet. I rather hope it is. I don't want to see her again. There has been no contact in a year, and that's fine by me! That episode is finally over, I'm happy to say, and I won't be losing any sleep over her absence in my life. Yes, you're right, she must be an incredibly lonely person. But I think she has brought it on herself.

My dad, William, is still around! He came down from Birmingham for Meggie's christening. It was good to see him. He brought his wife Patti with him; she's down to earth and a strong person, just what Dad has always needed in his life I suspect. In some ways she reminds me of my mum. She was a big laugher like Patti. It was good to see Dad so happy and see him smile; there was a time as a child when I wondered if he would ever smile again. He hasn't drunk alcohol for years now and takes care of himself, runs in the park and has even gone vegetarian. He had a cuddle with Meggie and he said she looked exactly like me and Meg when we were babies. It was good to talk with him about the past. But we didn't dwell on it. What's the point, he said, and I agreed with him.

Did I write about Meg a lot in my later letters? I'm sure I must have done. I convinced myself that she wasn't truly dead you see, because to me then, she wasn't. It went on for years, right up until last year which sounds crazy and you know, I think I was a little crazy. But now I'm better. Seeing Uncle Edward so upset that day I called round, something snapped in me, something broke, but in a good way. I think I must have come to my senses. With all that has happened, life for me has been an upward struggle. I've been climbing a mountain for all those years and now I'm finally at the summit, and everything is laid out before me in the right place and the view is breathtaking. That is how it feels.

Dearest Elizabeth, please write back to me

when you get the chance, though I know we are both busy people. I can't promise the prolific stream of letters I used to send, which is probably a relief to you (!) but I dearly would like to stay in proper touch from now on. It will be such a pleasure to resume our friendship.

Much love, Tina x

44

MAY 2015

'Hush, darling,' said Tina as she expertly unhooked her nursing bra with one hand. 'There's a beautiful girl.' Tina helped her baby to latch on, and she watched in fascination as her daughter's little mouth suckled greedily. Tina rocked herself and Meggie back and forth, back and forth in the rocking chair, the baby's wild suckling gradually calming and slowing to something more contented. Keaton, with the new perpetual grin on his face, watched as Tina fed their daughter. The night she was born, Meggie had been placed into her weeping father's arms. Tina had seen how much his child meant to him. Tina knew Keaton would be a good father, and do anything to protect his daughter. She had Keaton's dark hair, his triangular mouth shape.

Edward poked his head around the living room door and offered to make coffee. Simone wasn't up yet, he said, the lazy old thing. But she was tired. And when she did get up, they would make breakfast together for everyone. How did French toast and freshly squeezed orange juice sound?

It sounded wonderful, and she leaned her head back and closed her eyes. What an inspired set of choices she and Keaton had made over the

325

last year. He had been right all along to want a child, to believe in her ability to be a good mother. Yet Keaton was too grateful, sometimes, too in awe of her, too in awe of Meggie, and Tina occasionally had to tell him to shut up. It bothered her a little, this over-thankfulness, but it was all right. She put it down to his generous spirit. And of course for far too long she had put off motherhood and in doing so she'd quashed Keaton's dreams, and her own. She no longer cleaned houses; although she was still in touch with Judy and Sandra, and the Haynes family, and had visited them to show off Meggie.

And as for Meg — she had gone. Tina no longer spoke to her, and she no longer spoke to Tina. Tina had found a good counsellor, a colleague of Kath's, and she'd worked through everything from the beginning, which as she knew was a hard place to find, but worth the search. She discovered that her mother's absence had affected her more than she'd realised. But like Meg, Pamela was gone, long gone, and it was all right. Tina had made her peace with it.

It happened. It's over.

Tina clung to these words. They were her comfort, her mantra. She spoke them to herself daily. They were her favourite words, and they were true.

★ ★ ★

After breakfast, Keaton reluctantly left for work. He hated being apart from Meggie and Tina. He was talking about setting up his own business

326

from home, turning their last remaining spare bedroom into an office. Tina finished her letter to her cousin. She wrote Elizabeth's name and address carefully on the envelope, sealed it and, impulsively, drew a smiley face on the back. She'd pop Meggie in the pram to take a walk down to the post office. It was a beautiful late spring day, the sort of day that filled her with hope. She changed Meggie's nappy, dressed her in a fresh white onesie, and tucked her tiny resilient arms into a white cardigan. She placed her gurgling daughter in the pram, covered her carefully with a knitted blanket Simone had made, and took up her keys and handbag from the usual place in the kitchen. She popped her letter to Elizabeth in the basket under the pram. At the front door and about to leave, she looked down at her feet.

'Stupid woman!' she muttered to herself, and she went back into the lounge to find her sandals, which she thought she'd left by the sofa. In the doorway she stopped, and stared.

'Oh!' she cried.

'Oh?'

'I thought . . . '

Tina shook her head. No. It couldn't be. Not now. It's over. She put on her sandals. She felt herself being watched but she tried to ignore it. She moved back towards the hallway, where Meggie waited patiently in the pram, making her delightful little noises, slowly kicking off the blanket. Tina opened the front door, manoeuvred the pram down the single step, and turned back to pull the door shut behind her. But she stopped. She sighed.

'Are you coming to the post office with me?' she called back into the house. She hoped her call wouldn't summon Simone or Edward, who, Tina guessed, were in their comfortable little lounge, reading, or tending their houseplants, or maybe even beginning tentative packing for next week's cruise. Neither of them came to the door of their flat.

Tina walked towards the post office, proudly pushing the pram. Warm air whistled past her as she gambolled along, flip-flopping down the blossom-warm street.

'It's just like old times, isn't it?' said Meg, struggling to keep up beside her strong, striding sister.

'No. It's not,' said Tina.

'All right. Sorry I spoke.'

'So am I.' Tina stopped and turned to face her sister. 'Look, I don't mind you visiting me from time to time, but no more funny stuff. No more gloom and doom. No more whining about Keaton. No more whining about Lucia. Do you promise? It happened. It's over. It's all over. I mean it this time.'

Meg glanced into the pram. 'Your baby is adorable. My little niece . . . '

'You must leave her alone, Meg. I'm sorry but you must.' Tina leaned across her daughter, shielding her.

'I wouldn't hurt her!' Meg looked astounded.

'I know.' They were silent.

'I'm sorry,' said Tina.

'Ah, forget it. She's gone, right?'

'Lucia?'

'Who else?'

'She's gone,' said Tina. 'We don't hear from her. She doesn't hear from any of us.'

'Good. That's good. That's right, wouldn't you say?'

'Yes. It's right.'

'I'll say goodbye, then.'

Tina bowed her head. 'Thank you,' she said and continued her walk. She walked a lot these days. She was beginning to lose weight. She felt better than she ever had. She was doing so well and she was not going to look back, not even for Meg. Tattered blossom swirled around her feet, thrown about by the pram's tiny whirling wheels. She felt herself to be unaccompanied, save for the gurgling, kicking baby. She stopped and looked over her shoulder. Meg stood alone on the pavement where they had spoken, and she raised her hand and smiled. It was a beautiful smile, just as Tina remembered. Something in Meg's smile, the gesture, the distance, told Tina this really was goodbye. Tina raised her hand and smiled back. They nodded at the same time and turned from each other, and Tina picked up her pace and continued her walk to the post office.

Epilogue

JULY 1976

Lucia carried the tea tray out to the garden and invited Simone to join her at the table under the plum trees. Simone thought, *what harm would it do to sit and drink tea with Lucia?* She really ought to make an effort, because love her or loathe her, Lucia was her sister-in-law, and that was that. It might please Edward if they were to get along better; if they could be friends, even on a small scale. Simone intended to be Edward's wife forever. Her colleague at work, who made no secret of his attraction to her, could whistle. He was a nice enough chap, but he was not Eddie.

She and Lucia rarely spent time together. There had been an uncomfortable distance between them for many years, ever since that unfortunate business with the unwanted pregnancy. Probably it had all been for the best. But Simone could never think of it without a pang of regret for the child that could have — even should have — been. Should she have tried harder? Should she have offered to help with the baby? It was ironic, arranging an abortion for a vulnerable young woman and then not being able to conceive a child yourself. There was something poetic in it. God was wise.

Edward was indoors with Anne; the girls were playing. They'd had a fun shopping trip into town. Tina, so bookish, and Meg, so unbookish, were a delight. She was worried about Meg's new clackers: they were dangerous, but so popular. All the children seemed to have a pair these days. Meg had wanted a red pair but had contented herself with all that was left, which was blue.

Lucia was leading up to something, Simone could tell. She was fidgeting.

'What is it, Lucia?' asked Simone. Better to hear it and have it over and done with. It would be nothing important. On rare occasions Lucia had sought Simone's advice on clothes or hairstyles.

'It's about Edward,' said Lucia, quietly. She looked about her. There was nobody near. A breeze ruffled all the leaves.

'Yes?'

Lucia shrugged. 'My brothers are a bad lot,' she said.

'Really.'

'Yes.'

Simone sighed. 'What are you trying to tell me, Lucia?'

Lucia put down her cup, and looked about once again. The leaves rustled, the girls continued to play with Meg's new clackers. Clack-clack-clack.

'It's not so easy to say some things,' said Lucia.

'Just say it, whatever it is you want to say.'

'All right, I will. Edward interfered with me.'

Simone thought she might faint. A low rushing began in her ears. Her heart thumped hard. She clenched her fists. She wanted to hit this odious woman. 'You expect me to believe this . . . poisonous talk?' she said, spitting out her words like a wounded cat.

331

'No, I don't expect you to,' said Lucia, and she sounded bored. Bored! 'Nobody ever does believe this sort of thing.'

'There's a reason for that.'

'Yes. People don't want to believe. Even though it is the truth. There is no justice in that. Just because somebody is clever and handsome and nice, he cannot possibly be a bad man, people think. There are certain assumptions. But they just aren't true and I know they're not.'

Simone was silent. She felt tears brooding, and she felt panic. Lucia . . . Lucia couldn't possibly be lying, could she? How could she say these things about her own brother — who she apparently worshipped — if they weren't true? But if they were true, why the hell would she worship him?

'When?' Simone asked.

'When I was seventeen. He was drunk. It was only once. He got silly. He kissed me. He touched me. Then . . . other things.'

'What things?'

'He made me sleep with him.'

'Do you mean, he made you have sex with him? Tell me what happened.'

'Hush, be quiet. All right then. He had sex with me.'

'Against your will?'

'Yes.'

Simone was silent. She could not think.

'There's something else,' said Lucia. 'Something that's unspeakable.'

'Yet you speak of it.'

'Somebody has to.'

'Yes. Somebody has to. Go on.'

'The . . . the . . . that day in London.'

'What of it?'

Lucia said nothing. Simone stared at her, horror filling her heart, ringing in her ears, torturous.

'Lucia, are you lying? Tell me the truth because you have said the most damaging, desperate things anybody can say about another human being. Do you understand? Do you understand these accusations . . . they are the worst of all?'

Did Lucia waver? Did a shadow pass over her face? Simone couldn't tell. She couldn't see or think clearly.

'I understand,' said Lucia and she cried then, silent tears. There was feeling here. This was real. Something, if not true, not untrue. Simone rested her hand on Lucia's until she stopped crying. She kept an eye on the girls, who were still playing with the clackers. Edward was still indoors with Anne. Simone needed to think. She needed time to work out what any of this meant, if anything. She needed to assimilate, draw her own conclusions. Clack-clack-clack.

'Be careful, Meg!' cried Tina, her shrill voice rising in concern.

Simone stood up.

'Lucia, I need time. If what you say is true then . . . what in hell's name can I say? I don't know. The girls? Are they . . . are they safe?'

'They're perfectly safe,' said Lucia coldly. She stood up too. The women faced each other. 'I look after them and I know nothing bad will ever

333

happen. It was just one time. He was sorry after-wards. He begged me to forgive him. So I did. I forgave him and he promised me, promised on his life, that it would never happen again. I believe him. Nothing else has ever happened. He loves those girls in all the right ways.'

Yes, Simone thought. *That part is true. But the rest?* She didn't know, she couldn't tell. Lucia was an actress, no doubt. But she clearly remembered the teenaged girl's determination to be rid of the baby. Her assertion that it could not be born. That day they had chosen the material for the bridesmaid's dress. Her absolute conviction. It all made sense.

Did she not know her husband? Nightmarish thoughts and ideas clouded her mind; a mingled cacophony of panic and noise. And something illogical, out of keeping — she indeed was the one who could not have children. Thank God, who was more than wise, for that.

'You have forgiven him,' said Simone, 'yet you tell me of it.' She stared at her sister-in-law, who looked to the ground. 'Would it not be compassionate to say nothing? To me? His wife? And why now?'

Lucia merely shrugged. Simone swore at her, and walked down the slope, away from her sister-in-law, away from the swaying trees, away from the depths of their conversation. She called out to the girls, 'Show me these clackers! Show me how they work! I shall have a turn.'

Meg gladly demonstrated. Tina looked on in fear. 'You have to be careful, Tante Simone,' she said.

Simone nodded and wrapped her arm around Tina's shoulders. 'I am always careful.' Lucia walked past them, carrying the tea tray back to the kitchen. She disappeared into the gloom of the house and moments later, Edward appeared at the top of the steps. He crossed his arms and leaned against the doorframe and watched as his wife knocked the blue clackers together, slowly at first, her hand moving up and down, up and down, gaining momentum, faster, clack-clack-clack. Then higher, more rhythmic, quicker, and finally over her hands, flying, her face a picture of stern concentration and the girls and Edward looking on in awe, in trepidation, and the clackers flying back and forth, back and forth, back and forth, clack-clack-clack.

Acknowledgements

Bringing a novel into the world is always a team effort. I'm fortunate to have a wonderful bunch of people behind me. Thank you first and foremost to author Sarah Vincent for her advice, friendship and editorial input. I couldn't have done this without her. Also thanks to writer friends Isabel Costello, Louise Jensen and Rebecca Mascull for their unstinting support. Debi Alper and Emma Darwin taught me how to self-edit, and thank goodness they did: psychic distance anyone?! Big special thanks to Antonia Honeywell and all The Prime Writers — you know who you are. I promised to mention Benjamin Dreyer and Helen MacKinven who both came to my rescue on Twitter with the word 'incubator'. Many thanks to all at Troubador Publishing. Thank you to Antony Hitchin for the eagle-eyed copy edit, and thanks to Justine Cunningham for the thorough proof read. Big thanks to Jennie Rawlings for her amazing cover artwork. And finally, very special thanks to Hannah Ferguson, agent extraordinaire.

Thanks and love to the family I grew up with: Wendy, Stephen and Pete Tuffrey. Hugs and kisses to the family who are growing up with me: Oliver, Emily, Jude, Finn and Stanley. Finally, and once again, many thanks to Ian for his generosity and his ability to make all things possible.

We do hope that you have enjoyed reading
this large print book.

Did you know that all of our titles
are available for purchase?

We publish a wide range of high quality
large print books including:
Romances, Mysteries, Classics
General Fiction
Non Fiction and Westerns

Special interest titles available in
large print are:
The Little Oxford Dictionary
Music Book
Song Book
Hymn Book
Service Book

Also available from us courtesy of
Oxford University Press:
Young Readers' Dictionary
(large print edition)
Young Readers' Thesaurus
(large print edition)

For further information or a free
brochure, please contact us at:
Ulverscroft Large Print Books Ltd.,
The Green, Bradgate Road, Anstey,
Leicester, LE7 7FU, England.
Tel: (00 44) 0116 236 4325
Fax: (00 44) 0116 234 0205

Other titles published by Ulverscroft:

MRS SINCLAIR'S SUITCASE

Louise Walters

Forgive me, Dorothea, for I cannot forgive you. What you do, to this child, to this child's mother, it is wrong . . . Roberta likes to collect the letters and postcards she finds in second-hand books. When her father gives her some of her grandmother's belongings, she finds a baffling letter from the grandfather she never knew — dated after he supposedly died in the war Dorothy is unhappily married to Albert, who is away at war. When an aeroplane crashes in the field behind her house she meets Squadron Leader Jan Pietrykowski, and as their bond deepens she dares to hope she might find happiness. But fate has other plans for them both, and soon she is hiding a secret so momentous that its shockwaves will touch her granddaughter many years later . . .